ARCTIC ADVENTURE

"Hey, what's going on?' Roger yelled. 'Is it an earthquake?"

The snow beneath him was shaking violently. It had come alive. There was a deep growl. Then the head of a polar bear came up. The beast was angry because his sleep had been disturbed. With a mighty heave the great body rose, tossing Roger ten feet away head first into a drift.

He pulled himself loose and began to run. The great bear came lumbering after him. The boy staggered in the deep snow. He had once been chased by a grizzly in Canada. But this creature was big enough and strong enough to eat a grizzly.

SAFARI ADVENTURE

The animals that dared to visit the camp at night began to arrive. The grass around the bandas was kept watered, and attracted grass-eating animals. There was a distinct chomping, chewing sound. Straining their eyes, the boys could dimly make out stripes.

Hal brought out the binoculars and looked in the direction of the sound. It was remarkable how much better one could see with these things, even at night.

"Zebras," he said. "A whole herd of them."

ARCTIC & SAFARI
ADVENTURES

Willard Price

Illustrated by Pat Marriott

RED FOX

ARCTIC & SAFARI ADVENTURES
A RED FOX BOOK 978 0 099 48772 2 (from Jan 2007)
0 099 48772 1

Published in Great Britain by Red Fox,
an imprint of Random House Children's Books

Arctic Adventure first published in Great Britain by Jonathan Cape Ltd, 1980
First Red Fox edition 1993
Text copyright © Willard Price, 1980
Illustrations copyright © Jonathan Cape Ltd, 1980

Safari Adventure first published in Great Britain by Jonathan Cape Ltd, 1966
First Red Fox edition 1993
Text copyright © Willard Price, 1966
Illustrations copyright © Jonathan Cape Ltd, 1966

This Red Fox edition 2005

3 5 7 9 10 8 6 4 2

Papers used by Random House Children's Books are natural, recyclable products
made from wood grown in sustainable forests. The manufacturing processes conform
to the environmental regulations of the country of origin.

Red Fox Books are published by Random House Children's Books,
61–63 Uxbridge Road, London W5 5SA,
a division of The Random House Group Ltd,
Addresses for companies within The Random House Group Limited
can be found at: www.randomhouse.co.uk/offices.htm

THE RANDOM HOUSE GROUP Limited Reg. No. 954009
www.**kidsatrandomhouse**.co.uk

A CIP catalogue record for this book is available from the British Library.

Typeset in Bembo by Palimpsest Book Production Limited,
Polmont, Stirlingshire

Printed and bound in Great Britain by
Bookmarque Ltd, Croydon, Surrey

ARCTIC ADVENTURE

To
M.V.P.
always

Contents

1
Polar Bear

Roger sat down on a snowbank. At least he *thought* it was a snowbank.

He was tired. He had been helping his big brother, Hal, build an igloo.

An igloo was a house made of blocks of snow. This one was about twelve feet in diameter and rounded off on the top. It was nine feet high. That was high enough even for Hal, who was six feet tall.

Roger shivered. "It's as cold as Greenland," he called.

He had often heard people say that, even in New York. Why didn't they say "cold as Alaska" or "cold as Siberia"? He asked Hal about it.

"Because Greenland is about the coldest spot on earth," Hal said. "It's the closest to the North Pole. Besides it wears a cap of ice two miles thick. That's why you're shivering right now. Because you're in Greenland."

"Why did Dad send us here when there are so many nice warm places to go to?"

"Because a famous animal collector like Dad has to get the animals that zoos want to buy. And zoos have been asking for the wonderful animals that live up here – the polar bear, walrus, big bearded seal, sea lion, musk-ox, narwhal, wild reindeer, caribou, humpback whale, sea otter, Greenland shark . . ."

"Hey, what's going on?" Roger yelled. "Is it an earthquake?"

The snow beneath him was shaking violently. It had come alive. There was a deep growl. Then the head of a polar bear came up. The beast was angry because his sleep had been disturbed. With a mighty heave the great body rose, tossing Roger ten feet away head first into a drift.

He pulled himself loose and began to run. The great bear came lumbering after him. The boy staggered in the deep snow. He had once been chased by a grizzly in Canada. But this creature was big enough and strong enough to eat a grizzly.

Roger made for home as fast as his legs could carry him. Home was the igloo. Hal could have killed the animal if he had had a rifle. But he and his brother were "bring 'em back alive" men. A dead bear would be of no use to a zoo.

Roger plunged into the igloo. The great white bear followed him. Boy and bear were alone in the snow house.

The unwelcome guest rose on his hind feet to attack this impudent human. That was the bear's mistake. Standing up he was ten feet tall. Since the roof was only nine feet high, the enormous head crashed through the roof.

What a strange sight – an igloo topped by the head of a polar bear. But Hal and Roger had built well. Not well enough to prevent the monster from going through the roof, but well enough to catch the bear between the icy blocks so he could not get down to pull that rascal, Roger, to pieces.

Hal saw his opportunity. He ran into the igloo, snatched up a piece of rope, and tied the animal's hind feet together. The rope was strong with a wire running through it. The bear roared furiously and danced a fandango to loosen the rope, but it was no use.

The front feet dangled inside and Hal promptly gave them the same treatment – or tried to. The trouble was that the forefeet were the bear's chief weapons, so strong

3

that one swat of a powerful paw would send Hal to heaven and he wasn't ready to go there – yet. So Hal dodged the flailing feet. Luckily the big bear, with his head out in space, could not see where Hal was at any moment so his hammer blows failed to reach their mark. Hal dodged here and there – one wrong dodge and he would go to join his ancestors.

Hal finally got a loop over one of the bear's front legs. Then it was not too difficult to run the rope over the other leg and draw them together under a tight knot.

In the meantime Roger had been speeding to other igloos to get help, since two boys could not handle this thousand-pound monster alone.

An Eskimo is always willing to help, and it was only a matter of minutes before a dozen men were on hand. They weren't sure what they were supposed to do. One carried a big gun, and another came with bow and arrow. Hal, not proficient in the Eskimo language, could not tell them that the bear was not to be killed.

A handsome young man stepped forward and said, "I speak English. What do you want?"

"We want", Hal said, "to take this bear alive and put him in a zoo."

"A zoo? What is a zoo?"

"A place where wild animals are cared for and everybody can watch them."

"Yes. Very good," said the stranger. He turned to the men with the gun and the bow and arrow. He seemed to be telling them that this was no killing job.

"What is your name?" Hal asked.

The young man was embarrassed. "No Eskimo tells his name," he said.

"Why not?"

"Because to an Eskimo his name is like his soul. It is a spirit. And the spirit is angry if the man it lives with tells his name. Someone else can tell you. That is all right."

He spoke to the man next to him, who told Hal the name that its owner did not dare to speak. Their helper's name was Olrik.

Hal said, "Glad to know you, Olrik." And he clasped Olrik's hand. "How old are you? Or is that another secret?"

"No secret. I'm twenty. And you?"

"The same," Hal replied.

Roger had a question. "What's the Eskimo name for polar bear?"

"Nanook."

Hal said, "I have a notion that all of us including the bear are going to get along well together."

Olrik gave him a warm smile. Already they were friends.

"Now, about this bear," said Olrik, "have you a piece of cloth?"

Hal didn't quite see how one could tackle a polar bear with a piece of cloth. But he went into the igloo and came out with a scarf.

Olrik, hoisted to the roof by the men, tied the scarf tightly around the bear's head, completely covering his eyes.

It had a magic effect. The giant was conquered. He stopped twisting, squirming and roaring, and was as quiet as a lamb.

Then one of the cages that the boys had brought from home was placed directly in front of the entrance to the snow house.

An axe was used to break the blocks that held the bear captive. Nanook dropped to the floor of the snow house. With his legs tied and his eyes covered he could only hunch about blindly. But he presently found the outlet and stumbled into the cage. The door was promptly closed behind him.

"He's tired after all his struggles," said Olrik. "Polar bears sleep a lot. When he's asleep you can come in and take the cloth off his eyes and the ropes from his feet. But be very careful. If he wakes he'll be after you like a stroke of lightning. Perhaps you'd let me do it."

"No, I'll take care of it," Hal said.

"I will," chimed in Roger. "After all, he's sort of my bear. I sat on him."

Hal laughed. "So you think sitting on him gave you a special privilege? No, the folks back home would never forgive me if I came home alone."

But when both bear and Hal were sound asleep, Roger slipped cautiously into the cage, removed the blindfold and untied the bear's feet. The bear woke, but there was no stroke of lightning. Polar bears are intelligent. This one was intelligent enough to know that somebody was doing him a good turn.

He rolled over and went to sleep again.

2
This Strange Greenland

"Why do they call it Greenland?" Roger wanted to know.

"Perhaps because it isn't green," Hal answered.

"That's no answer," Roger objected.

"Yes it is. The Danes came and made it a part of Denmark. They wanted other people to come and live here. It's the largest island in the world. Almost 1,700 miles long and 800 wide. But it's no good without people. People wouldn't come if they called it Drearyland or Deadland or No-Man's Land. So they called it Greenland."

"But that was a lie."

"Not exactly. It's true that most of the island is covered with ice. And what ice! Eleven thousand feet thick. If you could go down a mile into it you would find ice a thousand years old. It just never melts — except that it gets a little slushy on top in summer. It's growing thicker all the time. Come back ten thousand years from now and you'll find it a towering mountain of ice."

"Thanks. But I don't intend to come back. I still think it should have been called No-Man's Land. Why Greenland?"

"Because," Hal replied, "there's a broad band of green from fifty to a hundred miles wide all the way up the west coast. There are no forests. Nothing grows more than ten feet high. But there are dwarf birches, alders, mosses, saxifrages, poppies, grass, and away up here where we are, not far from the North Pole, I've heard that they can grow broccoli, turnips, lettuce, radishes and gardens of flowers."

"I'll believe it when I see it," grunted Roger. "Why should these things grow on the west coast and nowhere else? It doesn't make sense."

"They grow because a branch of the Gulf Stream flows along this coast. It brings warm water from the Gulf of Mexico. Of course it's not so warm when it gets here. It may be about zero. But that's not so bad as on the savage east coast, where it can be terribly cold. So that's why most of the people live here, and only a few on the east coast. You might almost call that No-Man's Land."

Roger had to admit it. Big brother had an answer to everything. If he, Roger, ever learned half as much he'd be a wise man.

"Another thing gripes me," Roger said. "Why is it so dark?"

"Because this is still winter. All winter there is no sun. All summer the sun shines all the time, night and day. It never goes up in the sky. It stays down near the horizon. If you didn't have a watch, you would never know whether it was noon or midnight."

"But I have a watch."

"Even so, it's not easy. Suppose your watch says ten o'clock. Well, which is it — ten in the morning or ten at night?"

Roger remarked, "I never heard of anything so topsy-turvy. If this is winter, why isn't it pitch black? It's only a dark grey."

"That's because the sun is just out of sight, but it's close to rising. In a few days we'll have the sun. And a couple of weeks later you'll be sick of it — shining all the time when you want to sleep."

Roger laughed. Even this bad news couldn't get him down.

"There's one good thing," he said. "My polar bear. I'm going to feed him now. I don't know whether it's breakfast, lunch, or dinner — anyhow, I bet he's always hungry."

3
Roger and the Giants

Roger got along well with animals. Perhaps it was because he liked them, or perhaps because he was not afraid of them. Maybe he was too young – fifteen – for any beast to be afraid of him.

His polar bear, Nanook, stood five feet high at the shoulder if standing on all four feet. Roger was five feet tall. So the two were a match.

A few gulps by his four-legged friend and there would be no Roger. If he had shown fear that might have been the end of him.

But he spoke gently. And he petted the monster as if he were a pussy cat. His Majesty had never been so well cared for in his life. His mother bear had not petted him, and his father had threatened to eat him. This boy fed him every two days. Previously he had often been forced to go without food for a week or two.

Nanook had never learned the Eskimo language or English. But he understood the tone of a voice. Roger's voice flowed over him softly and he replied with the best imitation of a purr that he could manage.

One day Roger told his brother, "I'm going to let him out."

"If you do he'll take off like a blue streak."

Roger respected his brother's opinions. But he also respected his great bear. He very quietly opened the cage door. Nanook did not move. Roger got behind the half-ton of bear and pushed. He might as well have tried to push down a stone wall.

The bear looked back at him with big eyes that seemed to say, "What's on your mind, kiddo?"

Roger could think of only one other way to move this mountain of flesh and bone. Perhaps it would work. Perhaps it wouldn't. He walked out of the cage door and stood twenty feet away. Then he turned and spoke. Again, the tone of his voice was easy to understand.

The great Nanook stood still for five minutes, ten, fifteen. Roger was patient. Then the King of Greenland Beasts walked out and joined his friend.

From that time on the cage door was left open. The bear went in to eat or sleep. Sleeping was good there because the floor had been covered with thick caribou hides. That was better than sleeping in the snow with rocks pushing up against your ribs.

★   ★   ★

The young Eskimo, Olrik, came to tell them that Whiskers had been seen offshore. Whiskers was the mighty bearded seal. The Eskimos called him mukluk.

Hal had heard much about the mukluk. Hal's father, John Hunt, on his animal farm near New York, had said, "Get all the seals you can. Especially the giant bearded seal. It's twelve feet long and on average it weighs 800 pounds. An extra large one weighs twice that. Look out for the jaws. They could bite your head off. It pokes its head out of an ice hole to breathe. So do all the other seals. The difference is that you can get hold of the smaller seals and pull them out."

"But you could never pull an 800-pound seal up through a six-inch hole," said Roger. "So how do you get it?"

"Go underwater. Take scuba tanks and Neoprene wet suits. The water will be cold but Neoprene will keep you warm," said Hal.

So now, clad in the thick rubber Neoprene and carrying on their backs the tanks of air that they could breathe while searching for the monster, they joined Olrik and walked the short distance to the beach.

Roger glanced back and saw that his bear was following him.

"Stop him," Hal said. "Send him home."

"Easier said than done," objected Roger.

"You don't understand," Hal said. "Seals are a polar bear's favourite food. If he goes down with you and comes on a seal, he'll start eating it."

"I think I can teach him not to do that."

"He'll just be a nuisance."

"On the contrary," said Roger, "he may be just what we need to capture an 800-pound mukluk. He's stronger than both of us put together. But to help him learn, we'll start with something smaller."

Olrik set off for the nearby town of Thule to hire a truck in case the hunt for the giant seal was successful. Hal also asked him to bring some men to help.

The two boys walked out on the ice and stopped at a seal hole. The seals make holes and keep them free of ice so that they can poke their heads out and breathe. The brothers stood by the hole and waited. They did not budge an inch. The slightest scrape of a boot on the ice would scare away any seal.

At long last a black head came up through the hole. Hal grabbed it and tried to draw it out. Roger used his jackknife to make the hole larger.

"Great," said Hal. "A harp seal." The black lines on the

creature's back did look like a harp. "This is just a pup. That's good. He's easier to handle than his six-foot father."

Nanook, the bear, pushed forward. Was this to be his breakfast? Roger pressed his hand over the bear's jaws and he obediently backed away. Lesson one. The pup was dropped into a sack.

Later a ringed seal was caught. Again the bear was restrained. Lesson two.

After an hour they caught one more. This was a hooded seal, so called because his upper lip was so long and it flopped back over his head like a hood. Again, no lunch for Nanook. Lesson three.

All three valuable seals were in the bag.

Nanook was ready now to go down with the boys, and could be trusted not to sink his teeth into the great bearded seal if one should be found.

Roger already knew that the polar bear was a famous swimmer. It could swim six miles an hour and keep going non-stop for a hundred miles. No other bear could match this performance. Roger also knew that a polar bear could kill an 800-pound bearded seal with one swat of his paw. Roger must see that this did not happen.

Olrik was back with the truck – and half a dozen men.

"We'll be ready for you if you get a mukluk. Wish I

could go with you but I have no wet suit and no scuba. By the way, keep a sharp lookout for another big beast — the oogjook."

"Never heard of it. What is an oogeljerk?"

"The name is oogjook," said Olrik.

"Is it a seal?"

"A big one. Weighs as much as five men."

"Well, this oogleboogle," said Hal, "what's it's name in English?"

"Doesn't have one. But you'll know it when you see it. It twists and wriggles like a ballet dancer. It's unknown to most people here and perhaps even your father has not learned about it. But if you could get one he could probably sell it to a zoo for many thousands of dollars."

"All right," Hal said. "Here goes for the mukluk and the ooglebug."

He knew very well that the word was oogjook but he enjoyed playing with it. Olrik laughed.

Although summer was coming, plenty of ice remained on the sea. But near by there was a narrow lane of open water, and here the two boys and the bear slipped below the surface.

The water near the surface was cloudy with plankton, tiny living cells that were the food of the baleen whale.

16

But thirty feet down the water was as clear as glass. The temperature was close to freezing. The boys in their Neoprene suits didn't mind it.

Seal pups were much interested in the visitors, and swam all around them. They came close and nibbled Roger's hands. They cavorted and scampered like children let out of school. Hal's watertight torch lit up the lively dance of the little fellows.

But even the hungry bear paid no attention to them.

Fish in all colours swam about, and the sea floor was a fairyland with shells of all sorts, crabs with rainbow backs, and swaying sea fans rooted in the bottom and looking exactly like plants – but Hal knew they were animals. What a sight – an animal with roots in the ground.

Then a mukluk hove into sight. The bearded seal was known to be a noisy fellow. "Chuck-chuck-chuck" was his song, but sung so loudly that he could be heard plainly through the water. He came close and squinted with weak eyes at these curious creatures who had invaded his territory.

Hal at once threw a loop of rawhide rope over the big fellow's head. He and Roger began towing the monster to the open break in the ice.

They soon found that they were as weak as cats when it came to towing an 800-pound monster.

Instead of them towing him, he was towing them. His great fins were like broad paddles, and with very little effort he could pull these two-legged beasts far away under the ice.

The bear! Nanook could help. Roger searched for him. His large pet had disappeared. Roger looked up, and there was the bear at the surface getting a breath of air.

Of course Nanook had no scuba. He must go up to the surface for air. But why did it happen just now when he was so badly needed?

He came at last, peering about for his friends. Then he saw them far away and deep down, at the mercy of the big seal.

Nanook sank to join them, and was he welcome! Roger put the end of the line between the bear's teeth. It grew taut and the surprised mukluk paddled in vain. The boys swam toward the open water lane, and the 1,000-pound bear had no trouble in towing the bearded seal, whose whiskers trembled with astonishment as he was pulled into the water lane where the men waited at the edge of the ice.

He kept chuck-chuck-chucking as he was lifted up on to the ice and then slid up a ramp on to the truck.

"Great," shouted Olrik. "You did a fine job."

"We didn't do it," Hal said.

"Then who did?"

"Our four-footed giant. Without him the whole thing would have been a flop."

"Well, jump on the truck and we'll go to town."

"Not quite yet," said Hal. "We saw something else that may have been the oogjook you were talking about. We'll go back down and try to get it."

So they went down, and saw to it that their bear went with them. They knew now that they could do nothing without him.

What they had seen before was still there. It did look as if it weighed as much as five men, and it squirmed, wriggled and twisted in a crazy dance.

They lassoed it and gave the end of the rope to their big pet. He dutifully hauled it, still wriggling, to the waiting men, who put it on the truck and tied it down. The bag of smaller seals was also loaded.

"Where to?" Olrik asked.

"To the Thule air base," Hal said. "We'll charter one of those flying box-cars, I think you call it a skyvan, and we'll send it off tonight to our animal farm near New York. I'll telegraph Dad right now to watch for it."

He wired his father:

SENDING YOU TONIGHT BY SKYVAN HARP SEAL, RINGED SEAL, HOODED SEAL, HUGE BEARDED SEAL, AND AN OOGJOOK – DON'T LAUGH – THEY WILL ARRIVE AT YOUR PLACE TOMORROW MORNING. ALSO HAVE POLAR BEAR, BUT WILL KEEP HIM A WHILE. WE NEED HIM

LOVE, HAL

"There's one thing I don't understand," Roger said after they had returned to their igloo. "Won't those seals die because there's no water in that plane?"

"They'll be all right," Hal said. "Long, long ago seals were land animals. In a way they still are. They have no gills like a fish to get oxygen from the water. They have to come up to breathe. They took to the sea because they could find food there. But they no sooner eat than they pop out of the sea. You remember Glacier Bay, Alaska?"

"Sure."

"What did you see there?"

"Hundreds of seals, each one sitting on a floating block of ice."

"Exactly. They liked to spend most of their time out of the water. And you remember the great rocks offshore along the Oregon coast. What did you see there?"

Roger answered, "We didn't actually see the rocks at all, because they were completely covered with seals."

"Right. They like to leave the sea, except when they are hungry. So you don't need to worry about their one night in the skyvan. When they get to the farm they can use the lake if they want to because there are fish in it. But when we get home I'll bet we find them perched on the rocks, enjoying the fresh air."

4
Zeb – the Smart Guy

The hole in the roof made by the great bear had been mended. Now Hal, Roger and Olrik sat in the warm snow house, chatting comfortably.

"By the way," said Hal, "where did you learn English?"

The Eskimo answered, "In your country. I spent two years at Harvard. Later I'll go again and finish."

Hal was astonished. "I'll bet you're about the only Eskimo who has studied abroad."

Olrik smiled. "Many of our people have gone to England or America to study. Especially they want to learn English."

"Why English?"

"So they can get a job when they come back. Did you realize that we have six thousand Americans and English in Greenland? They run most of the industries here and the two big airports – one at Thule and one at Sondre Stromfjord. If an Eskimo wants a job he'll be more likely to get it if he can speak English."

"But Denmark owns Greenland. Aren't there a lot of Danes here?"

"Yes – and they're fine people – but they don't have the technical skill of the British and the Yanks."

"I heard," said a rough-looking fellow who had just come in. "You're right. We're the smart ones. You Eskimos are the dumbest people on earth. And I mean you."

He was looking straight at Olrik. Olrik said nothing.

Hal objected. "Hold your horses, Zeb. They told me your name. You were here with the men who helped after the big bear bust our roof. And I recollect that you stood behind and did nothing."

"Why should I mix with a pack of Eskimos?" blurted Zeb. "I keep better company than those ignorant blokes." Again he stared at Olrik.

"What was your college?" Hal asked.

"College of hard knocks."

"Do you know," said Hal, "that you're insulting a Harvard man?"

"What's that?"

"A man who has studied at Harvard."

"Don't know any jerk town named Harbard. Me – I'm from New York – biggest city in the world. And I've come here to get my pay."

"Pay for what?"

"Helping save your silly snow house."

24

"You didn't turn a finger to save anything. The Eskimos helped — just to be friendly — and they wouldn't take a cent. But I'll pay you to get rid of you." He pulled out a five-dollar bill and slapped it into Zeb's hand.

"Five dollars," grunted Zeb. "It ought to be fifty."

"I'll give you fifty — fifty punches — if you don't get out." Soft-spoken Hal was really losing his temper.

Zeb went out with a final threat. "I'll see you again — you four-flusher."

There was a shot. Hal was out at once. Nanook, who had been sleeping in the lee of the igloo, was on his feet growling. The rascal had tried to kill their pet bear. Hal and Roger felt Nanook's hide. There was only a scratch near the neck.

Zeb was gone. He was so poor a shot that even a target as huge as a 1,000-pound bear had lost only a few hairs.

5
Who Cares about a Caribou?

The boys cared when one day a caribou came sliding down the hill behind the igloo, broke the wall, and fell in.

A caribou in the house! That was just too much.

Was it bad luck or good luck? Dad had asked the boys to get a caribou. And now one had been delivered to them.

The caribou belongs to the deer family. He is sometimes called the northern deer. But he differs from the deer we are used to. He doesn't have lovely brown eyes, and he's not gentle and friendly.

This one began thrashing about wildly. For some reason, he didn't feel at home in an igloo. His magnificent antlers ploughed into the kettle, the lamps, the pans, the dishes, and sent them all flying.

"Let's get out of here, quick," said Hal.

They got out, but not before they learned that the sharp horns of the caribou don't feel too good when they penetrate tender parts of the human body.

To the caribou this was not a home but a prison which he would tear to bits. He was dangerous at both ends – he had his horns in front and his heels behind.

The caribou is famous for his kick. It can kill, and has killed many interfering animals including the two-legged kind that call themselves men.

"He'll rip the igloo to pieces," Hal said.

He was not exaggerating. The horns were tearing down the snow blocks on one side of the igloo and those terrible heels were turning the other wall into snow-dust.

The noise of clashing pots and pans brought Eskimos to see what was going on. Among them was Olrik.

"Why did you put him in the igloo?" Olrik wanted to know.

"We didn't invite him," Hal said. "He invited himself. What do you do in a case like this?"

"Darned if I know," said Olrik. "That's one thing Harvard didn't teach us."

Zeb arrived. He knew just what to do. He sneaked in over the fallen blocks of snow and grabbed the caribou's stubby tail. At once the beast kicked Zeb in the stomach and sent him soaring ten feet away to land on a sharp rock. Zeb bent double, clutching his midriff and whimpering like a baby. He complained to Hal.

"You've got to pay me for this."

The fellow always wanted money for doing nothing.

Hal didn't answer. He couldn't waste time on a crybaby.

The igloo was now completely ruined. The caribou plunged out straight for the boys. Hal seized the horns and was lifted eight feet off the ground. Down he came but he still hung on. There were plenty of horns to go round, so Olrik and Roger took hold and brought the animal to a standstill.

Zeb, holding his stomach with one hand and a whip in the other, said, "I'll teach the brute."

As the whip came down Roger caught it and pulled it out of Zeb's hand.

"You interfering upstart," Zeb cried. "What do you know about wild beasts?"

"Not much," Roger said. "But I know a whip is no good if you want to calm down a terrified animal."

Still holding a horn with one hand he used his other hand to stroke the neck of the excited animal and he spoke sweet nothings into a big ear. He kept this up for a good ten minutes, stroking, speaking softly.

It was the old Roger magic. The animal had given up struggling. His eyes were fixed upon the boy. After all, he was just a boy and not worth killing. And he didn't seem to mean any harm.

It was lucky for Roger that it is not difficult to tame a caribou. Thousands of them have been tamed by the Eskimos of northern Canada and Greenland. They have been harnessed and can pull a plough or a wagon as well as any horse or ox. In fact they are much better than an ox. One caribou can draw a sledge with two men on it at a speed of up to eighteen miles an hour. To become tame, all they need is a little understanding.

Roger noticed that the caribou's feet were as big as soup plates.

"That's so he can walk on snow without sinking in," Olrik said.

"What's that funny flat bone that looks like a shovel just above his upper lip?" Roger asked.

Olrik replied, "That's exactly what it is — a shovel. He uses it to push the snow out of his way so he can get at the lichen underneath. For most of the year lichen is his only food."

"What is lichen?"

"It's something that will grow where nothing else will grow. It doesn't even have to have soil. It will grow on rocks. It's sometimes called reindeer moss because it's a little like moss, and all members of the deer family including the caribou consider it a good food. It keeps on growing even under snow. It never grows large, not over a few inches. Some Eskimos eat it — I've eaten it myself. It's not half bad."

"Dad told us to get one of these caribou," Hal reminded his brother. "He said it was the best friend of the Eskimos. It gives them most everything they need. Their warmest blankets are caribou hide, and their shoes can be made of it because it's strong. Its blood makes a good soup. They cut open the stomach to get the moss — they think it's as lovely as cake. The caribou provides them with meat, cheese, clothes, tents, buckets and bedding. In northern Canada the caribou have been the chief support of Eskimos for thousands of years. Clothes made from caribou hide are as warm as toast. You've got this one feeling pretty good, so I think it's time to take it to the airport."

The great animal, nine hundred pounds of bone and muscle, was led by the horns a mile to the airfield, where it was placed in a box-car. After a few more animals were added the box-car would be mounted on an airplane, which would then be called a skyvan and would take off on a night flight to Long Island.

6
Terrible Journey

The two Yanks and Olrik looked at the ruins of the snow house that Hal had so carefully built.

There was not one block of snow standing on another. The caribou had done a thorough job.

"Are you going to rebuild?" Olrik asked.

"After we come back," said Hal. This was a surprise to Roger.

"Are we going somewhere?"

"I've been thinking about making a trip," Hal said. "Up on the ice cap. Now is a good time to do it. Tonight we'll just sleep out in the open in our nice, warm, caribou-hide sleeping bags. Tomorrow we'll hire ten dogs and a sledge and take off."

"You don't need to hire anything," said Olrik. "You can use mine. Provided you let me go along with you."

"We'd like nothing better than to have you with us," said Hal. "Of course we'll pay you."

"Of course you won't," said Olrik. "We Eskimos don't do things that way. Friends don't pay each other."

Hal saw there was no use in arguing. He knew Eskimo

32

custom. If your friend did something for you, you would do something for him. Hal already had an idea of what he would do for Olrik and his parents. He would build them a stone house so solid that nothing could pull it down. This Eskimo's family now lived in an igloo. Hal had seen stone houses in Thule. The chinks between the stones were filled with mud which froze solid and kept out the cold. The roof was made of the skins of wild animals all sewn together, and sod completely covered the skins. This layer of earth was about three inches thick and froze almost as hard as ice. In summer it thawed a little, just enough for grass and flowers to grow in it. And what you really had was a roof garden above your head.

But he wouldn't breathe a word of this to Olrik until it was almost time for them to leave Greenland.

During the night snow fell, but the boys were snug in their furry bags and drew the flaps over their heads. In the morning they were practically buried under four inches of snow. Olrik couldn't find them at first. He saw two mounds and cleared them away only to find large rocks. Then at a little distance he saw the snow move as if it were alive. He cleared it away as best he could and discovered two very lively and hungry boys.

They heard a yapping sound that told them the dogs and sledge were already there.

"The huskies are ready to go," said Olrik.

"Why are they called huskies?" Roger asked.

Olrik explained. "A husky man is one who is big and strong. So they call these dogs huskies because they are big and strong."

They kicked off the snow that covered their supplies and had a quick breakfast. Then they loaded the sledge with all that they would need, mainly food. Also they put on crates and cages for the animals they expected to find.

"Where do we sit?" Roger wanted to know.

Olrik grinned. "You don't sit. You walk. Unless you get sick. In that case, you ride. But you can't expect the huskies to go so fast if they have to haul a big fellow like you."

The harness for the dogs was made of strips of walrus hide. The huskies looked powerful. Every one of them weighed ninety pounds or more. Olrik said they were the finest in Greenland. They looked a little more wolflike than most dogs.

The sledge was four feet wide. The runners were the long jawbones of the Greenland whale. Roger admired them. He saw the bottom of each one was covered with ice.

"How did that happen?"

"I made it happen," said Olrik.

"How?"

"You turn the sledge upside down. Then you pour water on the bottom of each runner. It quickly turns to ice. The well-iced runners glide smoothly over ice or snow."

"Do the huskies have to be fed three times a day?"

"Not on your life," laughed Olrik. "They are fed only once every two days."

"But don't they get hungry?"

"They do. And it's when they're hungry that they run fast. If they are stuffed with food they slow down."

"But how can we walk or run without sinking into the snow?"

"I saw you had skis. I have a pair also. We'll put them on and then we can get along as fast as the huskies do."

"How quiet your dogs are. Even when they bark it's hardly a bark."

"No," said Olrik. "They have only two ways of speaking. One is a growl, and the other is a howl."

"A howl," said Roger. "That's what wolves do."

"Right. And I wouldn't be surprised if there's a bit of wolf in every one of these huskies. That doesn't mean that they like wolves. They're deathly afraid of them. Wolves killed seven of my dogs – killed them and ate them."

"I hope we don't meet any wolves," said Roger earnestly.

"We probably will. But we won't worry about that now. Are you ready to go? Better wear your skis. I have mine here. Then we won't stumble along so badly in the snow."

They took off for the great beyond. Roger's heart thumped with excitement. Even his big brother was thrilled to think of the adventures that awaited them. They were going to travel on the mighty ice cap. Under them would be ice not three inches thick as on a lake or ocean, not three feet thick, but two miles thick. It seemed impossible.

It was not easy to get from the lowland up to the ice cap. It did not slope gently down from high to low. Instead it ended in a steep cliff three hundred or four hundred feet high. To get up such a cliff with ten huskies and a sledge was impossible.

There were only a few places in all Greenland where the abrupt cliff gave way to an easy slope from low to high. Olrik knew where to find the nearest one. The huskies were happy, the humans enjoyed speeding along on their skis in the sparkling fresh air straight from the North Pole.

Suddenly Olrik said, "Now you are on the ice cap."

The wind had blown the snow away and their skis were sliding over ice but it was only two inches thick.

"Is this a joke," Roger demanded.

"No joke," said Olrik. "This is the edge of one of the two greatest caps of ice in the world. The other is in Antarctica. Now all we have to do is go up and up and up. The famous ice cap is only a few inches thick here. We will keep going until it is two miles thick. If anyone wants to go back, now is the time to say so."

Nobody said so.

The rise was so gradual that they could still ski.

They had followed a road through the low country, but now there was no sign of a road.

Roger asked Olrik, "Why don't we go up one of the roads?"

Olrik answered, "There's no road across the ice cap."

"I can see that there's no road here. But there must be somewhere. How do people get from one shore of Greenland to the other shore?"

"There's no road anywhere. There will be some day. Then automobiles will stream across from one side to the other of the great ice cap. They will pull caravans, or perhaps they will live in motor homes. They will stop where they please and have all the comforts of home. That day hasn't come yet."

"How about snowmobiles — like the ones we have in

America?" Roger asked. "Then you could go anywhere without roads."

"I know," said Olrik. "I've been there and I've seen them. They are all right but I hope they don't come here soon. I like my friends, the huskies. And I'd rather have the peace and quiet of the dog team than the noise and stink of engines. Besides, if your gasoline or petrol or whatever you call it ran out where would you be? There's no place up here where you could get more. With dogs you don't have to worry. They don't run on gasoline. They eat only once in two days and they are always cheerful and eager. Besides, you can make friends with them and you can't do that with an engine."

Poor Olrik. The time would come, and soon, when the old pleasant way of life would change.

Now they were going up a slope so steep that they had to remove their skis, put them on the sledge and walk.

It was a stiff climb but the huskies never hesitated. Olrik didn't seem to mind it, but Hal and Roger did a good deal of snorting and puffing. Even the brave dogs were tiring. Roger understood now why his dream of resting comfortably on the sledge and being pulled up the mountain was not practicable. For three hours they struggled on.

Now they were nearing the top of the great ice cap. It didn't look at all as Roger had imagined it. He had expected that it would be perfectly rounded, as smooth as the top of an old man's bald head.

But instead it was all hills and holes. The holes were great cracks in the ice, sometimes forty feet wide and hundreds of feet deep. The hills were drifts of snow that had grown higher and higher under the strong winds so that they rose into the air anywhere from twenty to ninety feet high. The snow had turned to ice so that they looked exactly like icebergs, except that they were not floating in the sea but two miles up in the air on top of the Greenland ice cap.

"We can go around some of them," Olrik said. "But this one ahead is so long that we can't take the time to go around it. We'll simply have to climb over it."

Olrik picked out the place where this mountain range of ice could be climbed. It looked impossible to the boys from Long Island. But the huskies were tackling it and set an example of courage for the other climbers.

Up they went, slipping, sliding, advancing two yards and falling back one, but keeping at it until they reached the peak.

Now, what a view they had! Away down there by the sea was the city of Thule. Around them they could count seventy nunataks, which was what Olrik called the pyramids of snow and ice.

Judging by the position of Thule, Roger guessed the direction of the North Pole.

"It must be that way," he said. "Hal, what does your compass say?" Hal got out his compass. The needle didn't point to the North Pole. Instead, it pointed south-west.

"What do you make of that?" said Hal. "This compass must have gone crazy."

Olrik grinned. He thought that the crazy one was Hal, not the compass.

"You're forgetting something," he said. "A compass never really points to the North Pole."

"Then what does it point to?" Hal demanded.

"To the Magnetic Pole."

"I remember now. The earth is a sort of magnet or bowl of electricity. The electric centre is down there to the south-west. But if you were in New York and looked at the compass you would be so far away from both poles that the compass would give you a pretty good idea of due north."

"But up here", complained Roger, "we just have to guess where the North Pole is. It seems to me we've got to do a lot of guessing. We have to guess whether it is morning, noon or night. Look at that silly sun. All summer it never goes up in the sky. And it never sets. It just goes round and round, low down all summer. And up here, summer is like winter."

He shivered inside his thick caribou coat.

"Here it is June," he said, "and it's a sight colder here than in New York in February. Everything is the wrong way around."

"Well," laughed Hal, "that's what makes it interesting. You wouldn't want to find Greenland just another New York."

They went down the hill of ice and wound their way in and out and over the nunataks.

A bitter wind came up. Winds could be terrific on the ice cap. Down at Thule they were not so bad. But two miles up winds could tear over the surface of the ice cap at more than 150 miles an hour.

Soon they were all chilled to the bone.

To make matters worse, it began to snow. But it was the strangest kind of snow the boys from Long Island had ever known. It did not come down in big flakes. The strong wind ground the flakes into a powder.

"We call it snow dust," said Olrik.

Like dust, it got into the parkas that covered their heads,

inside their fur coats, even into their sealskin trousers, into every pocket, into their boots, and, worst of all, into their eyes, and into their ears, and even their mouths if they dared to open them.

Roger was lagging behind. He was a strong boy but he couldn't keep up with his twenty-year-old companions. An especially strong gust knocked him over and he lay in the snow. Oh, how good it was to lie down. He didn't care if he never got up. He was dizzy, tired, and all his natural energy was whipped out of him by this awful wind.

Hal looked back. He could not see his brother because of the dense cloud of flying snow dust. He called, but the screech of the wind was stronger than his shout. He would have to go back and find his brother. That should be easy – he need only follow his tracks.

But he found no tracks. They had promptly been filled by snow. Now, which nunatak had they come around last? He wasn't sure. He was getting lightheaded.

"Wait a minute, Olrik. We've lost the kid."

Olrik was only a few feet away but did not hear him. But Olrik saw him stagger. At once he reached out to help him.

"I can't see anything," Hal said.

43

"I know. You're having a white-out."

"What's a white-out?"

"It's a dizzy spell because wherever you look there's nothing but white — white on the ground, white in the air, and a white sky. It's all very confusing. Some people have gone crazy in a whiteout."

"Well, I can't go crazy because I've got to find my brother. If he's tumbled down in the snow, he may freeze to death. Which way did we come?"

"I'm not sure. Fact is, I'm having a bit of a whiteout myself," said Olrik. "But I know who can find him."

"Who?"

"The huskies."

He turned the dog-team about. Perhaps they thought they were going home. They went back as they had come and stopped where Roger lay in the snow. He was unconscious.

Hal pushed and pulled the body. "Wake up," he said. There was no response.

Olrik was worried. "Is he dead?"

Hal pulled off one of Roger's fur mitts and put his finger where the pulse should be. He could feel nothing. The hand was stiff with cold.

"I'm afraid he's gone," said Hal.

"Perhaps not. He's so cold the circulation has stopped in his wrist. Try his temple."

Hal put his finger on a point about an inch in front of the boy's ear. At first he felt nothing. His own fingers were so cold that even if there were a pulse he might not feel it. He put his hand inside his own coat and warmed it up. Then he tried again. He found a very slow, weak throb in his brother's temple.

"Thank the Lord," he yelled. "He's alive!"

"That's great," cried Olrik. "Too many have died up here. Let's wrap him up in a couple of caribou hides and put him on the sledge. He ought to warm up and wake up. Perhaps he won't – but we'll do our best."

The boy was bundled up in a caribou skin with the fur side inside. Around this was wrapped another skin with the fur side outside.

"That's the way we do it to get the most warmth," Olrik said.

The huskies, who had thought they might be going home, were turned about and the trip was continued.

For an hour Roger lay there without moving, his eyes closed. Then warmth and life seemed to steal through his body and he opened his eyes.

"What am I doing on the sledge?" he asked. "Am I a

piece of baggage?" He tried to throw off the covers.

"Just try to be baggage for a while longer," Hal said. "We almost lost you."

"I don't remember anything," Roger said. "Get me out of here. The dogs have enough to pull without me."

"Don't move," said Hal. "Just pretend you are the King of Siam and this is your golden chariot."

"The storm is letting up," Olrik announced. "Already there's a bit of blue above. In half an hour we'll see the sun. Then we'll stop for lunch."

"How can you tell when it's lunch-time?" Hal wondered.

"By my stomach," said Olrik. "I don't really know whether it'll be lunch-time or dinner-time or midnight. Anyhow, something inside me tells me that it's time to eat."

7
Perils of the Ice Cap

They put up a tent. It was easier than building an igloo every time they stopped. The tent was not made of canvas. It was far better than that. Thick caribou hide with plenty of shaggy hair still on the outside would keep out the cold and would also shut out the sunlight in case they wanted to sleep. The floor was another caribou hide.

"How about the dogs?" Roger asked. "Don't they have to be unharnessed?"

"No," Olrik answered. "The harness is very light – it won't bother them. If a bear came around and the dogs were not harnessed they might run away and we'd never see them again. Or they might gang up against the bear and kill it. You wouldn't want that to happen."

"But won't they freeze to death if they can't run?"

"They know how to avoid freezing. Come and take a look at them."

He took Roger around to the side of the tent. There Roger saw one of the strangest sights he had ever seen in his life.

What he saw was a great heap of dog flesh. The weary

huskies had piled up on each other so that every one of them was kept warm by the dogs who pressed against him on both sides or the dogs beneath or above him.

"Pretty smart dogs to think of that way of keeping warm," Roger said. He was about to enter the tent when Olrik stopped him.

"First get rid of your snow dust," he said. "It's all over you. You look like a ghost. If you go into the tent that way and start your little stove, the snow dust that covers you will melt and soak into your clothes. Then if you come out your wet clothes will freeze and you will be dressed in ice."

All three began to brush off the snow powder that covered them, blow it out of their noses, take it out of their ears and eyes, dump it out of their pockets, and turn their pockets inside out.

It was only when they were free of the pesky snow dust that they dared enter the tent, light the small portable stove, and eat.

"All I want to do now is sleep," Roger said. Hal and Olrik were quite willing to do just that. Hal was the only one who carried a watch. He took it out and looked at it. It had stopped. Whether he had banged it against some icy nunatak or some snow dust had gotten into it, there was no doubt that it was useless.

"Well, it doesn't matter what time it is," Hal said. "We're all tired – let's sleep."

It was some seven or eight hours later that Roger woke and looked into the face of a polar bear. It had forced its head in between the flaps and seemed to be trying to decide which of these juicy morsels to eat first. Roger had no desire to be a bear's breakfast. His yell woke up his two companions and they stared with horror and disbelief as the great beast forced its way into the tent.

Olrik felt guilty. He should have brought a gun. But Hal had told him not to because they were not killers.

But the polar bear is a killer and could not live if he were not. He must kill if he wants to eat. What do three non-killers do if they face a killer?

Hal picked up the heavy frying pan and prepared for battle. Before he could land this heavy weapon against the bear's nose, the unwelcome visitor turned into one who was very welcome. The monster went straight to Roger and rubbed its great furry head against the boy's shoulder.

"It's Nanook!" cried Roger. "Put away the frying pan."

The bear lay down beside Roger, gargling something that may have been his effort to say, "Good Morning". Roger put his arms around the great furry neck. Both boy and bear were very happy.

"How did he ever find us?" Roger wondered. "Our tracks must have been covered with snow."

Olrik explained. "It takes more than snow to defeat a bear's sense of smell."

"I didn't know we smelled as bad as all that," said Roger.

"Bad or good, it's all the same to the bear. Two things brought him to you. One was smell — the other was love."

They fed the bear and then had some food themselves. The three of them went out — the four of them — the bear following Roger.

It was a sparkling morning — if it was morning. The sun was shining bravely. It had of course been shining all the time they were asleep. The thick tent-hides had kept out the light. Now there was no snow dust, no wind. The sky was a great dome of pure blue.

But there was one thing that bothered Roger. "We're supposed to be after animals and we haven't seen one — except Nanook."

"They were all in their holes during the storm," Olrik said.

"I don't believe there are any animals up here. How could there be? There's nothing for them to eat — not a sprig of grass, not a leaf, nothing."

"They don't need grass or plants," said Olrik. "They're all carnivores, meat-eaters."

"Where do they get the meat?"

"By eating each other. The bear eats the wolf. The wolf eats the wolverine. The wolverine eats the fox, and so on. All these animals eat birds such as the auks, the barnacle goose, the pink-foot goose, the white-tailed eagle, the Greenland falcon, the snow bunting, the snowy owl and the raven. So, don't worry, there's plenty of food for everybody."

"Well," said Roger, "I think they're pretty smart to find it."

"You're right. I saw a fox hole near that nunatak. Come and see how smart the fox is."

They walked over to inspect the home of the fox. The animal was not present.

"Look in there," said Olrik. "See that pile of birds?"

"They don't have any heads," said Roger.

"Exactly. Even a fox can't eat heads. These are all auks. The fox bites off all their heads and piles up the bodies in neat rows, covers them with gravel, and puts stones on top. Then, when winter comes, he has a fine supply of food to last him through the dark months."

Roger was astonished. "I thought animals didn't have enough brains to think about the future."

"Some, like the fox, can plan ahead better than some people do," said Olrik.

It was such a lovely day that it seemed nothing bad could possibly happen.

But then it did. There was a wild commotion on the other side of the tent. The boys ran to see what was going on. Three wolves were not eating birds for breakfast. They were attacking the dogs.

"But they wouldn't really kill the dogs, would they?" said Roger. "After all, the huskies and the wolves are cousins."

"A cousin can kill a cousin," Olrik said. "Last year wolves killed all seven of my dogs."

Roger popped into the tent and came out with a pan. He started beating it loudly and sang. It was a sound the wolves had not heard before. With ears erect, they stared at the boy with the pan.

"See? They're scared. They'll run away," cried Roger.

The wolves ran, but not away. They attacked the boy with the pan. They had meant to make the dogs their breakfast, but this two-legged nuisance seemed to have plenty of meat on him and would make a good meal.

Hal and Olrik rushed at the wolves, yelling at the top of their lungs. The wild animals did not seem to notice them. Their savage teeth dug into the face and hands of the boy and they began to tear off his clothing. The wolves were the great heavy polar variety and Roger, though strong, could not resist them. They pushed him down on the ice and he lay there, protecting his face with his hands.

Hal began to sing. That was a strange thing to do, but Hal had learned that wolves hate singing. But this time the wolves paid no attention to the song.

Then, around the tent, came the great Nanook. With a roar that seemed to shake the nunataks, he attacked the wolves. In quick succession he swatted all three and they fell in a heap. The swat of a polar bear's paw is quite as strong as that of a lion. A lion can kill with one blow, and so can the great bear of the north. Two of the wolves were dead, and the third went limping away, howling.

Would the bear eat the breakfast so conveniently placed before him? That would be only natural, but since Nanook had just had his breakfast he left the carcasses where they were to be buried by the next snowfall.

Hal helped Roger to his feet and took him into the tent. He applied antiseptic to the scratches on Roger's face, then covered them with tape. He bandaged the boy's hands. Roger did not wince or whine although he was in great pain.

He thought he was being an infernal nuisance to his companions. Yesterday they had been forced to put him on the sledge. Today he would refuse to be treated like a baby. His legs were all right. A scratch had closed one eye but he could see with the other.

He saw Olrik taking food supplies out of the tent and putting them in a pile covered with rocks large enough to keep off animals.

"Where do these rocks come from?" Roger asked. Olrik pointed to the high mountains far to the east. There was no ice on them since they were so far up in the air.

"Rocks keep falling from those mountains."

"How do they get here?"

"You ought to know after yesterday. The terrific winds they have up here can move rocks a few inches every year. That isn't much – but give them thousands of years and they can travel great distances."

"Why did you put all those tins of food under the rocks?"

"That's called a cache. A traveller across these wastes leaves a cache of food once in a while so that when he comes back the same way it will be waiting for him and might save him from starvation. We'll put down several more caches as we go along."

"But will we be coming back exactly this way?"

"Very likely. That's because the dogs want to get home. They'll follow the same route they came by. That's husky intelligence."

They took down the tent, folded it, and strapped it to the sledge. It was a fine day, although quite a bit below freezing. The sun stayed so low that it gave off very little heat. Everybody was happy, including the fifteen–year–old behind his plasters and bandages.

8
Thunder River

"I hear thunder," said Roger, and he looked up at the sky. There was not a cloud in sight. The sky was one great vault of brilliant blue.

And yet Roger heard thunder, and so did Hal.

Olrik said, "It's not up there. It's down below. Pretty soon you'll see what makes it. We're just coming to Thunder River."

They arrived at what seemed to be the end of the world. They looked down a steep cliff several hundred feet to a rushing river. Its loud roar echoed against the cliffs. The noise was tremendous. The boys agreed that Thunder River was a good name for this frantic torrent.

"How do we cross that?" Hal asked. "Is there a bridge?"

"No bridge," was Olrik's answer.

"Then how?"

"Swim."

"You're joking," said Hal. "Three of us plus the bear plus ten dogs and a sledge? Swim?"

Olrik said, "You can swim, can't you?"

"Of course. But not in that."

Four of the dogs had gone over the edge and were suspended by their walrus-hide harness. They were whining pitifully and struggling so wildly that the rawhide lines that held them might break at any moment and drop them to the bottom of the abyss.

Olrik saved them by backing up the other dogs so that the ones hanging in space were also pulled up and away to safety.

Hal was bewildered. "Where does all this water come from?"

"From far away to the south where it is warmer than it is here. This is melt water from that part of the ice cap."

"Why doesn't it freeze over?"

"It's running too fast to freeze."

"Well, what do we do now? Can we go around it?"

Olrik shook his head. "That would take us hundreds of miles out of our way. No, we'll have to cross it."

"But how do we get down this cliff?"

"We don't. We'll go along the edge until we find a slope that may lead us down."

The three boys and Nanook did as Olrik suggested. They found a place where the slope was gradual enough for the dogs to go down while the boys held back the sledge to prevent it from sliding forward and breaking the legs of the huskies.

Now they were at the edge of the river. It was a roaring tumult of water. It rushed by like an express train. Its waves leaped many feet into the air.

"It's quite impossible," Hal said. "I suggest we turn around and go home."

Olrik laughed. "You don't really mean that. I suppose you can both swim?"

"Yes, but not in that," said Hal once more.

"And the dogs can swim. And the best swimmer of all is the polar bear. So why not strip off your clothes and pack them inside the tent, where they'll keep dry."

Hal still had his doubts. He knew that his young brother had been pretty well beaten up by the wolves. Would he be able to stand the beating he would get from the waves of this wild river?

"Let's get to it," said Roger. He took off his clothes and stowed them away. Hal did the same and so did Olrik. As for Nanook, he didn't mind getting his overcoat wet.

Olrik drove the huskies into the wild turmoil of water and foam. The huskies swam as these brave animals were used to doing, and the sledge floated on the surface. Waves broke over it but did not penetrate the inside of the tent. Roger hung on to the tail of the sledge. He was battered, bumped and pummelled by the waves but never let go. Nanook swam beside him protecting him from the worst of the rushing waves.

Hal swam without hanging on. That was his mistake. As soon as he came out of a back eddy into the main current he was carried off like a leaf in a gale. In vain he tried to swim back up to the sledge. It was no use. He was being carried steadily down toward the ocean. He crashed against unseen rocks. The waves played with him as if he were a football. One wave tossed him to the next wave, and they all howled with glee. They were having a good time, but Hal was not. He looked back and saw that the rest of the company had all reached the other shore. Hal was perhaps the best swimmer, except for Nanook. But now he was losing his nerve, getting short of breath, swallowing too much water.

He tried to reach either shore, but the central current was too strong and held him firmly in its grip.

His eyes began to cloud over and his head ached. A little more of this, and he would be finished.

Then he was aware that someone was beside him. Was it Olrik, or was it Roger?

It was Nanook. This magnificent swimmer of the animal world would save his life. He placed himself on the downstream side of the exhausted Hal, and with the boy's body pressed hard against him he swam to shore. Hal found himself dumped on a bank of gravel and it felt like a bed of roses. He lay there almost unconscious until Olrik and Roger came to help him to his feet. The bear stood in front of him, looking up at him. Hal weakly reached down and took the bear's right foot in his hand.

"Thank you, pal," said the boy to the bear.

9
Frozen Whiskers

The boys put on their clothes. The dogs had done their work well. The contents of the sledge had been splashed a bit, but there was no serious damage.

Hal's voice rose above the thundering voice of the river, "Imagine — a river on the ice cap! Are there any others?"

"Half a dozen," said Olrik. "They all come from the south, where the deep snow that falls on the ice melts quickly and is in a great hurry to get to the sea. Hal, I want to show you what you just missed."

"What did I miss?"

"Sudden death."

Olrik led them around a corner, and there was a sight that made Hal's blood run cold — a waterfall plunged down more than a hundred feet and created new thunder as it crashed on rocks below.

Said Olrik, "You would have been mushed to a jelly on those rocks if Nanook hadn't got to you just in time."

"Good old Nanook," said Hal.

"I think this is a good place to put another cache," Olrik said. "We'll remember it's just above the waterfall."

Again, food was stored under heavy rocks.

Five miles farther on another cache was made. "That makes three," said Olrik. "Now if we run out of food we'll be sure to have some waiting for us in these caches."

Even Olrik could be wrong. It was not going to be as easy as he thought.

The weather changed, as it suddenly does on the ice cap. The sun disappeared behind a cloud. Up came the wind. This time there was no snow dust, but something worse. This was an ice storm.

The boys had been tramping over broken ice. Now the wind swept pieces of ice into the air and they cut painfully into their faces. They even ripped holes in clothing. The wind howled like a wild beast. The dogs were whipped off their feet. The boys could hardly breathe. It was bitterly cold, but the great effort of fighting the storm made them perspire. Hal had not shaved since leaving the lowlands, and he had a short beard on his cheeks and chin. Sweat covered his face and promptly turned to ice. Hal tried to wipe off the ice but did not succeed. Roger laughed as he looked at his brother.

"That's what you get for not shaving," he said.

Hal tried to answer but his iced-over face was so stiff

that he could not say a word. Even his lips were frozen together.

He took off his mitt and put his hand over his mouth in order to melt the ice. It didn't work, because his hand was frozen.

He had been told that his hands would unfreeze if he rubbed them in snow. That was fine. The only trouble was that there was no snow. There was nothing but these flying pieces of ice as sharp as fragments of a broken window. Like knives, they cut his face and the blood oozed out only to be frozen at once and make him look more wild than ever.

Roger had done what he saw Olrik do. Olrik had twisted his parka around so that it covered his face. Now he could not see, but he placed one hand on the crossbar at the back end of the sledge and trusted the dogs to keep going in the same direction. Roger imitated Olrik and got along pretty well.

However, Hal had one advantage. He was the only one who saw the small Arctic fox who stood gazing with wonder at the strange things that were passing him. Hal scooped it up and popped it into a crate on the sledge.

That was easy, but he didn't have as much luck when he tried to snatch a wolverine. It bit him viciously but his frozen hand didn't feel the pain. He managed to get hold of it and toss it into another crate.

The wolverine is a bunch of black hair with teeth. It is very cunning and cruel. It has no friends. If it is caught in a trap, it will run away and carry the trap with it. The Eskimos are superstitious about it. They think it is an evil spirit. They are afraid of it because it is so powerful and they try to get its power by wearing a bit of wolverine fur next to their skin.

It is about the size of a bulldog and looks a little like a black bear, though much smaller. It is believed to be the most powerful animal of its size in the world. There are great numbers of this little rascal in the Arctic. It finds food in places where no other animal would look for it. It eats squirrels, hares, foxes, grouse, and birds when it can catch them. It lives in under-ice dens.

Hal had never seen one in a zoo and was sure that his father would be glad to have this unique beast to sell to some zoo-keeper who would appreciate such a strange animal.

Mr Frozen Face, the only one who could see, saw something else of great interest. He could not take care of this so quickly. He reached for the reins and stopped the dogs.

Olrik mumbled through his parka, "What's up?"

"The best of luck," said Hal. "Four baby bears."

There they were, four little fellows crowded close together to keep warm, and whimpering under the onslaught of flying ice. At a little distance was their mother, lying in the ice, stone dead.

A female polar bear usually has twins, but sometimes gives birth to quadruplets, four little bears. These were exactly what Hal wanted because there was a great demand for polar bears. And it was good that they were small. Any zoo would rather have a small bear that would live for twenty-five years than a big bear whose life was nearly over.

Olrik and Roger lifted their parkas just enough to watch Frozen Face pick up the orphans, one at a time, and tenderly put them in a little house of their own. Because the bitter wind sang through the crate, he covered the small creatures with a caribou mat.

The wolverine in the next crate made a violent effort to get at these small balls of meat and fur, his favourite food, but he didn't succeed.

When the ice storm died down the tent was again erected, and after a sleep they planted a new cache of food to await their return journey. Hal's icy face melted and he once more looked like a human being instead of a pillar of ice.

10
Dance of the Hobgoblins

A strange thing happened that day. A black cloud blotted out the sun and yet light came from the sky.

A very strange light, with many colours, red, yellow, green, blue, grey and violet.

"What in the world is that?" Roger asked.

Olrik said, "You are looking at what the dictionary calls the aurora borealis, but some Eskimos who never saw a dictionary imagine it to be a dance of hobgoblins."

"What's a hobgoblin?" Roger wanted to know.

"It's something that doesn't exist – like a devil or an evil spirit. Many people are afraid of it. They think it means that they are going to have trouble."

"We never saw this in Long Island."

"No, you are not likely to see it anywhere except north of the Arctic Circle."

What a show it was! Quivering rays of colour shot here and there. They bounced up and down as if they were dancing. They waved like a curtain blown by the wind. Every moment there was a change.

Sometimes they wound about like a serpent. Sometimes

the colourful little devils danced around in a circle. Sometimes there was a faint whistling sound. It was all very weird and Roger shivered.

Hal said, "You would think you were looking right up into heaven."

"The Eskimos don't think of it that way," said Olrik. "Their heaven is not up in the sky – unless they have become Christians. The old Eskimo tradition is that heaven is down in the centre of the earth where it is nice and warm at all times. Hell is up in the sky. It is bitterly cold. It sends down freezing storms upon the earth. Many of man's troubles come from the sky. Terrible winds come from there. Hail, so big that people must go indoors to get away from it, comes from above. The devil called Thunder and the other devil called Lightning come from there. Even the sun refuses to go up there. If you have led a bad life you'll go up there when you die and you will freeze solid and stay frozen through all eternity. If you have led a good life you will go down to that lovely, warm, comfortable place beneath the earth and you will be cosy and happy for ever."

Hal wished that he had a camera with a colour film to make a picture of this wild dance of the sky devils. But he didn't think of them as devils. He knew that the whole performance was electrical and rarely seen anywhere except in the polar regions. Once in Long Island he had noticed a white glow in the northern sky but there was no red, blue, green and so forth in it, and no dance of the hobgoblins. After all, to see some of the world's greatest performances you had to go to this savage land of ice and snow.

11
Musk-Ox in Evening Dress

"I think we can go on for about another five sleeps," said Olrik. "Then we'll turn around and go back."

Roger was puzzled. "Five sleeps! I suppose you mean five days."

"Well, I could hardly say that," said Olrik, "since we have only one day all summer long. The Eskimos don't count in days. They count the number of times that they sleep. They sleep when they are tired. But it's always daytime. The sun never quite sets until summer is over. The whole summer is just one day. But whenever we feel we have had enough we put up our tent and sleep."

"Why do you figure on five sleeps?"

"Because then our food will be almost gone. We will have just enough to get back to the last cache we set up. That was the fourth cache we made. There will be food enough there to carry us on to the third cache. What we get there will take us to the second cache. And then the first cache, and after that, Thule."

So they set out to do five more "sleeps" before turning back toward home.

"How's that hand of yours?" Olrik asked Hal.

"Still frozen solid," Hal said. "It doesn't hurt a bit. I know it'll hurt like fury when it starts warming up. I kept it out of the sleeping bag to keep it frozen so that I could get some sleep."

"It musn't stay frozen too long," said Olrik, "or the rot called gangrene will set in and you'll have to have your hand amputated."

The idea that his hand might have to be chopped off was not pleasant. Hal knew that a good snow rub was necessary. But as far as the eye could see there was nothing but ice.

Olrik looked at the sky. "Cheer up. Pretty soon it's going to snow."

It did snow before sleep time. Hal promptly gave his hand the snow treatment. He would have preferred to keep it frozen, because then it didn't hurt. Now it began to give him terrible pain.

"Good," said Olrik. "That means circulation is coming back. The blood is beginning to flow down into your hand."

"I don't understand it," Hal said. "Snow is cold, and yet it is warming my hand."

"Snow is not as cold as it seems," Olrik said. "Animals like to be covered by snow. They burrow into snowbanks to keep warm. When our dogs lie in a heap they are happy if they are buried in snow."

When Hal found that he could move his fingers he discontinued the snow bath and tucked his aching hand under his caribou jacket, where it could get the heat from his body. Here it gradually stopped hurting and felt like a hand once more, not a chunk of ice.

They travelled on for three sleeps, then came upon a treasure.

"A musk-ox!" exclaimed Olrik. "There used to be a lot of them in Greenland. Most of them have been killed, so now they are extremely rare. We are in luck."

The amazing thing about the musk-ox was its great coat of shaggy hair, hanging so low that it almost touched the ground.

"It reminds me of Mother," Roger said.

"Is that any way to speak of your mother?" Hal protested.

Roger explained. "Whenever Mom went out to a party or a concert, she wore a long evening dress that reached all the way down to her feet."

Olrik laughed. "You have a good imagination, Roger, if you can compare this beast to your mother."

"But what's the use of all that hair?"

"It's a lot better than a lady's evening dress," said Olrik. "It keeps the animal warm even when the temperature is way down below zero. It really consists of two coats — two heavy layers, and inside them there is a lovely undergarment of beautiful wool softer than cashmere. And there's one other thing the long evening dress is good for. If the musk-ox has a baby it can conceal the youngster behind those heavy curtains of fur."

Hal sniffed the air. "What's that strange smell?" he asked.

"It's not a bad smell and it's not a good smell. What is it?"

"Musk," said Olrik. "The lady is not only wearing evening dress, she is using perfume."

"Well," said Hal, "it doesn't exactly smell like perfume."

"Perhaps not," said Olrik, "but the manufacturers of perfume couldn't get along without it. In almost every bottle of perfume there is some musk."

"Do they get it only from the musk-ox?"

"No – some other animals secrete musk – the civet, musk-rat, otter, and the musk-deer."

The musky musk-ox showed no inclination to run away. Instead it acted as if it might charge at any moment. It tossed its great head around, made threatening grunts, and lowered its curved, sharp-pointed horns dangerously.

"But I'm sure the lady would be too much of a lady to attack us," Roger said.

"Don't be too sure," said Olrik. "It happens that this lady is no lady. This is a bull. He would like nothing better than a fight and he could kill us all in a few minutes."

The bull was angrily pawing the ground.

Hal didn't wait to be flattened under that quarterton of wild beast. He drew his sleep gun from the sledge and sent a dart into the animal's neck. The medicine in one dart was not enough to put the beast to sleep but at least it would calm him down. The bull turned and began to wander away. Hal's lasso whistled through the air and the loop settled over the great head just behind the horns. Hal fastened the end of the line to the sledge and Olrik snapped the long whip over the dogs. The ten huskies began to pull and the musk-ox, half asleep, staggered along behind.

After five sleeps they all turned about and headed for home.

They got one more fine animal – a wandering reindeer. This was a polar reindeer, quite different from the reindeer of Lapland. It did not bite them and was easily captured. It was graceful and beautiful. Unlike the musk-ox it had no curtains reaching to the ground. Its body was well formed and its horns were magnificent. This was a male. The female also has horns, but not so large.

"You judge reindeer antlers by the number of points," said Olrik. "I've made a careful count and find there are sixty points in this animal's fine set."

"Does the reindeer have any enemies?" Roger asked.

"It doesn't like wolves," Olrik answered. "And its worst enemy is the raven."

"How can a raven do any harm to a big reindeer?"

"It swoops down and pecks out its eyes."

"You said the animals on the ice cap live by eating other animals," Roger said. "But I don't believe the musk-ox and reindeer eat other animals. So how do they live on the ice cap?"

"They scratch away the snow from the rocks and eat the lichens that grow on them."

Like the musk-ox, the reindeer was attached by a long line to the sledge and walked along behind.

Click, click, click went his feet.

"What's all the clicking about?" Roger asked.

Olrik answered, "The bones in the reindeer's feet rub together and make that noise. All the little animals hear that sound and get out of the way. I don't know of any other animal on earth that clicks as he walks along. There's one other way that the reindeer is different. He has flat feet as big as pancakes."

"I'm getting hungry," said Roger.

"We're all out of food," Olrik said, "but we don't have to wait long. As soon as we get to the first cache we can eat."

12
Starving Is No Fun

After the last sleep there had been no breakfast. There would be no lunch. Some hours later they should get to the cache.

The dogs ran twice as fast as usual because they were going home. But even this was not fast enough for the stomachs of the hungry boys. Then Roger had an idea.

"Don't reindeer pull sledges in Lapland?"

"So I've heard," Hal said.

"Well, we have a reindeer. Why can't he pull instead of being pulled?"

Olrik said, "I should have thought of that. Hal, you have a bright kid brother."

He stopped the team. The huskies were not harnessed two by two as in Canada where the whole outfit must be narrow to get through the trees. On the ice cap there were no trees – so the dogs were spread out in a sort of fan. Each dog could see straight ahead instead of having nothing to look at but the rear of the dog in front.

The reindeer was brought around and placed in the

middle of the fan, five dogs on one side of him and five on the other.

Then Olrik cracked his whip and away they all went like the wind. The boys could not run so fast, so they climbed on to the sledge.

This did not slow things down in the least. The reindeer was so strong and swift that he was almost equal to all the dogs put together.

The musk-ox kept up well in spite of the wind that caught his side curtains and sent them flying up in the air.

As for the great thousand-pound bear, he could have been excused for being slow because of his weight. But he was not slow. All his life he had been forced to run if he wanted to eat. Even now he stopped for an instant to put his teeth into a lemming, and again to catch an Arctic hare, yet he at once regained his place beside the rushing sledge.

So it was not surprising that they came in sight of the cache sooner than they expected. The boys shouted and the dogs howled. Soon they would fill those aching stomachs.

But as they came nearer, Olrik began to worry. The stones he had put over the food had been disturbed.

Something or somebody had been tampering with the cache.

He hauled his team to a stop beside the cache.

It was empty.

Not one scrap of food remained.

"Look," said Hal. "Aren't those bear tracks?"

"That's just what they are," said Olrik, "and the tracks go that way."

Nanook was sniffing the tracks. Then he began to follow them. Behind a big clump of ice he found the thief.

At once there was a battle royal. The other bear was as big as Nanook. But he was loaded down with food and his reactions were slow. Nanook gave him a thorough lambasting, tearing out his fur, bloodying his nose, biting off his tail.

But that didn't get the food back. Roger called Nanook. His huge pet came at once. The other bear stumbled off. He had been taught a lesson. He would think twice before robbing another cache.

Olrik, who was as hungry as the others, tried to be cheerful.

"Never mind," he said. "Let's hope we have better luck at the next cache."

But when they arrived at the spot they saw wolf tracks

all about. A pack of wolves had been here. However, the stones still stood up, so the food must be under them.

Then Olrik noticed that just one stone low down had been pulled away. The hole was big enough for wolves, one at a time, to crawl in and steal their dinner.

He pulled down the other stones and saw that all the supplies had vanished.

Hal and Roger could have stormed at Olrik for not building better caches. They didn't. They knew that Olrik had done his best, and now he was just as hungry and unhappy as they were.

"Sorry," said Olrik.

"Not your fault," said Hal.

Having eaten nothing, they were even more weary than usual. So they put up their tent and went supperless to their sleeping bags.

The animals did better. The dogs, the musk-ox and the reindeer all scraped away the snow and ate the lichen that grew on rocks.

Roger heard them scratching and chewing, and crawled out to see what was going on.

Lichen! They were all eating lichen. It must be good.

He scraped away some of it and put it in his mouth. It was bitter. Manfully, he swallowed it. His indignant stomach threw it up. It would rather be empty than try to digest such fodder.

Roger thought he would have some fun with his brother and Olrik. After sleep he said, "You don't need to be hungry any more. You've got tasty food all around you."

"What do you mean?" demanded Hal.

"Lichen. It's on all the rocks. You'll love it. Just try it."

They were hungry enough to try anything. Their faces twisted as they tasted the bitter lichen. They swallowed it, and up it came.

Hal glanced at Roger. "You son of a gun. If I weren't so weak I'd wallop you so hard that you couldn't stand up."

"I'm glad you're weak," said Roger.

Surely, by the time they reached the cache above the waterfall, their bad luck would turn to good. But a crack between the stones was just large enough to admit an Arctic fox. His tracks as he came were light, and heavy as he left loaded down with a good meal.

Now they had to cross Thunder River. The reindeer was unhitched. Roger had said he wanted to ride it.

"You'll both sink," said Olrik. "You and the reindeer."

But Roger remembered what he had read about reindeer. Every hair of the reindeer was hollow and was full of air, which meant that the reindeer couldn't sink even if he tried. His body was so high out of the water that Roger rode across without getting wet.

Hal and Olrik put their clothes inside the waterproof tent. Olrik drove the dogs and sledge across, and Hal swam.

The line that held the musk-ox broke and the beast in his heavy evening dress was swept down toward the falls. If he went over the waterfall he would be killed on the rocks below.

The best swimmer of all, Nanook, gripped one end of the trailing dress and swam against the strong current to the other shore. The bewildered musk-ox clambered out on the sand, making his own waterfall as the river water poured out of his masses of shaggy fur.

The dogs were used to going without food for many sleeps, but the boys slept the sleep of utter exhaustion.

Feeling more dead than alive, they lay on the sledge until the final cache was reached. Here there were no animal footprints. But there were human prints, of heavy boots. And the cache was empty.

Somebody had stolen the food. How could any man be so mean? Whoever it was could be charged with murder if one of the starving boys fell dead.

Nothing was left in the cache except a slip of paper. Hal picked it up. It was a picture of Zeb. Zeb was in the habit of carrying a bunch of pictures of himself and handing one out to anybody he met. He had dropped this one by mistake.

The boys went on to Thule, where they made straight for an eatery.

"Don't eat too much," Hal warned them. "Our stomachs aren't used to food. They'll just throw it up, unless you eat very little. A couple of hours later, you can eat a little more. After another hour, some more. Take it easy, or you'll have trouble."

They felt like devouring everything in the place, but they followed Hal's advice and went easy. Then they had food put up for them to eat later.

Off to the airfield to put their haul of animals into the box-car. The snow-white Arctic fox, the wolverine, the four small polar bears, the great musk-ox, the beautiful polar reindeer. The airport hands slid the box-car on to the flat deck of the skyvan and Hal wired his father to expect the shipment.

Not until this was done did they think of making a home for themselves. They went back to the ruins of their igloo and began building a new one.

Zeb strolled over, not to help, but to look on.

"What did you do that for?" said Hal.

"Do what for?" said innocent Zeb.

"Steal everything in that cache."

"You're out of your head," Zeb replied. "I don't know anything about any cache."

"Oh, you don't? How about this picture?" He pulled out Zeb's photograph.

"Well, what's the matter with that?" said Zeb. "It's a pretty good picture of me, isn't it?"

"Yes, it is," said Hal. "It's the picture of a thief and a killer. I picked it up in the cache. You should be arrested for attempted murder. But since you're only a half-wit, we'll just give you a good spanking."

"Spank me?" yelled Zeb. "Do you think I'm a baby?"

"That's just what we think. Heave ho, boys." And all three, Hal, Roger and Olrik, grabbed Zeb, laid him face down over a snowbank, and gave him such a hard beating that Zeb would never forget it as long as he lived.

13

The Man Who Ate His Foot

"What did he do?"

The question was asked by one of the Eskimos who had gathered to see the spanking.

"Just tried to kill us," Hal said. "Stole our food from the cache."

"He should go to prison for that."

"He doesn't know any better," said Hal.

"Empty up here?" said one man, tapping his head.

Hal nodded. He noticed that the Eskimo who had just spoken was on crutches. One foot was gone.

"What happened to your foot?"

"I ate it."

"You're joking," said Hal.

"It was no joke," replied the Eskimo, a fine-looking fellow, strong, and taller than most of his people. "You know what a bad place it is – up there on the ice cap. I went for days without one scrap of food. My right foot froze solid. There was no feeling in it at all. I couldn't give it the snow rub – the wind had blown away the snow. If I didn't do something, gangrene would crawl up my leg and kill me. So I took my snow knife and chopped off my foot."

"Wasn't that very painful?"

"I didn't feel it at all. All I knew was that I would die if I didn't get something to eat. So I ate my foot."

"I don't blame you," said Hal. "My hand froze. If there hadn't been snow to warm it I might have done what you did. By the way, where did you learn English?"

"In school. We had to learn Danish and English."

"And the Eskimo language?"

"We learned that from our parents."

"So you speak three languages!" said Hal. "You're way ahead of me. I speak only one."

The idea that an Eskimo could be smarter in any way than a Yank was hard to believe.

"What's your name?" he asked, forgetting that an Eskimo never gives his name. A man close by said, "His name is Aram."

Hal shook hands with Aram. "What do you do now?"

Aram said, "I teach in the school that used to teach me. I'm lucky. I get a good salary and my folks are rich. All I lack is one foot."

There was one thing a man on crutches could not do. He could not help build an igloo. Hal had been working while talking and with the aid of Olrik, Roger, and the Eskimos, the new snow home was ready for use.

"Aram, you will be our first guest. Come into our palace."

Roger went in with them, but Olrik said, "You must excuse me. I've got to get my dogs home and feed them."

Hal, Roger and Aram sat down on the double thickness of caribou hide that covered the ground. How good it was, after all the danger and agony of the desert of ice over which they had travelled.

"Many people have starved to death up there," Aram said.

Hal said, "The only food we found was lichen, and we couldn't keep it down."

"I know a man", said Aram, "who ate his trousers, made of caribou hide. And another who ate his seal-skin mittens. And two men who had to eat their dogs. And one who ate his sleeping bag. And a party ate the walrus hide that they had wrapped around the runners of their sledge. And one ate his boots, and went on barefoot over the ice until his feet froze. And two men ate the fleas and lice that they picked off their dogs. And one ate his own clothes made out of animal skins. And one kept alive seven days by eating those little animals you call lemmings, along with leather scraps and bones."

"How could anybody eat bones?" Roger asked.

"You should try it some time," said Aram. "It can be done if your teeth can stand it. Inside the bones there is marrow and it is good food. If you can't break the bones with your teeth you can crush them between two rocks."

"I ate a couple of mice," said Hal, "but I didn't like them any more than they liked me."

"You were lucky", Aram said, "that your dogs didn't eat each other."

"They weren't quite that hungry", Hal said, "because we cut up a walrus hide into pieces so small that they swallowed them without chewing. I had heard that they lie in the stomach for days before they are completely digested. So the dogs did a little better than we did."

"If you eat your dogs," said Aram, "you are apt to come down with a disease called trichinosis and it will kill you."

"That's the last thing we would do, eat our fine huskies," said Hal.

Aram said, "Another thing that can kill you is sweat. Running along, you are apt to sweat. The sweat turns to ice. Your whole body is encased in ice like a suit of armour. At first it's painful. Then it becomes comfortable and you get drowsy as the circulation of your blood slows down. And then you die."

Hal said, "Aram, what would you say is the most dangerous thing on the ice cap? Is it the bear, or the wolf, or what?"

"No," said Aram. "The most dangerous thing is man. Many crimes have been committed on the ice cap. There are no police up there. The fellow called Zeb nearly finished you off."

Hal laughed. "Well, he didn't succeed. And I'll bet his backside feels so bad now that he's sorry he tried. Now, let me serve you something a little better than mice, lice and old boots."

He took a pan from the little stove and filled three bowls with a rich, delicious soup he had bought at the Thule eating place.

They relaxed in the cosy igloo and Hal murmured, *"Home, Sweet Home."*

14
Ghosts Get Angry

Aram took them to see his parents.

"They are very good people," he said, "but you mustn't mind their old-fashioned ideas. They never went to school. They live in the farthest north where people have not changed their ways in a thousand years."

Hal and Roger went with him to the airport, where Aram kept a small plane. Boarding it, they flew past Thule and on to the shore of the polar sea. There was nothing between this land and the North Pole.

Here, at the edge of the world, the igloos were better built. Farther south the art of igloo building was dying out since so many Eskimos now lived in stone and sod houses.

Aram took them to a beautifully built igloo with a large window made of a sheet of transparent ice.

The boys were warmly received by Aram's father and mother. They did not speak English, but Aram translated everything they said.

"An old man is happy that you have come to see him," said the father.

Roger was puzzled. He asked Aram, "Who is the old man he speaks about?"

"Himself," said Aram. "Eskimos are very modest. They think it is rude to say 'I' or 'me'. So they speak as if they were talking about someone else."

The mother spoke and her voice was very low and sweet.

"My mother," said Aram, "wants you to know that an old woman is surprised that you have come so far to see people who are not worth bothering about. And she asks if you would like some fresh blubber. Say yes."

Hal nodded and smiled. "Tell her that her visitors would be delighted to have some fresh blubber."

Roger objected. "Hey, what are you getting us into? Blubber is the fat that animals up here have under their skin to keep out the cold. Who wants to eat a chunk of stinking fat?"

"You do, tough guy," said Hal. "Be polite, or we'll kick you out. Smile and bow."

Roger smiled and bowed. He didn't do it too well. He took the blubber and tried not to wrinkle his nose in disgust as he swallowed the greasy stuff as quickly as possible.

Aram's mother was delighted. She said gently, "An old woman who is no good would be proud to have a son like this one. He is half Eskimo already."

The father said, "An old man thinks you must be very happy to get away from your country where it is so hot and there is no snow for a sledge."

Roger wanted to say, "Baloney!", but Hal replied, "Yes, in New York all summer we don't have one bit of snow. And it's so hot we have to turn on what we call 'air conditioning' to cool the house."

The old folks shook their heads sadly. Father said, "An old man thinks you were very lucky to come here. In your country you don't even have the North Pole."

Hal said, "I've heard that the Eskimos never punish their

children. How do you make them behave? Surely you spank them once in a while."

The old man turned to Aram. "Were you ever spanked?"

"Never," said Aram. "Perhaps I should have been."

"No," said the old Eskimo. "Striking a child just puts an evil spirit into him. The air is full of evil spirits trying to get into us."

"He means ghosts," Aram smiled. "The Eskimos believe that everyone who dies becomes a ghost and tries to do mean things to the living. If anyone gets sick, it's an evil ghost that is making him sick. So they think. There is no doctor up here – only the medicine man. He sells you all sorts of things that are supposed to keep off the ghosts. Perhaps they will show you some of them."

He spoke to his parents. At once they began to lay out all the things they had bought from the medicine man – they called him a shaman – and the boys were bewildered by the vast numbers of things that the shaman had insisted they must have to keep off bad ghosts.

A seal's eye to fend off the evil eye.

A rabbit fur against frostbite.

A bear's claw to keep off the evil spirit called lightning.

An ermine's tail against the wild dance of devils in terrible storms.

A caribou tooth to avoid starving. ("Just what we needed when we had no food," said Hal.)

The paw of a wolverine to keep you from going crazy.

The head of a fox so no one could play tricks on you.

The ear of a deer so you could hear well.

The skin of a lemming against sickness.

And many more.

Surely the cloud of ghosts that were supposed to fill the igloo had no chance to do harm so long as they were held off by all these ghost-stoppers.

No wonder the shaman got rich, selling these worthless objects to people who trusted him and believed everything he said.

"Every month when the moon is great," said the old man, "the shaman goes up to see the man in the moon who will tell him what to do next."

The mother gathered up a large pan of food. She said, "An old woman will take this to our neighbour, who has nothing to eat." She went out, and came back presently with an empty pan.

When had the boys from Long Island seen anyone take a good dinner to a neighbour?

Never.

No matter how ignorant these people were, their hearts were true and kind.

They would not let the boys go without feeding them well. Meat was served to each of them. It was raw and it was rotten. And it smelled.

The mother said, "We have been keeping it a long time. Now it is ripe and ready to eat. Some white people cook it. That spoils it. An old woman hopes you will like it."

Roger's stomach almost threw up its blubber. The odour of the rotten meat made him want to hold his nose. His hand started to go up, but Hal caught it in time.

"It won't kill you," he said. "Eat it, and like it."

"I'll bet you're not going to eat yours."

"Watch me," said Hal.

He put a gob of it in his mouth. His face took on an expression of utter agony. He sneezed, and his delicious meat sprayed out all over the caribou floor. The old woman at once cleaned it up, and put it back on Hal's plate.

Roger laughed until he thought he would burst.

Hal began to apologize. "It's nothing," said the mother, Aram interpreting. "You're just not used to it. I did the same thing when someone gave me cooked meat."

Hal and Roger downed the meat. It stayed down. They were very proud of themselves.

A young man came in. He seemed very unhappy.

"Something awful has happened. My wife had a baby."

"Is that awful?" Aram's mother said.

"No. The awful thing is this — the baby has no teeth. It's our first baby. Should we throw it away? How can it eat without teeth?"

"Your wife will nurse it," said Aram's mother.

"But it would be bad for it to grow up without teeth. I think we will throw it into the sea. Perhaps the next baby we have will have teeth."

He was just going out when the old man called him back.

"I don't think you understand," he said. "Look at Aram. He had no teeth."

"No teeth? It's strange that he is still alive. How does he get along without teeth?"

"He has teeth now. Show him your teeth, son."

Aram bared his teeth.

"How did he get them?" said the worried young father. "Some people put caribou teeth in their mouth."

"Those didn't come from any caribou. And he didn't have them when he was born. But they grew up later."

"That doesn't make sense. You're just trying to comfort me. Our baby wasn't born without hands. He wasn't born without a nose, or without ears. He has legs, and ten toes. He's all there — except teeth. That's bad — and you can't tell me it's good. I think I'll dump the brat."

"You'll do no such thing," said Aram's mother. "Just be patient. The teeth are there, but they haven't come up yet. Give them time. It's your wife you should be thinking about just now — not your baby. I will go and see if she is all right."

She looked at Hal and Roger. "I'm sorry. Perhaps you will come again." And she was gone.

15
Flight to the North Pole

Hal looked out through the ice window to the polar sea.

"Just think," he said, "the North Pole is right over there."

"I can't see it," said Roger.

"Neither can I. It's seven hundred miles away. Peary spent years trying to get across that 700-mile stretch by dogteam. He didn't get there until 1909. The first man to get to the North Pole."

"Now you can get there in two hours," said Aram.

"You don't mean it," Hal said. "No dogs could cover seven hundred miles in two hours. Besides, the sea is all broken up by drift ice. And there are wide lanes of water between the floes."

"Floes?" said inquisitive Roger. "What are floes?"

"You're looking at them," said Hal. "Those pieces of floating ice are called floes."

Roger saw one that was as flat as a raft and about twelve feet wide. "Are they all like that?"

"Some are smaller. Some are much larger. I've heard of a floe that was as big as the state of Connecticut."

"Gee!" exclaimed Roger. "The North Pole right there and we can't get to it."

"Yes you can," said Aram. "I'll take you."

"You're kidding," said Hal.

"No I'm not. Button up your caribou coat and come along. Next stop, North Pole."

He led them out to his plane. They climbed in, still doubting that Aram could do what he promised.

Away they flew, over the floes and the open water between them, with no worry about dogs and sledges that had made the journey so difficult for Admiral Peary.

Within two hours they came down on a great expanse of ice.

"Meet the North Pole, gentlemen," said Aram.

"But there's nothing here," said Roger as he stepped down.

"And there never will be," said Aram. "There is no land under this ice – nothing but water fourteen thousand feet deep. What you are standing on is just a great ice floe. And like all floes it drifts."

"But", said Hal, "I understood that Peary planted a mast here with a flag to prove that he had reached the Pole."

"Right," said Aram. "But the floe where he planted his mast and flag floated away. And another floe came, and

100

another, and another. Floes are always on the move. The wind blows them along, or a current carries them. I suppose thousands of floes have passed over the Pole during the seventy years since Peary was here."

"So there's been nothing here since Peary's time?"

"Oh yes, other people have tried. They can't get it through their heads that nothing will stay at the North Pole. The Russians put a weather observatory here. It drifted away. Another expedition brought ten tons of building material and put up a station. When they came back, it was gone."

"But there's a station at the South Pole and it doesn't float away," said Hal.

"It can't move," said Aram, "because there is land beneath. Here there's just water."

"Anyhow," said Roger, "it's great to be here on the very tip-top of everything. You just can't go any farther north than this."

"Yes," said Aram, "this is the end of north. Nor is there any east or west here."

"How do you make that out?"

"Well, just think a bit. There's no direction here but south. It's south to Greenland, isn't it? And it's south to Canada. It's south to Alaska. It's south to Norway. It's south to Great Britain. And that brings you back to Greenland – we will go south to get there. Anywhere you turn, you are looking south."

A big plane roared overhead. It did not stop. "Where's it going?" Roger wondered.

"It's a Japanese plane," said Aram. "It's going from Greenland to Japan. Our trading post buys a lot from Japan."

"But why does it fly over the North Pole?"

"Because that's the shortest way. The trip around the world to Japan would be twice as long."

"I can't imagine that," said Hal. "I'll have to look at a map."

"A map won't help you," said Aram. "It's flat. The earth is round, like a globe. Drop in at my school. We have a globe there. You can measure the distances – over the Pole, or around the earth."

"So there's a lot of traffic over the Pole?"

"Dozens of planes every day." Aram laughed. "It's as busy as Times Square, or Fleet Street. And it's not just the planes that go this way. Since the submarine *Nautilus* passed under the North Pole in 1958, many subs do the same every year. Since the water is more than two miles deep, there is plenty of room under the ice for a sub to go full speed without bumping into anything more than a fish or two."

"Or a whale or two," laughed Hal.

"They don't come this far north," said Aram.

There was a crashing sound as their floe was struck by other floes, hurled against it by the waves.

"I think we'd better get going," said Aram, "before this floe breaks up under us."

He flew them back to their igloo. The next day Hal visited Aram's school and examined the globe. Aram was right. The shortest way to many lands was over the North Pole.

No longer was it a place of mystery. Many explorers had given their lives in the struggle to reach it. Without any effort, thanks to Aram, the boys had stood where Peary had stood, *on the top of the world*.

16
The Walrus Said . . .

"The time has come," the Walrus said,
"To talk of many things:
Of shoes — and ships — and sealing-wax —
Of cabbages — and kings —
And why the sea is boiling hot —
And whether pigs have wings."

So Lewis Carroll wrote about the walrus.

The Eskimos call it "the sea horse".

That makes two sea horses in the ocean. The walrus is one. The other is the little fellow two or three inches tall who always stands up on his hind feet and who has a head that looks exactly like the head of a horse.

The Eskimos also call the walrus "The Old Man of the Ice Floes".

And he does look like an old man as he sits on his floe, his tusks almost three feet long hanging straight down. At a distance, the white tusks look like a long white beard.

John Hunt had asked his sons to capture a walrus. To do this it was necessary to use a kayak.

"What's a kayak?" Roger asked his big brother.

Big brother knew a lot, but he had never been in a kayak.

"It's a sort of canoe," Hal said. "But it's quite different from the canoes that we have used for hundreds of miles in our travels. It's not made of wood like the canoe. There's hardly any wood in north Greenland – so they use sealskin."

"What good is that? Couldn't a walrus punch a hole in it with one of his tusks?"

"You guessed it. That's a risk we have to take. If that happens, I'll meet you at the bottom of the sea."

They hired two kayaks. The owner told the boys how to use them. "A kayak takes one person only. You notice that all the top of it is covered except for one hole where you get in."

"It's as good as a canoe," Roger said.

"It's a lot better than a canoe. If a canoe upsets, you drown unless you are a good swimmer. If a kayak upsets, you just flip it back up and you are not even wet."

"How come? How can you go upside down and not get wet?"

"You wear this sealskin coat. No water can get through it. The hood is watertight. The collar fits tightly around your neck. The sleeves are tight-fitting. Best of all, the

105

lower edge of the sealskin fits into this ring around the manhole so that not a drop gets into the kayak even if it is upside down."

"That's wonderful," Hal admitted. "But if you are upside down, how do you get right side up again?"

"You must hang on to your paddle. One stroke of the paddle, and up you come."

"Great," said Roger. "I can't wait to try it."

Hal was anxious about what might happen to his eager brother.

"Take it easy," he said. "Watch me. I'll try to do it right and you copy me."

The kayaks were only ten feet long and far lighter than any canoe they had ever carried around a waterfall or rapids. They carried them over their heads to the water's edge, launched them, and carefully stepped in, making sure to lock themselves into the ring around the manhole so no water could get into the kayaks.

Then they paddled off, searching for "The Old Man of the Ice Floes".

Usually a walrus hunter carried a harpoon, since his purpose was to kill the beast. But the boys had a much harder job. Their father would have no use for a dead walrus. They must take it alive. Each boy carried a lasso.

The Eskimo owner of the kayaks stood on the shore watching the boys hunting for a 3,000-pound walrus with nothing but two pieces of rope.

"They are just like children," he thought. "We Eskimos are much wiser than these children from the hot lands."

And the "children from the hot lands" considered themselves far better than the ignorant folk of the Arctic. Who was right? It was hard to say.

Hal had his doubts about this adventure. To take a walrus with a rope was like trying to catch an elephant with a piece of string.

Finding a walrus was the easy part. There were dozens of them, each on a cake of ice, singing their hearts out. Well, not exactly singing. The sound was more like the bellow of a bull or the bark of a bloodhound. Anyhow, it tore the air apart with noise. As the kayaks came near, they slid off their icy pedestals and disappeared under water.

"They're all gone," said Roger.

"Never mind. They have to come up to breathe."

"How long can they stay down?"

"About nine minutes."

"What do they do down there?"

"Use those sharp tusks to dig up the bottom for shellfish."

"Do they swallow them, shells and all?"

"No. I've read that they crush the clam shells between their flippers, then drop the pieces of shell and eat the clam."

"But clam shells and oyster shells are like iron. How could they break them with a pair of flabby fins?"

"Not so flabby," said Hal. "A walrus could take your head between its fins and turn it into a pancake."

"It must be as strong as a horse. No wonder they call it a sea horse. How deep does it go? Thirty feet?"

"More like three hundred feet. A man is apt to get the bends if he goes down a hundred feet without a scuba. The walrus does three times as well. But if he doesn't come up for breath, he dies. Watch. Here they come now."

Up they came, poking their black heads out of the water and whistling a tune as they inhaled – not once, but a dozen times until every crevice of their lungs was full of air.

They were annoyed to find the kayaks still there and roared their disapproval. A big bull charged Hal's kayak and upset it. Hal forgot what he had told Roger not to forget. Surprised by this sudden attack, he let go of his paddle. It was a strange feeling, his head hanging three feet under water, as he held his breath, paddling desperately with his hands to turn the boat upright.

It didn't work. His hands were not as good as a paddle.

He groped about but could not find it. He was getting dizzy. He could not hold his breath any longer. What a way to die, upside down!

But if there was any dying to be done he was glad that he was to do it, not his kid brother.

What was the kid brother doing all this time?

He had brought his kayak up beside Hal's and was trying to roll Hal's boat over. He couldn't budge it. Hal's weight kept it down.

Hal was a good swimmer. But he was locked into the kayak. Roger realized that a kayak, however good, had its drawbacks. Once in it, it was a devil of a job to get out of it.

Hal's paddle was drifting away. Roger passed his paddle down. It poked Hal in the ribs and woke him from his stupor. He grabbed the paddle, and with one stroke he turned his kayak and himself right side up. Roger captured Hal's drifting paddle.

The bull had been waiting for his chance to make trouble. He was more than the usual length of twelve feet. Some bulls were twenty feet long, and this was one of them. He was twice as long as a kayak.

What a prize, if they could take him before he took them.

Hal's head was not working well, and no wonder after his terrible experience. It was up to the "kid brother" to do the thinking for both of them. Roger had an idea — but would it work?

As the bull came near, he struck it on its tender nose with his paddle. The bull sank. Soon it rose, bellowing, and again Roger gave it the sore nose treatment before it had a chance to breathe.

Again, down went the bull. But he *must* have air. So he was up again almost at once. Another resounding crack. And down went the breathless sea horse.

Hal saw what Roger was trying to do — make the animal go weak for lack of air — and he joined in.

Finally the great beast's eyes closed and he gave up struggling. Two boys had conquered him, simply by preventing him from filling his lungs.

Now they had to act fast. The bull might recover, and defeat them after all. They threw both lassos over his head and towed the unconscious monster to shore.

Many men had gathered to see the show. They knew the boys and liked them. They saw what was needed and had a truck with a drag behind. The drag, a sort of raft, was pushed under the walrus while still in the water — then they started the truck and pulled the drag and its ton-and-a-half load all the way to the airport.

The walrus did not recover until he was safely stowed into a skyvan, ready for the trip to Long Island.

17
Roger and the Killer

A voice outside the igloo called: "Somebody wants to come in."

"Who is it?" said Hal. He got no answer. Then he remembered – no Eskimo would give his name – that would offend the name-ghost.

If it was Zeb, Hal certainly did not want him to come in. But Zeb wouldn't say "Somebody". So it must be an Eskimo.

"Somebody may come in," Hal said.

Olrik entered. He was amazed to see the brothers dressed in their Neoprene rubber diving suits. Each carried a scuba breathing tank on his back.

"What's up?" said Olrik. "Going for a swim just for fun? Or business?"

"You might call it business," Hal said. "We got a telegram. Dad wants a killer whale."

"A killer whale! Why, you poor dopes – you'll get murdered. We Eskimos know the killer whale. He's about the most dangerous visitor we have in these waters. Many of them have just arrived. Everybody is staying off the ice for fear of being gobbled up by a killer whale."

"Perhaps they come so seldom that your people have never really become acquainted with them. Have you ever seen one?"

"Can't say I have. But there are a lot of stories. Some of our own friends have been killed by those brutes."

Hal said, "No one can see very well under water. Perhaps what got them was a shark."

"But surely you know the reputation of the killer whale," said Olrik.

"Yes, it has a terrible reputation," Hal replied. "It is only about thirty feet long and can kill a whale a hundred feet long. It has twenty-four teeth as sharp as razors. It bites a whale on the corner of its mouth, makes it open its jaws and then it proceeds to eat the tongue. For some reason that makes the whale almost helpless. It begins to bleed to death. The killer goes on until it has filled its six-foot-long stomach and then other killers come in and do the rest."

"Well then," said Olrik, "if you know it's so terrible why go down after it?"

"Because it happens to be one of man's best friends. People call it a whale but it isn't. It is a big dolphin. And dolphins never attack men. They seem to think that we are their cousins."

"I'm no cousin of any killer," said Olrik.

Hal went on, "I wish I could introduce you to a killer whale."

"You want to get me murdered?"

"Certainly not. But I know you'd be safe. I know he would like you."

"You're right. He'd like me so well he'd eat me up."

"Not a chance. In all the zoos where they have dolphins they are the best performers. They can do no end of tricks. They are very easy to teach. The elephant is a fine animal and has a great brain. But the brain of a killer whale is seven times as large as the brain of an elephant."

"That doesn't mean anything," said Olrik. "A big brain that thinks of nothing but mischief is not as good as a small brain that behaves itself."

"That is true, Olrik," said Hal. "But now if you will excuse us we're off to see if the big brain can also behave itself."

"Well," said Olrik, "it's been nice knowing you. I suppose I'll never see you again, so here's goodbye."

"Not a long goodbye," said Hal, "but just a short one. See you at lunch."

It was now mid-summer, yet there was plenty of ice. They walked out on the drifting floes, jumping from one to another. If their jump was a bit short they would go into the sea long before they intended to. When they were far enough out to know that they were over deep water, they slid down into the sea.

The water was cold, but their rubber suits kept them as warm as toast.

They looked about with great care. It was not a killer whale that they were looking for just now, but a shark. The shark was no friend of man.

As bad luck would have it they glimpsed one which was coming their way. They shot up like two bolts of lightning and clambered up on to a floe.

Olrik, on the shore, was amused. "They're running away from the killer whale already."

He expected to see the snout of a killer whale rise above the surface. Instead he saw the jaws of a shark shoot out of the water, reach for the boys, sink again.

The floe that they were on was drifting with the current. Not until it had floated a quarter of a mile did the boys once more drop into the sea.

No shark was in sight, nor was a killer whale.

They could see a great object like a submarine coming their way. It had its huge mouth wide open. Hal guessed that it was a Greenland whale.

It was a whale with no teeth.

How can any animal get its food if it has no teeth?

There are two kinds of whales — those with teeth, and those without. The toothed whales include the beaked whale, the white whale, the goose-beaked whale, the sperm whale and others. On the other hand the whales without teeth are the humpback, the finback, the grey, the sei, the right and the blue. Largest of all is the blue whale, one hundred feet long, the largest animal in the world, equal in size to 150 oxen or twenty-five big elephants.

How do these monsters live? Simply by swimming along with their mouths open and taking in anything that gets in the way — the tiny living things called plankton, also crabs, lobsters, shrimps and what-not.

This might seem like small stuff for such a huge animal, but they succeed in putting away about a ton of food a day — and without taking one bite. What an easy way to live!

The Greenland whale, swimming along with eyes shut and mouth open, was as surprised as Roger was when the boy was scooped up by those great jaws. He could not be chewed because there were no teeth. He could not be swallowed because the throat of the animal was too small. He was just stuck. His feet dangled out of one side of the mouth and his hands out of the other. And if there was any bellowing to be done, Roger did it. But if you try to howl inside a whale's mouth, you might as well save your breath. You cannot be heard.

The whale stopped. He was very much annoyed by this squirming thing in his mouth. He tried to get rid of it but it was stuck fast.

Hal sympathized with the whale, as well as with his brother. There was nothing he could do. He was unusually strong, and weighed more than his own father, but what chance did he have against this monster that weighed perhaps a hundred times as much?

He grabbed Roger's feet to pull him out. He could not move him one inch. He went to the other side and took

hold of Roger's hands. These he pulled lustily but with no effect.

He looked around for help.

It came in the shape of a young killer whale, not more than fifteen feet long, who saw the two boys and came to the rescue. He thrust his head into the great mouth and closed his jaws on Roger. The sharp teeth were not too comfortable but they did not penetrate the heavy rubber suit. With a thrash of his tail the killer whale propelled himself backward and pulled Roger out of the jaws of death.

The Greenland whale made off with all speed because he was no friend of the killer whale.

The whale who was not a whale was apparently reluctant to leave. He rubbed his head dog-fashion against Roger and then, in order not to have any favourites, he gave Hal the same treatment. When they rose to the surface he was with them.

Their faithful friend, Olrik, had a truck and drag waiting for them. The young killer whale was hauled on to the drag and the boys got into the truck. Away they went to the airport.

"We'll have to hurry," Hal said. "No whale or dolphin is any good until he is in the water. His lungs are in his chest. The weight of his body presses down so hard that he cannot get enough air into his lungs and will suffocate. He may be dead before we can get him into a skyvan. Those tanks we saw at the airport – could we have one put into the skyvan at once?"

"It's in already," Olrik said. "I knew you'd need it. It's twenty feet long, about five feet longer than the animal. And it's full of water."

"Bless you, Olrik. I don't know what I'd do without you," said Hal gratefully.

The killer whale was still alive when it was put into the tank. It would never need to kill again. It would be fed as soon as it arrived at Long Island, and then it would be tanked to the zoo that had ordered it. There it would be happy, learning the various acts required of it more quickly than any other swimming animal because as the scientist Dr Lilly had said, "Dolphins learn as fast as humans."

18
His Tooth Is Nine Feet Long

"Now we are asked to get a narwhal," said Hal.

Roger's forehead wrinkled. He thought he knew animals pretty well but he had never heard of this one. "What's a narwhal?"

"It's one of the most peculiar animals on the face of the earth. It's found only in the Arctic, so most people have never heard of it."

"What is it — a whale?"

"No, it's not a whale."

"A fish?"

"No, it's not a fish."

"Well then, what is it?"

"It's a narwhal."

"Don't beat about the bush. What the dickens is a narwhal?"

"Something like the unicorn."

"All right then, what's a unicorn?"

"Something that isn't. It doesn't exist and it never did. But people two thousand years ago believed in it. It was supposed to be a kind of horse, but the odd thing about

121

it was that it was thought to have a horn protruding many feet in front of the head. So it was called a unicorn – *uni* meaning one and *corn* from the Latin *cornu* meaning horn. The explorers found a horn of solid ivory, the very best. Only animals produce ivory, therefore they decided that this must come from a real unicorn. They told the world that they had proof that the beast called a unicorn really existed. Actually it was the tooth of a narwhal. It was nine feet long."

Roger said, "You can't tell me that any animal has a tooth nine feet long."

"We'll see, when we get one. A very peculiar thing about the narwhal is that it has only two teeth. The one on the right side is just a small tooth, the one on the left is nine feet long – sometimes ten."

Roger shook his head. "I still don't believe that there's anything on earth like that. I've been in a lot of zoos and never saw one."

"Most zoo men don't know anything about it. The New York Aquarium in Coney Island had a very small one. It was said to be the first narwhal that had ever been captured alive. It refused to eat fish. But it did like milk shakes. It gained twenty pounds in a week on milk shakes. That was in 1969. If it grew up it would be twenty feet long by this time. I have no idea whether it lived or not. But up here they come and go, sometimes a thousand of them at a time."

"So perhaps we won't see one of them or we may see a thousand."

"That's the way it goes," said Hal. "The Eskimos kill them for their meat, which is delicious. Olrik told me that the Eskimos once killed a thousand narwhals. They left the meat on an ice floe and a gale came along and swept it out to sea. The meat was lost to the bears."

"Are the horns any good?"

"They are ground into powder and sold to the Chinese, who think they are wonderful medicine. And tourists who come to Greenland like to take home a foot or two of horn with a carving on it done by some talented Eskimo artist. A fine carving on pure ivory brings quite a lot of money."

Olrik came to tell them, "Now's your chance to get a narwhal. They haven't come in thousands as they sometimes do, but there are at least a hundred offshore."

"A hundred is more than we need," said Hal. "Just one will do."

"Well it won't be easy to get one. They swim like lightning. But if anybody can get one I know you can.

I'm so sure of that that I'll have a truck and a drag ready when you come ashore with it."

Hal and Roger went out in their two rented kayaks. Olrik was right — there were a hundred or more narwhals having a grand time leaping over each other, poking each other playfully with their horns, shooting down to the bottom to scratch up halibut. Those that were at rest stood upright in the water, their horns standing straight up above the surface so they looked like dozens of posts, all about nine feet high. Suddenly the posts would disappear and the water would boil with the antics of these lively animals. They treated the kayaks like new playthings. They bumped them into the air and they actually slid across the front deck and the rear deck but never touched the boy who occupied the hole in the middle.

Hal tried repeatedly to catch one with his lasso but it only slid on to the horn and was shaken off again.

Roger did better, without trying. A rollicking narwhal plunged his horn through the sealskin sides of the kayak so far that it came out of the other side. It barely missed Roger himself. It tore a hole big enough to let the water in, and the kayak with Roger inside it began to sink. Once locked into a kayak it is very difficult to escape. The narwhal also was trying to get out, but without success.

Hal brought his kayak up beside Roger's. "Break loose," he said, "and scramble out of there fast."

Roger was already up to his neck in water. Hal threw his lasso over the boy's head and hauled him out.

"Lie flat on the deck behind me," he said.

Roger had never been noosed before but he was glad to be rescued from a watery grave. He grabbed the gunwale of the sinking kayak and held on with all his strength. The narwhal had given up struggling to get free. Hal paddled toward shore and Roger never let go of the kayak and its horny passenger.

Olrik was ready with truck and drag. "That's a new way to catch a narwhal," he said.

Hal paid the kayak owner a little extra for repairs to his boat. A patch of sealskin over each hole would quickly restore the boat to its proper condition. The narwhal was transported to the airport.

The news travelled fast through the city of Thule and the paper the next morning praised Hal and especially Roger for doing what had never been done before in Greenland. It was easy to take a narwhal dead, but a fifteen-year-old boy had taken one alive.

"It's all nonsense," said Roger. "I didn't catch him. He caught himself."

19
Monster with Ten Arms

"Somebody wants to tell you something very important."

"That sounds like Olrik," said Hal. "If your name is Olrik, come in. If your name is Zeb, don't."

Olrik came in. He said, "Have you heard about the sea serpent?"

"No," said Hal. "The last time I heard about a sea serpent was when I was eight years old. My father told me there was no such thing."

"Then it probably isn't a sea serpent. But it's Something very strange. The whole town is worried about it. Women are weeping because they have lost their children. Men are sharpening up their harpoons to kill the Something."

"What is this Something like?"

"It's like a snake. It reaches up out of the water and grabs whatever it can find on a floe. It takes a seal, or a baby walrus, or a seagull. That wasn't so bad, but when this Something began to take down boys and girls and even grown-ups who had come to watch, everybody got excited and they want you to do something about it."

"It must have powerful jaws", said Hal, "to pull men and women as well as children down into the sea."

"It has no jaws, no fangs, no mouth, no eyes. In fact, it has no head. Where its head should be, it has a hand. It's a very powerful hand and even when it closes on a strong man he can't resist it. Down he goes into the ocean."

"A snake that has a hand where its head should be," said Hal. "Sounds pretty fantastic."

"Come and see for yourself," said Olrik.

"We sure will. We can't tell much by looking at it from a floe. We'll have to get on our diving suits and go down. Perhaps it's something that a zoo would like to have."

The Eskimos on the ice floes watching this strange Something were glad to see Hal and Roger. They were astonished when they saw that the boys carried no weapons, no harpoons, nothing but a coil of rope.

"Don't go down there," someone shouted. "You'll get killed."

"He may be right," Hal said. "No need for both of us to go down. You stay here."

Hal sank into the sea. Roger waited until his brother was well out of sight, then he joined him.

What they saw was no serpent. It was more like a lot

of serpents. Hal counted them. There were ten. And all of them sprouted from one body. Judging by its size, Hal reckoned it must weigh a thousand pounds. The most terrible thing about its appearance was its huge black eyes, almost a foot in diameter. It had terrific jaws, large enough to take in Roger at one gulp. With its tentacles stretched out it must measure fifty feet from tip to tip.

Hal knew what it was. It was the giant cuttle, which has various other names such as giant squid, devilfish and cuttlefish.

It was quite at home in all oceans, including the Arctic, and was so strong that it could drag down a large boat. It was the world's largest invertebrate, that is, an animal without a backbone. It was carnivorous – nothing but meat would satisfy it. And here, before its nose, were two fine chunks of meat.

But it had evidently dined so well that it was not hungry. Instead it was startled and a little frightened by these two animals that did not seem to be afraid of it.

It waved its tentacles about, and it was easy to see that on each one there were four rows of cups, each cup full of sharp edges like knives. In fact that was why it was called a cuttle. Cuttle is a very ancient word meaning knife. When these suction cups were clamped on any prey the knives began their work and the victim was dead long before it reached the monster's jaws.

Every tentacle did look like a snake, but it ended not in a head but in a sort of hand which could firmly clutch and hold any living object.

Hal had learned that this peculiar beast had a shell – but the shell was not on the outside, but inside the body. Though inside, it protected the heart and other organs.

Disturbed by the boys, the peculiar beast spouted a cloud of ink into the water which entirely concealed him from sight. That was why it had still another name – the pen-and-ink fish.

Hal feared that the cuttle behind the cloud of ink would now swim away. It would swim backwards, forcing itself

along by jets of water from its siphons – a method copied by the makers of jet planes. Men had learned something very valuable from this remarkable Something.

Hal and Roger burst through the ink cloud, determined that this marvellous creature should not escape. The monster, preparing to swim, brought all its ten arms in close to the body. Hal slipped his lasso over the head and back over the body. Then he pulled it tight, imprisoning not only the body but the ten "serpents". Roger helped to adjust the loop and got for his pains a slash from a tentacle with its dozens of knives. The result was that his Neoprene suit was badly cut and would need a lot of repairs before it could be made waterproof again.

His skin had been badly gouged and the blood that came from the wounds made another cloud, this time of red, beside the black cloud of the cuttle's ink.

The boys then carried the end of the heavy rope up to a floe, where it was seized by a dozen men. Inch by inch the prize exhibit was drawn out of the water and began its journey to the airport.

20
Living under Ice

They walked the streets of Thule – Hal, Roger and Olrik.

"Quite a town," said Hal.

"Sixteen streets," said Olrik, "and a radar tower fifty feet higher than the Empire State Building."

"All I see is shops, shops, shops," said Hal. "Where are the people who live here?"

"The big bosses live in these houses. The working men live under the ice."

Hal stopped and stared at Olrik. "You don't mean that."

"Of course I do. Haven't you been down under?"

"No. I've had all I can handle on top."

"Come with me," said Olrik. "I'll show you the under-ice city."

Outside Thule they reached a hole in the ground. A stairway took them down to the strangest town they had ever seen.

It consisted of immense metal tubes twenty-six feet in diameter. These tubes were the streets of the town. The floor was made of planks. Along the side of the tube were cabins where the working men lived.

"But why don't they build the cabins up on top?" said Hal.

"Because they would soon be buried in snow. Once they were up above, and the snow completely covered them. So they went below where the snow can't get at them."

There was not a glimpse of daylight but there were plenty of electric lights. "It's like being in a submarine," Roger said.

But this was much larger than any submarine ever built. There were several dining-rooms. There was a library. There was a game room with table tennis. There was a radio room. There was a gymnasium, and a theatre where, Olrik said, you could see the latest American films even before they were shown in America.

"How far down are we?" Hal asked.

"Thirty-six feet below the surface," said Olrik, "and getting deeper every time we have a snowstorm."

"Doesn't the snow on top keep it very cold down here?"

"On the contrary, snow keeps it warm. It's a very good insulator."

Men who happened to be off duty were having a good time – looking at films, playing games, reading, singing, talking politics, protected from any bad weather that might happen to be outside.

The boys came out into a snowstorm. A chill wind was blowing. They had to admit it was much better under the ice.

A few days later Olrik took them to another under-ice city. It was called Camp Century and it was even larger and better than the first. Main Street was a quarter of a mile long. It was covered by iron sheets above which was snow many feet deep. When rain came the snow turned to ice.

"Those iron sheets will be removed after a time," said Olrik.

"Doesn't the snow fall in?" said Hal.

"No," said Olrik. "After the snow becomes hard it is able to support itself."

Main Street was very busy. It was so high and wide that tractors and trucks that Olrik called weasels were able to pass through without difficulty. There were fourteen cross streets. They were lined with cabins made of plastic.

"We think plastic will be used a lot in the ice-sheet stations of the future," Olrik said. "It makes good, tight little houses."

In the centre of the town there was a nuclear power plant to provide all the electricity needed in the little city.

"Sometimes it is too warm," said Olrik.

"Do you get cold air from above?" Hal asked.

"No, from below."

"How could you do that?"

"Holes have been bored forty feet down into the ice and fans bring up the cold air."

They visited the quarters of the officers. They were large, lovely rooms with leather-covered armchairs, mahogany chests, decorated lamps, thick carpets and everything else that an officer could desire.

This modern town under the ice was designed for one hundred and fifty men, but Olrik said it would soon be enlarged to accommodate a thousand.

Some of the rooms that Hal and his companions visited were twenty-four feet wide and two hundred feet long. One of these was a laboratory in which experiments were being made to improve still further this unique city under the ice.

21
Hal Rides an Iceberg

"Would you like to go to the iceberg coast?" Olrik said one morning.

Hal was surprised. "You mean Greenland's east coast? That's eight hundred miles away. By dog team it would take twenty-five days to get there."

"I see you have been reading up on it," said Olrik. "You're a pretty thoroughgoing chap. You always look before you leap."

"Cut the compliments," Hal said. "All I know is that we have no chance of getting to the east coast. It must be wonderful. Most of the world's icebergs are born there. But we can't afford to spend twenty-five days to get there and twenty-five days back."

"Well then," said Olrik, "how about half a day to get there and half a day back?"

"Dream on," laughed Hal. "You can only do that by plane. And we have no plane."

"Yes you have, if you want it. You know I work at the airport part time. A fellow I know is going to fly over to inspect a mining operation. I asked him if he could take you along. He would be glad to have your company. It's lonesome flying alone. The young fellow is called Pete. He'll be leaving at eight this morning. It's nearly that now. Get on some very warm clothing because it's mighty cold over there."

They dressed warmly and accompanied Olrik to the airport, where they met Pete. He shook hands with them.

"Glad to have you along," he said. "Hop in."

They climbed aboard. Something above them began to whirr.

"So you fly a helicopter," said Hal.

"I fly almost anything," said Pete, "but a helicopter is best on this trip because landing on the cliffs of the east coast is sometimes pretty difficult."

"I understand," said Hal. "The helicopter lets you down easy. You don't need a runway."

"That's right," said Pete. "It's pretty wild over there. Nothing but cliffs and glaciers. No runways. No trees, no grass, nothing but ice and snow and precipices. It's a bad place to live, a good place to die."

Now they were crossing the great Greenland ice cap. "They say", Hal remarked, "that this ice cap is millions of years old. The oldest part of it, of course, is at the bottom. What would happen if the whole ice cap melted some day during a warm spell along with the one at the South Pole and became just a part of the sea?"

Pete answered, "If they melted, it would raise the level of the sea 245 feet."

"Think of that!" said Hal. "All the cities along the coast from New York to Buenos Aires would be drowned."

Roger said, "Has anybody ever bored down through the ice cap to the bottom?"

"No, they bored a hole fifty feet deep and found that the snow there had been laid down in 1879."

"Why don't they bore deeper?"

"Because the ice cap is twisting like a snake. If you should bore a straight hole today it would be a crooked hole tomorrow. It would be so twisted that you couldn't possibly get to the bottom of it. Nobody can imagine how this ice cap moves about. There are a few stations on the ice sheet but you don't know where to find them. They wander here and there. The moving ice carried one station 550 feet in a year. Another station moved half a mile south. The ice cap is alive and kicking. It has a mind of its own."

Roger looked off to the north-east. "Do those black clouds mean it's going to snow or rain?"

"Those are not clouds," said Pete. "They are mountains.

They're called the Watkin Mountains. They are 12,200 feet high. And the mine I am going to see is bored right into the side of one of them. I'll take you to the iceberg area and leave you there while I go on to the mine. I'll be there two or three days, then come back and pick you up."

"That's all right with us," said Hal. "We have a tent and our sleeping bags, and provisions."

As they neared the east coast they could see the ocean covered with icebergs. Hal remembered how a mighty iceberg such as these had sunk the great ship *Titanic* in 1912. It was the largest ship in the world and it was making its first voyage. Its captain believed in speed, he couldn't wait for anything, because he wanted to break the trans-Atlantic record. The sea was very calm and the night was clear and cold. The captain knew there were icebergs ahead but he depended upon a sharp lookout rather than reducing speed.

The lookout wasn't sharp enough. Faster than any ship afloat at that time, the *Titanic* ploughed head-on into an iceberg which split the ship open as if it had been a walnut. Water rushed in and the ship began to sink. Down to their death went 1,500 passengers.

Perhaps the captain had thought that his mighty ship

could plough right through any iceberg. He was sadly mistaken. The berg was just chipped a little, while the ironbound ship became in one moment a pile of junk.

The captain was severely criticized for his carelessness but that did not bring 1,500 people back to life.

Another careless fellow was the captain of the ship *Californian*, which was only ten miles away but did not respond to the distress signal and simply went on its way without offering any help to the sinking ship and people.

Looking down from the helicopter the boys could see rivers on their way to the ocean. These were not rivers of water but rivers of ice.

"Those glaciers are very deep," Pete said. "Some of them almost a thousand feet from top to bottom. One is seven hundred miles long – the longest in the world. Of course being solid ice, they move very slowly, about a hundred feet in a year. But they finally get to the edge of the cliff overlooking the sea. They don't stop there. Pushed from behind, the glacier keeps going right on into the air. It may ooze out anywhere from a hundred to five hundred feet. But it has nothing to hold it up, so finally, with a terrific crash, it falls three hundred feet to the sea. And that means a new iceberg."

Roger was excited. "I want to see that."

"You'll see it. And you'll hear it — the cracking and groaning and thundering of the glacier and the terrible crash when it falls into the water throwing up fountains in every direction."

"And that's what they call calving," said Hal.

"Yes," said Pete. "It's a strange way to describe it, but it means that just as a cow gives birth to a calf so the glacier gives birth to an iceberg. I must say an iceberg is a mighty big calf."

Pete couldn't land his helicopter where he wanted to. The 100-mile-an-hour wind so common on this coast blew the helicopter out over the sea and a wind current carried it down almost to the water. Pete worked hard to get his machine up again into the air. He circled a couple of icebergs, always in danger of striking one, and finally got the flying machine up above the cliff. There he brought it to a wobbly landing.

Hal and Roger piled out with their tent, sleeping bags and provisions.

"Good luck," cried Pete, as he turned his plane to the north and took off for the mine.

Roger shivered. "What makes it so awfully cold here?

It's much colder than it was on the other coast and that was cold enough."

Hal replied, "There's no north-flowing current here as there was on the other coast to warm it up a little bit. On this side there's nothing but cold current coming from the north."

Roger drew his parka around over his face. His breath made his face damp. He pulled his parka away in order to see. At once the moisture on his skin froze and his face was encased in ice. Even his eyelids were frozen together. He could dimly see through his lashes.

"Why did that happen?" he wanted to know.

"It's a lot colder here than on the ice cap," said Hal.

"I'll run around and get warm," Roger said.

"You'd better not. You will sweat and the sweat will turn to ice. Then you'll be covered from top to toe with ice."

Crash, crash, crash. More and more icebergs where there were plenty already.

"What good are icebergs anyhow?" Roger said. "Why don't the engineers find a way to prevent them?"

"They have tried," said Hal. "They have shot them with cannon. They have bombed them. They've drilled and blasted them. They have painted them black to make them

142

melt more quickly. All these measures have failed."

"But surely they must melt after a while."

"Yes, after a while. But it's a good long while. An iceberg will last more than a year. Very large icebergs take much longer to melt. Some bergs are seven hundred feet high and weigh eight million tons. They may last for years. Storms make them crash into each other and chip off ice. But not enough is chipped off to have any great effect."

They put up the tent and anchored it firmly so that the wind would not blow it away. Then Hal said, "Let's take a walk."

"Where?"

"Out on this glacier."

"But the glacier will take us out and drop us into the sea."

"I think we can get off in time," said Hal. "It only moves very slowly."

So they walked on the groaning, grinding glacier, which was not as smooth as they expected. It had many furrows and ridges and holes. Roger got tired and went back to the tent. He crawled into his sleeping bag to warm up. He took a nap – then was roused by a scream louder than the crashing of icebergs.

He jumped out to see what was going on. He saw his brother falling through space. Hal had gone out too far on the glacier as it reached out over the sea, and when it broke off he went down with it. There, far below, was Hal floating away on an iceberg.

What could Roger do? Even if he could get down the 300-foot cliff he could do nothing. Hal's berg was already too far away.

"If only I had a boat," Roger thought.

There must be someone, somewhere, living on top of this cliff. Roger ran north through deep snow. He did just what Hal had warned him against. He began to sweat, and the sweat turned to ice. Now he was an ice man and could hardly move his joints. There was no sign of a house or hut or igloo. No one was fool enough to live here.

He turned about and ran south. All he accomplished was to make more sweat which turned into more ice on his body.

He looked out to sea, hoping he could signal a ship. There was no ship to be seen. No ship was likely to sail into this ocean of icebergs.

He must do something about this coat of ice he was wearing. It was getting more and more difficult to move.

He went into the tent and lit the little camp stove. Then he took off all of his clothes and stood as stiff as a statue while his icy armour began to melt. When it had turned to water and run off him he dried himself with a towel and dressed. Then he went out and looked but he could not see Hal now. His iceberg had floated too far away.

He felt like crying but he was too old to cry. He was a big boy and a big boy should be able to do something. But he was helpless. He went back inside and got into his sleeping bag.

He could not sleep. Every time he was about to drift off he thought someone had left him all alone at the North Pole.

"Never mind," he told himself. "When Hal gets beyond the iceberg area some ship will come along and rescue him."

If only Pete would come back now rather than wait two or three days. Pete would know what to do. He could fly south and perhaps he would find Hal.

But it was four sleeps before Pete came back.

"Hal is way off somewhere floating on an iceberg. He hasn't had any food for four days and he must be just about dead."

"Let's go find him," said Pete.

They flew away in the direction that Hal's iceberg had floated. They did not find the floating boy. They searched among all the icebergs but caught no sight of him.

Roger, with sinking heart, said, "Let's go outside the iceberg area."

They went outside and within an hour they came upon a small fishing vessel and there was Hal upon its deck as neat and fat and chipper as ever.

The helicopter came near and hovered above the deck. A rope ladder was lowered and Hal climbed to the helicopter. He waved his thanks to the captain of the fishing boat.

Roger's first question was, "Did you get anything to eat?"

"I was three days without anything to chew but the iceberg," Hal said. "Then we floated outside the ice pack and this fishing boat took me in and fed me."

Roger was happy – and angry.

"You gave me the heebie-jeebies," he said.

Hal smiled, "Sorry, my boy, that you had to eat alone while I starved on an iceberg."

Roger was too glad to get his brother back to do any more grouching.

They flew back to the cliff and struck camp, climbed aboard the helicopter again, and in four hours were in their own igloo, where Nanook gave them a warm and sloppy reception, standing up on his hind feet and licking their faces as if they had been away for a year instead of only four days.

22
Hurricane

"We've got to get a polar bear to send home," said Hal.

"We already have one," said Roger. "Nanook."

Hal said, "We'd hate to part with Nanook. He's a member of our family. I mean this little family that we have in our igloo. Nanook and you and myself. And he's so fond of us I doubt he'd be happy without us."

"Where would we go to get another? Up on the ice cap?"

"We might go miles without finding one," said Hal. "I think the best place to get one is Hudson Bay. They say there are plenty of them in a town called Churchill."

Roger laughed. "We go to town to find a polar bear?"

"I know it seems strange — but that's just where you would find a lot of them. Right in town on the main street."

"You're kidding. Where did you get that crazy idea?"

"From an article in the *Smithsonian*. That's the official magazine of the Smithsonian Institution in Washington. It's the national museum of the United States. I think we can believe anything they say."

"But how do we get there?"

"A brig is sailing for Churchill tomorrow. We'll be on it. Don't expect any luxuries. It's no ocean liner. Usually a brig just carries sails. But this one has both sails and engine. I think it will get us there without trouble."

It wasn't Hal's fault that he was making a wrong guess. He couldn't foresee the coming hurricane.

Two hours after they boarded the little vessel, the sky exploded. A terrific wind had come up. It was so violent that it threatened to carry away the sails, so they had to be brought down. The wind shrieked and wailed. A violent ice storm attacked the little vessel.

There was a grinding and thrashing sound as millions of tons of ice under the force of the gale beat upon the small ship. Ice floes ten or twenty feet thick screeched and roared as they attacked the brig.

No boiler factory could produce such a racket. The Arctic Ocean has been called the silent sea, but there was no silence aboard the *Happy Waters*. Hal and Roger, side by side as they clung to a mast in order to avoid being blown away, could not hear each other speak.

They wanted to go down below and get into their bunks, but then they would miss the show. It wasn't every day that you could see a hurricane in action. Everybody else was below except the captain.

They were ploughing through Melville Bay, which has the reputation of being the most dangerous in the Arctic. It was full of icebergs. They did not soar seven hundred feet high like those on the east coast. But even icebergs twice as tall as the ship presented a great danger. The brig was strongly built but the best hull can't stand a million tons of ice leaning against it.

Since only one-eighth of an iceberg shows above the surface, the seven-eighths below the surface is very likely to cause trouble. Time and time again the brig was nearly upset by the part of an iceberg reaching out below her keel. Once she tipped so far to starboard that all the passengers below fell out of their bunks. Sometimes the brig stuck fast and only the screaming wind was strong enough to move it onward.

The gale was roaring like a lion. The captain tried to bring his ship around into the lee of an iceberg where it would get less wind. He had no sooner done this than the iceberg that sheltered the brig was pushed into another berg and the ship was squeezed between them. Since both bergs slanted, the ship was hoisted up in the air until she was raised ten feet above the raging sea.

There she was, no longer tipping and teetering, but so still that the passengers put their heads up to see if the

151

boat was in some harbour. They were astonished to see their craft stuck up in the air above the dashing waves. Now for a little time at least the ship was still and they had a chance to get over their seasickness.

But this was not getting them to Churchill. And the captain was distressed for fear the pressure on both sides would break the hull. Then everything and everybody would go down to the bottom, where there was perfect peace and death. For twelve hours the ship remained suspended in the air.

The passengers complained about the bothersome bergs.

Hal told them, "There's only one nice thing about bergs. That drink you are swallowing wouldn't be half as good without icebergs."

"You're off your head," said one gruff fellow. "What do icebergs have to do with a drink?"

"The ice in it is the very best. Greenland exports iceberg ice all over the world. Every summer at least ten Greenland icebergs are cut into small chunks and shipped abroad. They have a trade name, 'Greenland Iceberg Rocks'."

The passengers grinned and rattled the "Rocks" in their glasses. For the moment they were amused, but soon became grouchy again.

One complained to the captain. "Why don't you do something?" he asked angrily.

"If you tell me what to do," said the captain, "I'll do it."

"Well," said the man, "it's perfectly simple. Just push one of the bergs away and the ship will drop into the water."

The captain smiled. "Suppose *you* push it away. I'm sure it doesn't weigh more than a million tons."

Finally the hurricane passed and the powerful wind that had held the two bergs in place relaxed. The ship slid into the sea, and the voyage continued. Passing through Hudson Strait, the brig crossed Hudson Bay to the small town called Churchill.

23
City of Polar Bears

Hal and Roger walked into a small hotel on the Churchill waterfront and asked the man at the desk for a room.

"Yes, I have one room left. Number eight on the ground floor. You'll find it easily. The door is open."

They found the open door and walked into their room. But the room was already occupied. Hal stopped and stared. He could hardly believe what he saw.

"I'll be hornswoggled," he said.

Sitting on a low stool was a polar bear.

"Let's get out of here – fast," said Roger.

"Wait a minute," Hal said. The bear did not even look at them. He seemed to be very much at home. He did not move.

The boys went back to the office. "There's a bear in our room," said Hal.

"Don't let that bother you," said the proprietor.

"Why shouldn't it bother us?" Hal demanded.

"Just let him be. Sooner or later he'll walk away."

"Is it a tame bear?"

"Far from it. He's as wild as they come. He could kill

you with one swat if he didn't like you. In Churchill we are very careful not to annoy our bears."

"You mean that the bears come first?"

"Always. You see, we have more bears than people.

The population of Churchill consists of sixteen hundred people and two or three thousand bears. But not all the year long. Sometimes no bears at all – sometimes thousands. I can promise that if you stay a few months you will find no bears in Churchill."

"A few months!" exclaimed Hal. "We can't stay here more than a few days."

"Then you may as well prepare to enjoy our bears. We like them. Sure, they kill a few of us every year. But most of them are all right if you just leave them alone. If you get a polar bear cross he's far more dangerous than a grizzly. So, go easy."

They went back and peeked into their room. The bear had gone.

They flopped down on the beds to rest a while after the hard trip on the brig.

Then they went out to see the town. In the main street there were more bears than people. Why did the police allow this?

"It's too small a town to have a police force," said Hal. "But there's a Mountie."

"What's a Mountie?" asked Roger.

"A member of the Royal Canadian Mounted Police," said Hal.

The man who was called a Mountie because he was mounted on a horse, leaned down when Hal spoke to him.

Hal asked him, "What do you do when one of these bears makes trouble? Do you shoot it?"

"Never, unless we have to," said the Mountie. "There's a law that protects the bears. There are only about twelve thousand of them still left in Canada. We don't want them to disappear entirely. If you kill one you go to jail – unless the bear has already killed you."

"So your main job", said Hal, "is to protect the bears, not the people."

"Of course we protect the people. But there's no danger that they will disappear from the earth. So our main concern is to look out for the welfare of the bears. There's a Bear Patrol truck that keeps moving all day and all night around Churchill to see that the bears don't hurt people and the people don't hurt the bears."

"One more question, officer. We represent an agency to provide wild animals to zoos. Would there be any objection to our taking one of your bears for a zoo?"

"Of course not. It would get better care in a zoo than it does in the wilderness. Just how you are going to manage it I can't imagine. But apparently you are bright fellows and you will find a way."

The boys continued their walk. They were hungry, having had very little to eat on the brig. They found a small restaurant and went in. Of course there was a bear in the restaurant and everybody seemed to think this was quite proper. Bears had the right of way. A waiter served the bear a chunk of meat and demanded no payment.

The bear ate, and then, as if wishing to entertain the diners, he stood up on his hind feet. He was so tall that his head bumped the ceiling. This did not please him, and he growled. He came down on all four feet and walked out, shaking his head. Why couldn't people make their ceilings high enough so a bear could stand up? He didn't think much of people.

After lunch the boys took to the street again. They saw a bear at a window. He was not looking in the window. He was inside, looking out. This surprised the boys, but no one else looked twice. On one door they saw a sign, "Club Members Only". A bear tried to push his way in. A guard just inside yelled, "You're not a member. Get out of here." The bear walked away.

It happened to be Sunday and a church service was going on. A bear walked in. He proceeded solemnly up the aisle to the altar. The boys, looking in, saw one man who knew how to get rid of a bear. The organist produced such a terrific burst of music that the bear stopped in his tracks, trying to decide whether to eat the organist or escape from this terrible noise. The organist didn't look too tasty, so the visitor turned about and left.

Some people used firecrackers to frighten away a bear that became too inquisitive. One bear, terrified by the explosion within a few inches of his nose, took refuge in a bus. The boys saw their big chance. They closed the door of the bus. There were no people inside.

There was a driver in front protected by a heavy glass partition between himself and the rest of the bus. Hal spoke to him.

"Do you own this bus?"

"I do."

"Have you ever been to Long Island, just outside New York?"

"I used to live in New York."

"We want this bear for a zoo. The Mountie says we can have it. We'll pay you a hundred dollars if you'll take this bear to Long Island and deliver it to the Hunt Wild Animal Farm. If you don't know where it is, anybody there can tell you."

"Make it two hundred and I'll do it," said the bus owner. "In advance."

"Two hundred it is, but not in advance. How do we know you will really go through with it? I'll wire my father, John Hunt, who owns the farm, to pay you two hundred dollars upon arrival."

159

"That's fair enough," said the bus owner, and he lost no time in getting under way.

Hal sent this telegram to his father:

ONE THOUSAND-POUND POLAR BEAR COMING TO YOU BY BUS. UPON ARRIVAL PLEASE PAY DRIVER TWO HUNDRED DOLLARS PLUS FIFTY DOLLAR TIP IF THE BEAR IS ALIVE AND IN GOOD CONDITION

They spent the night in the small hotel and then flew back to Greenland, having no desire for another battle with the icebergs of Melville Bay.

They embraced their own Nanook, and were thankful that it was not this dear friend that they were forced to part with.

"We'll stick by you," Hal said, "as long as you want to stick by us."

24
Off to Alaska

"Why are you leaving Greenland?" Olrik complained. "Don't you like it here?"

"Of course we like it," Hal said. "But we have done about all we can here. We have taken many animals and they have all been shipped home. Dad told us before we started this trip to go on to Alaska when we were finished here."

"What could you expect to find in Alaska that we don't have in Greenland?"

"Well the Arctic moose, for example, the largest moose in the world. And the fighting fur seal, the sea lion, the sea otter and some kinds of whales that don't come into these waters. And the blue bear, the black bear, the grizzly. And the magnificent bighorn sheep. And, most important of all, the giant Kodiak bear, the greatest bear on earth."

"That sounds wonderful," Olrik admitted. "But we sure will miss you."

"We'll miss you a lot," said Hal. "You have been our best friend in Greenland. You lent us your fine dog team. You went with us on the ice cap and did everything in your power to help us. When we caught the walrus and the killer whale and the narwhal and the giant cuttle, you were right there on the shore with a truck and drag ready to take them to the airport. We would have had a hard time getting along without you."

"Shucks," said Olrik. "I just enjoyed tagging along."

"Will you tag along with us now? There's something in Thule I want to show you."

In the town Hal stopped before a brand new house. Hal had hired workmen to build it and they had done a good job. It wouldn't be called a house in New York, but it was a house, and a good house, compared with an igloo or tent.

The walls were made of rocks fitted together and any cracks between them were filled with mud. The mud had frozen and would stay frozen in this land so close to the North Pole, where the temperature almost never rose above the freezing point. The flat roof was a criss-cross of bones from the skeletons of whales, covered by sod six inches thick. In the sod wildflowers were already blooming.

"A very good house," said Olrik. "Whose is it?"

"It's yours, you numskull — for you and your family."

"I can't believe it," said Olrik. "My folks will love it. Every year we've had to rebuild our igloo. A solid rock house with a whalebone roof will never have to be rebuilt. Of course we'll pay for it – a little each year until it's all paid for."

"Nonsense," said Hal. "You have already more than paid for it by all the things you have done for us."

Hal and Roger went to see Aram, who had flown them to the North Pole. Aram was still on crutches, and would perhaps stay on crutches the rest of his life. He refused payment for the North Pole trip. His father would not take anything. His mother said, "The spirits of all our ancestors fill this room. So long as we do good deeds they will not harm us. What we have done for you is very little and you will please forget it."

Hal respected the old woman's fear of the spirits and left no money. He went to the doctor at the air base. He ordered and paid for a peg leg for Aram so that this brave young man would not have to go all the rest of his days on crutches.

Special attention had to be paid to Nanook. They were determined that he should be with them in Alaska. There was regular air service to Alaska by cargo plane, but Hal had difficulty in convincing the authorities that a 1,000-pound polar bear should be considered as cargo.

"You say he is tame," said the pilot. "But perhaps he is just tame while you are around. He has never been in a plane before. I'm not going to make a flight to Alaska with a possible killer behind my back. I'll take him only on one condition – that you two go along with him in the cargo compartment."

"We were planning to go in a comfortable passenger plane," said Hal. "We wouldn't enjoy very much going along with the boxes and bales in the cargo room. But if we have to we will do it."

"Where do you want to be landed – at Fairbanks, or Anchorage?" said the pilot.

"No," said Hal. "Those are too far south. We want to set up our camp at Point Barrow first."

"But that's the wildest part of Alaska. Point Barrow extends into the Arctic Ocean. It's only thirteen hundred miles from the North Pole. It's the most northern part of Alaska – the most northern part of the entire United States."

"Just what we want," said Hal. "Our job there is to find Arctic sea animals. What better place to find them than the Arctic Ocean side of Alaska? Is there an airfield at Point Barrow?"

"Yes, we go there almost every day. Flying over the top of the world, it takes only five hours."

"You mean you go over the North Pole?"

"Very close to it. Just a little to the left. It's the shortest way. We land at Point Barrow – then we go on south to the cities. You ought to go to Anchorage. It's on the southern edge and not as cold as everywhere else. It's a fine city. You'd like it."

"I'm sure we would," said Hal. "But this is not a pleasure trip. For one thing, we want to go to the Brooks Range near Point Barrow."

"The Brooks Range! Why, those mountains are eight thousand feet high. You'll freeze to death."

"Yes," said Hal, "sometimes nine thousand. But if the animals can stand it, we can."

Nanook did not show the least fear in this strange house in the sky so long as the boys were with him. It was a thrill to know that they were passing so near the very top of the world. After only five hours they came down on the airfield at Point Barrow.

The two boys and Nanook walked down to the little village of Barrow. Here they got food, rested overnight in a little lodging house, and set out early in search of anything they could find.

25
The Well-Dressed Sea Otter

The boys and Nanook stood on the beach. Behind them was Barrow village. Before them was the Arctic Ocean.

Not far out was a dark lump.

"What can that be?" Roger wondered.

The dark lump put up a long neck and a head that carried a pair of very bright eyes and long whiskers.

"It's a sea otter," exclaimed Hal. "Look at the size of it. It's twice as big as the otters we've seen down south. I'd say it's about seven feet long. That's the first animal we're going to get in Alaska."

Nanook was interested. He was growling softly. Did he think that this was going to be his dinner?

"What's so great about a sea otter?" Roger asked.

"One thing is that it loves fun more than almost any other animal. Life is just one round of games for the sea otter. Then it has the finest and most expensive of the world's furs. It's coming closer. See how well dressed it is."

The otter's coat was brown with a big orange spot like a headlight under the neck, and beautiful glints of gold and silver on its sides.

Hal said, "Women used to pay 2,500 dollars for one skin, and it took several skins to make a coat."

"You say 'used to'," said Roger. "Don't they still?"

"No more," said Hal, "unless they want to go to prison. So many used to be killed that the sea otters almost disappeared altogether. So a law was passed to put a stop to the killing, and now there are millions of sea otters here and in the Pribilof Islands near Alaska."

The otter was going through all sorts of acrobatics. It was having a very good time. It leaped up four or five feet, then turned and dived straight down. It came up again with a rock oyster held in one flipper that was bent like a hand. The other flipper held two stones.

The animal lay on its back and placed one stone on its chest. It put the oyster on that stone. Then it brought the other stone down with its full strength and broke the shell into fragments. Then it ate the oyster.

Roger stared. "I never saw anything like that in my life. Did somebody train it to do that?"

"No," said Hal. "All the otters do it. It gives you some idea of their intelligence."

"Is the otter like a fish? Can it stay down under water if it wants to?"

Hal said, "It's just like you. It has to come up for air. The only difference is that it does much better than you or I could. Without a scuba we could stay down no more than three minutes. The otter can remain under water for ten minutes."

"In the winter, when the water is frozen over, what does it do?"

"It comes out on land before the water freezes. It's too smart to stay under the ice and be drowned. It may waddle across country to some lake that has no ice over it because there is a hot spring at the bottom. Or it may decide to stay home."

"What do you mean, home?"

"Its home may be right here among these bushes. It digs

a tunnel, about thirty feet long, and lines it with leaves, grass, and moss so that it will be comfortable."

"Then you can trap it by closing the front door."

"No, there's a back door also, deep in the bushes."

"By jiminy," said Roger, "it thinks of everything. Has anybody been able to tame it?"

"Yes," said Hal, "I have read that in India and China it is trained to catch fish for its master, or drive the fish into the net. If it likes you it can become very affectionate. But you have to keep away from those sharp teeth. If you annoy it it may give you a very bad bite. But you would have no trouble. All animals seem to like you."

Now the otter was afloat on its back, sound asleep.

"Look," said Roger. "Something is crawling up on its chest."

"It's a baby otter," said Hal. "The big one must be its mother."

The mother otter woke and nursed her young one. She cleaned the pup with her teeth and her tongue. Just for the fun of it she tossed the pup into the air and caught him again on her chest. The little one squealed for joy.

The mother had several ways of speaking. She could squeal, she could bark, she could growl.

A shark was prowling about. The mother otter tucked

her young one under her arm and dived. When she came up she hugged the shore and put her baby up on the beach out of reach of the shark.

Roger began talking to the mother in the quiet way he always used when speaking to animals. The intelligent animal decided she was safer on the shore with these humans and a bear rather than in the water at the mercy of a hungry shark.

She joined her pup on the beach.

Hal said, "Take the pup in your arms, Roger. Then we'll walk slowly toward the airport. I'm sure the mother will follow wherever we take her pup."

And so it was that the best dressed of all the mammals was the first to be captured by the take-'em-alive men in Alaska.

Here, as in Greenland, there were cargo planes available and one was made the home of the mother and youngster, to be joined by other animals before the flight to Long Island.

26
Battle of the Giants

Why is everything so large in Alaska? Alaska itself is the giant of the fifty American states. Texas is an enormous state – but Alaska is twice as large as Texas. It would take three Californias to make an Alaska. Mount McKinley is North America's highest mountain at 20,320 feet. Alaska actually has sixteen mountains higher than any in the lower forty-eight states!

The world's biggest moose, the world's biggest bear, the world's biggest animals of many kinds are all in Alaska.

And on this particular morning the boys set out to find a sea lion fourteen feet long, twice the length of the seven-foot sea lion of the California coast. Alaska's fur seal is the biggest and strongest of its kind.

Hal and Roger were out early, carrying – not a gun – but a net and a lasso. They arrived at the beach just in time to see the fight. A big sea-lion bull was tackling a giant fur seal.

"Why do they call it a sea lion?" Roger asked.

Hal said, "The scientist who discovered it, Steller by name, called it the lion of the sea because it looked so

171

much like the African lion with its huge neck, massive shoulders and golden eyes. Also, it was as big as a full-grown lion. The one you see right there probably weighs a ton. The sea lion is said to be smarter than a lion – and it's a lot more intelligent than the average seal. The circus that wants an animal to do tricks chooses a sea lion because it can be trained very easily. Even the young one is born smart. It doesn't start blind like so many animals, but has its eyes wide open, can swim without learning how, and weighs a hundred pounds before it is two months old. You might say it is grown up when it is born. It starts out with excellent vision and good hearing. It can dive to more than a thousand feet – and a big adult can't do any better."

The fur seal sprang out of the water like a dolphin, his whiskers waving in the breeze, and came down with a mighty thump upon the back of the sea lion.

Roger laughed. "Makes me think of two boys playing leap frog," he said.

"Yes," said Hal, "but these two fellows are not playing games. They'd just like to kill each other, that's all."

The lion twisted out from under his enemy and gave the fur seal a terrific blow on the head with his powerful flipper, which was almost as strong as iron.

Then it was whiskers against whiskers. Each got the other's whiskers between his teeth and pulled. The result was a terrific roar of pain on both sides.

Pulling loose, the sea lion grabbed the fur seal's head and ducked it down under the water. There he held it tightly so that his enemy should die for lack of air.

The fur seal wrapped his long, strong hind flippers around the lion's head and pulled it down under.

"Now they'll both die," exclaimed Roger.

But the fur seal's wives came to the rescue. The boys hadn't noticed them before. Hal made a quick count. "There are thirty of them."

"And all of them are wives of this one bull?"

"That's right. Sometimes a bull has as many as fifty wives."

With a great deal of squeaking the wives swam under the two males and hoisted their heads into the air.

The wives got small thanks from their bull. Instead, he roared at them as if he were saying, "Get out of the way. This is no business for females."

Hal said, "He reminds me of some men who don't appreciate what their wives do for them."

Now there was a furious struggle between the lion and the bull. At one moment it looked as if the fur bull would slaughter the lion. All eight flippers of the two beasts were going like windmills. One thinks of a flipper as being as weak as a wing. Instead it is as dangerous as an axe. With all these axes flailing both animals were getting badly gouged. That didn't matter so much in the case of the sea lion because, like the African lion, his hide is not good enough to be made into a fur coat. But in the case of the fur seal it was a serious matter, since the fur of this animal is almost as valuable as that of the sea otter.

The boys didn't care to mix into this fight and perhaps get killed.

"Where do these fur seals come from anyhow?" Roger wondered.

"From the Pribilof Islands up past Russia."

"Russia! Why that's a million miles away."

"No," said Hal. "The line between Russia and Alaska runs up through Bering Strait. If you walk out on the ice to that line and reach over and shake hands with somebody you are shaking hands with a Russian. Russia is as close as that to the United States."

"If they were so close why didn't they grab Alaska?"

"They did just that. Peter the Great, Emperor of Russia, told Vitus Bering to find out what lay east of Siberia. Bering was the first white man to set foot upon Alaska.

The young United States knew nothing about it. Canada knew nothing about it. The Russians took it over. Many years later they sold it to the United States for seven million dollars. Now it is worth billions instead of millions."

Hal saw a black fin coming toward the two fighters.

"That's a killer whale," he said. "I'm afraid it's all up with the lion and the bull. The killer whale has a keen appetite for seals and sea lions."

But it was not all up. Frightened by the murderous whale, the two enemies quit fighting each other and prepared to face the killer whale. This was a battle they were not likely to win. If they ever needed help, this was the time.

Nanook was growling ferociously. He didn't like killer whales. He started toward the water and the boys let him go. The great bear swam out and sank his teeth into the lip of the killer. That gave courage to the lion and the bull and they joined Nanook in an attack upon the killer whale.

The killer would be killed himself if he didn't get away fast. He decided to seek his dinner elsewhere. With a swish of his great tail, he brushed his three tormentors toward the beach.

Nanook had so often seen the boys capture animals that he instinctively knew what to do. He pushed both animals up on to the beach. Hal promptly dropped the noose of his lasso over the head of the sea lion and Roger captured the fur seal in his net.

Hal said, "We'll give them time for their nerves to quiet down a bit before we take them to the airport."

"But won't they die — out of the water?"

"In ancient times", Hal said, "they were both land animals. Even now they like to be out of the water just as well as in it."

"But can they walk — without feet?"

"Their fins aren't quite as good as feet for walking," admitted Hal, "but they can waddle along. First, let them rest."

The fur seal was looking at Roger with big, beautiful brown eyes.

"He looks as intelligent as the sea lion," said Roger. "And his face looks exactly like a bear's face."

"You guessed it," said Hal. "He's a cousin of the bear. Steller called him a 'sea bear'."

"How big he is!"

"I suppose he weighs about five hundred pounds. All the same, he can move fast. Look at those big strong shoulders and the lightning movements of his neck, and his big ivory teeth. They are like the teeth of a sperm whale. Notice how they curve back so that they can hang on to anything they close on. He has a terrific bite, and yet he never chews anything, just swallows it whole. Now he's beginning to dance around. That's the way fur seals are — very lively, full of fun."

"Well," said Roger, "we'll have to give them the fun of a waddle to the airport."

And waddle they did, with Nanook following close behind. The people of Barrow had never seen such a sight — a parade of two boys, two ferocious beasts, and the great white bear acting as policeman to see to it that these mighty fighters should waddle in peace to the airport.

27

The Whale That Sings
The Whale That Whistles

"This is going to be a big day," said Hal. "Get on your Neoprene suit. We're going down."

"What's up?" said Roger. "I mean what's down?"

"The humpbacks and the belugas. A lot of both of them have just arrived. They are down there, waiting for us."

"What are you talking about?"

"I'm talking about two kinds of whales that Dad wanted. They've just arrived from Hawaii – hundreds of them. The humpback is the most astonishing of all whales. You'll understand when you see him and hear him."

"Hear a whale?" said Roger. "Whales don't make any sound."

"That's what you think," said Hal. "You'll put your fingers in your ears when the humpback sings. You've heard many sounds under water but nothing like the song of the humpback. So I've been told – I've never heard it myself. This will be a new experience for both of us."

"What did you say the other one was he wants us to get — a belly something?"

"Not belly. Beluga. It was named by the Russians. It comes from a Russian word meaning white. It's the only snow-white whale in the sea. It also is very musical."

"Does it sing?" asked Roger.

"Not exactly. It whistles."

When they came down, dressed in their rubber suits, the Eskimo landlord said, "What are you after today?"

"Whales," said Hal.

The landlord smiled. "You are joking. Two boys against a whale! Everybody in town knows how smart you are. You have caught many animals. But when it comes to catching a whale — that's another matter. You probably don't even know the ceremony."

"Ceremony?" Hal asked. "What ceremony?"

"All the women of the town must close their mouths and keep quite silent. If they speak the whale will swim away. They must not move. If they do the whale will thrash about and escape. Also, for good luck, you must wear a magic charm with the picture of a whale on it. We Eskimos know these things."

"I respect what you know," said Hal. "But perhaps all

that ceremony is for Eskimos, not for us. Don't tell your women to keep quiet for our sake."

"But you can't do this all alone."

"No," said Hal. "We're going to have help. I saw the chief of the Coast Guard yesterday. They will have one of their big boats above us where we go down. If we get into trouble, they will help us. Anyhow, we're not after the big ones. The zoos would rather have young animals who have a long life ahead of them."

"But even a young whale will be stronger than a dozen men. Even if you catch it, it will struggle and get away."

"That's why we have this," said Hal. He held a gun.

"You can't use that," said the landlord. "There's a law against killing whales."

"I know," said Hal. "But this isn't to kill a whale. There's no powder in it — only a spring. Instead of firing a bullet it shoots a dart full of sleep medicine that will simply pierce the skin of the whale and put him to sleep."

"You can't fool me," said the landlord. "A gun is a gun. And a gun kills. I'll have to tell our policeman what you are up to."

"Go ahead," said Hal. "Perhaps he can help us."

"He'll help you into the town jail."

Hal smiled. "Tell him first to talk to the captain of the

Coast Guard. He knows that we're not interested in killing anything or anybody – even you. Now, if you will excuse us, we must get along."

Hal and Roger walked to the Coast Guard station, where the men knew very well what the boys were up to and admired them for their courage.

A sleek, clean little vessel carried them around Point Barrow to the western side, where the water boiled with the frolicking whales. One monster who happened to be under the boat raised it up several feet into the air, where it teetered for a moment and then fell with a great splash into the sea.

The skipper said to Hal, "How about it? Want to change your mind? There's a riot going on down there. You're taking an awful chance."

"I don't think it will be too bad," said Hal. "Whales are not like sharks. They have no reason to attack us. By the way, where do you suppose they all came from?"

"From the warm waters down south. They spend the winter there. When summer comes it's too warm for them and they come up to the pleasant cool waters of the Arctic. Just as a precaution, give me the name and address of your folks so we can notify them if you get killed."

Hal grinned. He didn't expect to get killed. But he gave

the skipper what he had asked for. "John Hunt, Hunt Wild Animal Farm, Long Island, New York."

The boys adjusted the scubas on their backs, then stepped over the starboard gunwale and sank into the water.

The peaceful giants made room for them. They gathered around in a great circle and sang. Hal had never heard such a song before. Roger could not believe his ears. The gentle monsters let loose with an underwater concert such as the boys had never heard in any opera house.

Some of the notes slid from high to low like a police siren. Some were trilled, some were burbled. Sometimes there was a distinct melody. Some sang soprano, some mezzo-soprano, some alto and some bass.

Underneath it all was a boom-boom like the sound of big drums and the rat-a-tat-tat of snare drums. The big whales thundered, the little ones squeaked. Music boomed, echoed, swelled, a medley of glorious sound. It was a fanfare of trumpets, trombones, clarinets, oboes, bassoons, saxophones and flutes – not to mention the deep thunder of the pipe organ.

Since it came from huge lungs, the roar was deafening.

Hal remembered that the *National Geographic* had published a recording of the songs of humpback whales.

And now they were listening to the whales themselves doing even better than the record.

But what was that whistling sound? Somebody or something was whistling a tune. Hal pointed to a smaller whale all in white. It was one of the belugas, sometimes called white whales. Evidently it could not sing, but it whistled its heart out.

Why were the humpbacks called humpbacks? Like the killer whale, which carries a fin on its back projecting upward about five feet sharp and strong, the humpback also has a fin on its back but quite different in appearance. It was low and thick and looked more like a lump than a fin. And some had no lump at all.

The humpback was oddly shaped. Hal could understand why it was called the most remarkable of all whales. It had an enormous head and its jaws when open were big enough to swallow a Jonah. Its two swimming fins were unusually long. Its various parts were awkwardly joined together like the segments of an ant. The front section was huge, but then the body tapered down to a narrow tail.

It went through all sorts of crazy movements. It loved to stand on its head with its tail projecting up out of the water. It could curl up like a doughnut. It would furiously splash the water with the large flukes of its tail. And all the time it sang as lustily as the calliope on a Mississippi steamboat.

The big ones were 50 feet long. Hal had read that the heart alone of such a monster weighs 430 pounds. The young ones, who were singing high soprano, were about 12 feet long. Even they weighed about 3,000 pounds. Hal, picking out one of them that looked good to him, used his sleep gun. The dart penetrated the young one's skin. The sleep medicine circulated through its body. It had not been hurt in the least but it quit singing and drifted lazily to the surface. A hawser was cast from the deck of the vessel and Hal looped it around the neck of the whale.

So far, so good. Now they must get a beluga. Roger straddled the back of one of the white beauties and Hal gave it a shot of sleep. The men on the Coast Guard boat laughed when they saw Roger and the whale pop up out of the water.

Roger caught the rope thrown to him and put the noose over this sleeping beauty.

The boys climbed aboard and the two sleeping whales were towed around the Point to the airport, where airfield employees loaded them into tanks for the flight south. The cargo plane left at once in order to get to Long Island before their big passengers woke up.

The boys returned to their lodging house. The landlord laughed.

"So, you had to give up," he said. "I knew you couldn't do it. The women moved and talked and you didn't wear any whale charm, so, of course, you failed."

Hal smiled. "I hope we fail as badly every time," he said.

28
A Sheep Can Kill

They were climbing a mountain of the Brooks Range. It was difficult because the ground was covered with slippery snow.

Behind them was a sledge, pulled not by a dog team but by a boy team. The two boys did not mind much since it was light and there was nothing much on it but a folded-up tent and some provisions.

But an icy wind was blowing. The higher they went, the colder they got.

Roger stopped and beat his mittened hands together to get them warm. "It's as cold as Greenland," he complained.

"We feel it more than we did there because we are climbing," Hal said.

Every time they inhaled the cold air they shivered. It was hard to breathe. The deadly chill started at the feet and went up through the body, numbing the stomach, the kidneys, the heart, turning the nose and chin white with frostbite.

"What did we come here for anyhow?" Roger demanded.

"To get a sheep," said Hal.

Roger stared at his brother. "You mean we're going through all this just to get a sheep?"

"Not the kind of sheep you're thinking about," said Hal. "We're not after the sort of sheep the farmer has in his pasture."

"Is there any other kind?"

"There sure is. I'm hoping to find a bighorn. It's twice as big as a farmer's sheep. It's strong and wild and dangerous."

"Why do they call it a bighorn?"

"Its horns are the heaviest part of it. They are thick and solid and they go around in a complete circle. One bunt of that great horny head and you are done for."

Roger's sharp eyes saw something moving. "It's a man – a man with a gun."

Hal said, "Wherever there's a man with a gun there is trouble."

"He's coming this way," said Roger.

The man who joined them was a heavily built brute, with a mean face and a mean gun.

When he joined them he said, "Hello you guys. I'll bet we're after the same thing. A bighorn. Sorry to disappoint you, but if we see one, I'll be the one to get it. You see, I'm a sharpshooter."

"Where are you from?" Hal asked.

188

"Wyoming. I'm a bit famous down there. Perhaps you've heard of me. My name is Alec."

Hal at once thought of the term "Smart Alec", which according to the dictionary was applied to anyone who was a braggart and felt himself very clever.

"Sorry to meet you," said Hal with a smile. "I'm afraid we'd better give up right now."

"Well," said Smart Alec, "you can tag along if you like and see how I operate. It will be a good lesson for you – to see how an expert does these things."

"I'm sure we will learn a lot," said Hal. "Just why do you want to kill a bighorn?"

"To put the head and horns up on the wall in my house. I already have the living-room wall covered with antlers, but I think there's perhaps room for one more."

"So you've done a lot of killing," said Hal.

"Killing is my middle name. I'm afraid of nothing that walks. Why should I be afraid of a dall sheep? That's another name, you know, for a bighorn."

"You may find", said Hal gently, "that the dall is no doll."

"Never mind. I don't care what it is. The worse it is, the better I'll like it. I always get away pretty well with a tough job. After all, the Bible says man is superior to any beast."

"When did you last read your Bible?"

"I don't read it. Somebody told me. And he was right. No animal on earth is as good as me."

Hal said, "How about the ones that have sharper eyesight than any man, sharper hearing, better sense of smell, don't go to war and kill millions of their own kind? They don't smoke themselves into cancer and they don't get drunk. They don't neglect their young ones as some human parents do and don't go around shooting men in order to put their heads up on the wall."

"I can see that you're a couple of mollycoddles," said Alec. "I'll go along with you to protect you from the sheep. You'd never make it alone."

Hal noticed that the stranger had given his own name, but didn't bother to learn the names of the two he had met. He was thinking only of himself.

They proceeded up the mountain. Since Alaska is farther south than the polar part of Greenland, the sun was much higher than it had been in the far north, and stronger. Its reflection on the snow was painful and the three began to feel as if they had sand in their eyes, or hot knives. They were in danger of going snow blind. Roger began to wish that they were animals who didn't mind the glare.

Hal had known beforehand that their eyes would suffer. He drew out of his pocket a piece of walrus hide and some string.

"Wait a moment," he said. "We'll have to make three pairs of goggles." He cut out three strips two inches wide and about seven inches long. He put one of the strips over Roger's eyes.

"What's that for?" asked Roger. "Now I can't see a thing."

"I just wanted to find out if it was a good fit," said Hal. "Now I'll finish the job."

He took the strip and cut two slits in it, one for each eye. Then he put the strip back over Roger's eyes and tied it fast around his head with the string.

Now Roger could see through the slits and the glare was gone.

"Now I'll make one for you," Hal said to Smart Alec.

But Alec would have none of that. "What do you think I am, a child? Don't try to baby me or I'll punch you on the nose."

"O.K.," said Hal, "but I'll baby myself." And he made a pair of walrus goggles and put them on. He could see through the slits, but there was no longer any sun-pain. "You'd better let me make one for you," he said to Alec.

But Smart Alec was indignant. "That's all right for kids,"

he said. "I mean, if you have weak eyes. Mine are strong. I'm no weakling."

He trudged on, with his eyes almost closed. Now and then he stumbled. He was evidently suffering intense pain. Hal felt sorry for the boob. He knew that the eyes of Smartypants must feel as if they were full of needles. Alec could hardly see where he was going. Hal took his arm, but Smart Alec shook him off. He was a fool, and a fool is too proud to accept help.

They came upon a small herd of caribou. Most of them passed by, but one big bull stopped and pawed the ground angrily. He had magnificent horns reaching above his head four feet high. Hal had seen plenty of caribou, but none like this king of the snows.

Smart Alec could also see the towering horns. "I've got to have those antlers," he said and prepared to shoot.

Before he could do so, the bull lowered his horns, drove them into Alec's stomach, and lifted him twelve feet high. Now Smart Alec did not sound very smart. He howled with pain. No wonder, with those sharp prongs slicing through his hide.

Hal wanted to do something to help, but before he could think what to do, the bull started off with the herd. Every time he put his foot down with a jolt, the Smartie yelled blue murder as the sharp points dug further into his anatomy.

The climax came when the bull stopped at the edge of a cliff and dropped him twenty feet into a snow-bank, screaming as he fell.

Hal went and helped him up. Alec was crying. "I'm full of holes," he said. "Got to have some antiseptic. Those antlers have poisoned me. I'll get gangrene and die."

"No you won't," said Hal. "Those antlers are as clean as a surgeon's knife. They're always up in the clean air — never get dirty — except that now they have some of your dirty blood."

"How come you know so much about animals?" said Alec.

"It's my business," Hal said. "Now pull up your coat and your shirt and let's see what's happening."

The skin was punctured here and there and blood was oozing out. But as soon as it reached the surface it froze solid and stopped the bleeding. So the frigid climate did what a doctor could not do.

Smart Alec did not feel very peppy. "I want to go home."

"Perk up," said Hal. "You're not badly hurt. Don't forget — we're after a bighorn."

They came upon one an hour later. It stood proudly on a big rock. It was a magnificent fellow with great heavy horns that curled around and came back to where they had started. Smart Alec raised his gun. Smarter Hal had just brushed away the snow and picked up a small pebble. He threw it at the bighorn and when it struck the animal moved a few feet and the bullet missed.

All Alec had done was just annoy the animal and it now stood up on its hind feet and came toward him. It was taller than he was, and a great deal stronger.

Hal brought out his sleep gun. "I thought you didn't believe in guns," said Alec.

"I believe in this one," said Hal, and he fired.

The dart pierced the skin of the big sheep. He came down on all four feet and began scratching at the dart. He got it loose but the medicine had already gone into his body and was at work. Since he could wander away before the sleep medicine took effect, Hal lassoed him and held fast.

Roger drew the sledge up beside the animal. When the dall began to teeter Hal pushed it over and tied it fast on the sledge.

"Well, you won that round," said Alec. "By the way, what's your name?"

Hal told him.

Alec looked at him with more interest than he had shown before. "I saw something in the papers about you. You take animals for zoos."

"That's right," said Hal. "What's your business in Wyoming?"

"I have a ranch. Wyoming has some wild life too. And a fair number of zoos. I've a notion to imitate you — but on a small scale. Perhaps we can pick up some animals alive for our zoos."

"That's the best thing you've said yet," said Hal. "Good luck to you."

They parted on good terms. The Hunts with their trophy went down to the mountain's base, where a truck waited to take them to Point Barrow.

29
The Moose and the Mouse

"Send me the biggest moose you can find," John Hunt telegraphed to his sons.

Hal knew where to find the largest moose in the whole world. "This means a trip to the Kenai Peninsula," he said.

"I know where that is," said Roger. "But it's too far away. We're on the north edge of Alaska. Kenai is on the south edge. Aren't there moose right around here somewhere?"

"There are moose in many parts of Alaska, but the really great ones are the Kenai moose. That's where we'll have to go to find the big boys."

Early the next morning they were on the plane that would carry them south from the Arctic Ocean to an even greater ocean, the Pacific. They knew the pilot and co-pilot because they had so often visited the Point Barrow airport to arrange for shipment of their animals to Long Island.

"Hope you enjoy the trip," said the pilot, Ben Bolt. "If you want to come up in the cockpit now and then it will be quite all right. You can get a better view there of what's ahead."

What was ahead was quite thrilling. First the plane had to soar ten thousand feet high to clear the mountains of the Brooks Range. Then down, only to rise again to get over the Endicott Mountains.

Over dozens of lakes, then up again to cross the Ray Mountains.

Now below them was the great Yukon River. They were no sooner over that than they must climb again over the Mooseheart Mountains.

Then came the most thrilling experience. They passed over Mount McKinley National Park. They flew close to Mount McKinley, highest mountain in North America, but did not attempt to fly over it. They did fly above the other mountains of the Park, Mount Brooks, Mount Hunter and Mount Foraker.

Then over lakes, lakes, lakes — what a wet country Alaska was! Over a great glacier, over Cook Inlet, then down to the airport in the small town of Kenai.

Hal and Roger were in the cockpit when a big moose appeared in the middle of the runway. The moose is a proud animal, and very stubborn. He does not make way for anybody. Everybody must make way for him. He rules the animal kingdom in the north, just as the elephant in Africa is all-powerful. There, if you see an elephant in the road, you must stop and wait – perhaps for hours – because elephants "have the right of way". In Alaska "moose have the right of way".

The moose continued to stand there as solid as a rock while the plane rushed toward him. The pilot did his best to bring the plane to a halt. It was no use. Plane and moose met with a sickening crunch. The whirling propeller tried to turn the moose into a hamburger. The plane came to a sudden stop throwing everyone forward. The moose must have been badly hurt, but no sound came from him because a moose does not cry as lesser animals may do.

Airport hands helped to disentangle propeller and moose, then turned the plane about and let it move slowly to another runway. In the meantime the moose remained exactly where he had been just as if he were not a living animal, but a granite statue.

"Now you get an idea", said Ben, "of what a job you are going to have if you try to capture a moose."

"That one wasn't big enough," said Hal. "Where can we find a really great one?"

"At Moose Pass," said Ben. "But first you'd better have lunch with us and we'll tell you what you are up against. You may change your mind about trying to capture a moose."

As they ate Ben told them what he had learned about this animal during his twenty-five years in Alaska.

"Right here you will find the biggest moose on earth," said Ben. "There are moose in Europe, but there they call them elk and they are about half the size of the Alaskan moose. The bull moose in Kenai weighs about eighteen hundred pounds and is much taller than any horse. Up to the top of his horns he may measure as much as twelve feet."

Hal looked up. "This room measures about eight feet from floor to ceiling," he said. "The moose is four feet taller! No wonder he's the animal king of Alaska."

"The moose belongs to the deer family," said Ben. "But did you ever see any antlers on a deer as wide as these — six feet across? He puts about fifty pounds of food every day into his stomach."

"What kind of food?" Roger asked.

"Wood," said Ben. "He doesn't kill any animals. He eats no meat. He eats trees — the leaves, twigs, even the trunks. The Indian name for him is *musee*, which means wood-eater. From *musee* we get the word moose."

"You mentioned Moose Pass," said Hal. "Do we fly there?"

"No. You had better hire a wanigan."

"What in heaven's name is a wanigan?"

"It's a sort of van. It is usually pulled by a tractor. When it is used on snow it has runners. But there's no snow here, so it is fitted with wheels and it has a motor of its own. You'll have to have a wanigan to bring back your moose – if you get one. I'll take you to a wanigan garage."

The boys rented a wanigan, said goodbye to their aviator friends, and set out on the road to Moose Pass.

Half-way there they encountered a moose. Of course he stood in the middle of the road. Remembering that moose have the right of way, Hal stopped the wanigan. For half an hour they waited. Some men were working at the side of the road. One of them called, "I'll move him for you."

He picked up a stone and threw it. It struck the moose on his nose. The nose of a moose is like no other nose on earth. It is a foot long, and very tender. The animal uses it as if it were a hand. The nose picks leaves from a tree and stuffs them into the mouth. It is the moose's pride and joy and he resents any interference with it.

This moose got the idea that the stone had come from the wanigan. He did not stay still one moment longer. He came bellowing and snorting like a steam engine.

Hal backed the wanigan down the road but the angry moose, with a speed that one would not expect from so large a beast, overtook the car. A moose is accustomed to standing on his hind feet to reach high branches. This time he stood on his hind feet, and with his powerful front feet pushed the wanigan over into the ditch. There it lay upside down with its engine still whirring. The upside-down boys crawled out and retreated into a field. The moose, having punished those he considered his tormentors, wandered away, his big nose trembling with anger.

The road men were Eskimos and, true to their nature, came at once to help. Together with the boys, they got the wanigan right side up and back on the road. The boys, feeling a little shaken, thanked the men and went on their way.

Eventually they came to a point where the railroad crossed the road, and near by was a small railway station. They went in to rest and get any information they could from the station master. On the wall they saw a sign which read, "NOT RESPONSIBLE FOR ANY DELAYS CAUSED BY MOOSE."

"You boys want a ticket?" said the station master.

"No," said Hal. "We just came in to get some information

about moose. We noticed the sign on the wall. Evidently you have trouble with moose getting on the track."

"Yes," said the old station master. "We've killed a lot of them. You've come to the right place for information. I know about all there is to know about the moose. It's a very strong animal, and if you eat it it makes you strong. The left hind foot of a moose is a cure for epilepsy. Bones from the antlers will take away headache. If you grind part of an antler up into powder it will be an antidote for snakebite. The hoof of a moose will cure six hundred diseases."

A young man who had heard all this laughed. "The old geezer has a lot of superstitions," he said.

Hal said, "But the moose is really a very remarkable animal."

"Yes it is. It is born with its eyes wide open. Seven days after birth it can outrun a man. The female adult moose weighs a thousand pounds and the bull moose weighs almost twice as much. Its antlers are unique. They look like big soup plates. With its terrific front feet it can trample to death bears, wolves, cougars, coyotes and wolverines. You wouldn't imagine it could get so strong eating nothing but asters, ferns, lilies, duckweed, burrweed, duck potato and all kinds of wood. It also eats the leaves and twigs of aspen, balsam, birch, maple and mountain ash. It's so big and clumsy-looking, yet it can slip through the woods without a sound. In spite of its diet of lilies and such it can get very dangerous. It crashes headlong into cars and yesterday one charged a locomotive. That was a bit too much for His Majesty."

"He died?"

"Yes, he died. But there are plenty more. Are you especially interested in moose?"

"Just now, yes," said Hal. "We want to take one alive for a zoo."

"It would be easier to take one dead."

Hal laughed. "I don't think we'll try to pick up the bones along the railroad tracks. Where are the live ones?"

"A good place to find them is around Kenai Lake. I'll go with you if you like."

"Great. My name is Hal. This is Roger, my brother."

"I'm Ivak – part Eskimo, part Montana."

The wanigan bumped over a fair road to the lake. Sure enough, there were several big bulls here, some on shore, some in the water. With them were some cow moose. They were smaller than the bulls, and had no horns. Also there were calves, hornless as yet, but bright, lively and strong.

"You notice," said Ivak, "that nearly all of them are inside that big circle where the grass is trampled down. That is called a mooseyard. Where there are many moose, you'll always find a mooseyard. It's a sort of meeting place, where they get together and enjoy each other's company. And they don't like to have any other animal come in and try to join the club."

"What magnificent antlers they have," said Hal. "They don't go up very much like the antlers of a deer. They go out — one set from the right side of the head, and the other from the left. Each one looks like a huge platter or a soup tureen. How would you describe them?"

Ivak said, "To me they look like big shovels. They can carry things on those enormous plates."

"What kind of things?" Roger asked.

"Bushes, plants, weeds — anything they want to eat later on. And you notice they have a fence all around the plate to hold things in."

"You mean that row of spikes? They look sharp and dangerous."

"They are the weapons of the moose. If any enemy comes around, the moose lowers its head and plunges those spikes into it and kills it. You see that some have only a few spikes, perhaps a dozen – and others may have as many as forty – all of them as sharp as needles."

"Why is there so much difference?" Roger asked.

"Nature plays tricks," said Ivak. "One moose is not exactly like another. They are like people – all different. Just as a lady may wear a different hair-do, so each moose has a different horn-do."

"What are those moose doing out in the lake?"

"Watch and you will see them disappear beneath the surface. They go down after water plants. They scrape up the plants with their horns. There's one that has just come up. He has a load of plants on his platters. When he is ready to eat them he will shake the plants off on to the ground and use his long nose to push them into his mouth."

"Look!" said Roger. "There's a grizzly. He's coming right into the mooseyard."

"That's very bad manners", said Ivak, "for any other animal to burst into the private club of the moose. He'll get what he deserves."

A huge bull moose was attacked by the grizzly. Every grizzly thinks himself very important. He is used to conquering any animal who interferes with him. This grizzly stood up on his hind feet in order to get his

teeth into the neck of the moose. All he got was the
goatee or whiskers that hung from the moose's throat.
He spat these out and tried again.

If a grizzly bear can stand on its hind feet, so can a
moose. The moose stood erect, battered the bear's face
with his front feet as a boxer does with his fists. But the
rock-hard hooves of the moose were much more terrible
than the gloved fists of a boxer.

The grizzly who had invaded the private domain of the
moose was thoroughly punished. His face looked like a bowl
of mush. Still he fought. Evidently more severe measures
were necessary to punish this rascal. The moose lowered his

head and used the deadly spikes on his antlers to punch his enemy full of holes.

The impudent grizzly, who probably never before had met an enemy he could not conquer, fell away and crawled out of the mooseyard.

"I think that's the moose we want," said Hal. "He's the biggest one of the lot."

Ivak grinned. "Do you think you can do better than the grizzly?"

"Yes," said Hal, "but without fighting."

"This is something I want to see," said Ivak. "Perhaps you are going to use your lasso."

"No," said Hal. "The lasso is no good in this case. He would break it."

"Then you are going to use gentle persuasion? You won't get far with that."

"We'll see," said Hal. "Roger, do your bit and I'll do mine." He went outside the magic circle, where he had seen a hole made by field mice. He stepped very softly, not wishing to alarm any mouse that might be at home. He lay down beside the hole and waited.

In the meantime, Roger was doing his bit. He walked slowly toward the giant moose. The moose had learned to be afraid of guns, but this visitor had no gun. He had no pistol, no stick, no knife. The great moose, master of the mountains, was not in the habit of running from anybody or anything – except a gun.

Roger came close and began speaking in soft tones. It was a friendly voice and the speaker was only a boy, so what was there to be afraid of? He let the boy pat his great neck.

Hal came, carrying in his hand a wriggling mouse. He walked very slowly, keeping his hands out in full sight so that the moose would understand that he had no gun. Then, very gently, he placed the mouse on the foot-long nose of the moose.

The little eyes of the mouse studied the moose, and the great eyes of the moose were fixed upon the mouse.

Neither was afraid of the other. By a dip of his nose, the giant could have slipped the mouse into his mouth and swallowed it.

He did not, for several reasons. First, the mouse was too small to do him any harm. Second, he never ate other animals. He was a strict vegetarian. He ate no meat. But the main reason was that he had never before been visited by a friendly little mouse. It was quite evident that he liked the little beast.

The mouse crawled up the nose and on up into the

antlers, where he lay down in the soup bowl or shovel or platter or whatever one might want to call it. Some leaves remained in the bowl and they happened to be to his liking. He munched on them and was very happy. This was better than a hole in the ground.

But a mouse can never stay still for very long. The little fellow noticed the wanigan. He crawled out of the shovel, and down the nose, and dropped to the ground. He also had a nose but nothing in comparison with the nose of the great moose. The mouse's nose, though small, was very keen and he smelled some food that the boys had left in the wanigan. He went in to investigate.

The great moose stood for a long time gazing at the wanigan. He was evidently waiting for his small friend to come out.

When he did not, the moose walked slowly to the wanigan and looked inside. After thinking it over, he climbed up into the wanigan making the floor creak under his weight of almost a ton.

Hal, very quietly, let down the sliding door at the back of the wanigan. Before it completely closed Roger thrust in a big bush for the wood-eater to dine upon during the trip to Kenai airport.

The boys thanked Ivak for his help, then climbed into

the cab, which was separated by a partition from the quarters occupied by the moose and the mouse. They drove back to the Kenai airport and made arrangements for the transport of the mighty moose to Long Island and, on the next day, flew back to Point Barrow and their faithful Nanook.

30
The Wild Williwaw

They were climbing Castle Mountain when the williwaw caught them.

"I'm afraid we're in for it," Hal said. "Here comes a williwaw."

"What kind of an animal is a williwaw?" Roger asked.

"It's not a wild beast," said Hal. "It's a wild storm. It's a hurricane and a typhoon and a tornado all mixed up together. It's born in the Aleutian Islands and it sweeps across Alaska tearing down houses and killing cattle."

"Doesn't sound too good," said Roger. "What can we do about it?"

"Nothing much. Just try to stay alive. Lucky we didn't bring our big tent. It would be blown away. The pup tent we brought will be better."

"Let's get it up in a hurry," said his young brother.

You don't carry anything more than you have to when you climb a mountain. The pup tent was light and small. It was just long enough for the one sleeping bag they had brought. The bag was large enough for two, providing that you didn't mind being jammed together like a couple of sardines.

They anchored the tent to the ground with large rocks. Surely the wind wouldn't be strong enough to blow away 100-pound rocks.

Hal had wisely placed the tent with its back end toward the wind.

"That's about all we can do," he said. "See those black clouds racing in from the west? They're full of wind. Let's get inside."

They crawled into the pup tent. Hal laced the flaps securely.

"You get into the bag first," he said. "Then I'll try to squeeze in beside you."

The wind struck with the force of a thousand hammers. The pup tent was ripped loose and sailed away toward Canada. The rocks on the side toward the wind rolled in upon the sleeping bag.

"Ouch!" cried Roger. "Get off my chest."

"I'm not on your chest," said Hal. "That's just a couple of hundred pounds of rock."

"Why did you pile them on me?"

"The wind did that without my help. Just be patient. The wind will blow them away again."

The next gust picked them up and carried them off as if they had been cardboard boxes instead of rocks.

"I suppose we'll go next," said Roger.

"Perhaps not. We're heavier than rocks. This rock weighed about one hundredweight. You and I together weigh about three hundred pounds."

To make matters worse, the black cloud sent down a deluge of rain. The bag was waterproof, so the boys pulled its flap over their heads.

"It can rain all it pleases," said Hal. "We're snug and warm."

But the rain soon turned into hail. The hailstones were as big as the biggest marbles.

"They're knocking the breath out of me," complained Roger.

"Lie face down," said Hal. "Then your lungs will be protected."

It was no easy matter to twist into a face-down position. Hal got a few smart blows from the elbows of his squirming brother. He himself had a stronger rib cage and could stand the pummelling he got from the bullets of the sky. He put his arm over his face.

The wind was roaring and screeching like a banshee. How long would this go on? Hal didn't know the habits of a williwaw. He had heard that the willies, as the

Alaskans call them, come rushing down the valleys and mountainsides like devils bent on destroying everything man had made. If any planes were in the sky they would not remain there. They would be dashed to pieces against the mountain peaks.

Surely, he thought, this furious blizzard could not last long. It would peter out before evening and they would be home in time to have a good night's sleep.

But the williwaw had no intention of petering out. It became worse as night arrived and it continued until daybreak.

"I'm hungry," said Roger.

Hal said, "I'm afraid you'll just have to stay hungry. We didn't bring any food because we expected to be in Barrow for supper."

Roger was angry. "You were a big boob not to bring anything to eat."

"O.K.," said Hal. "I was a big boob. Perhaps you were a little boob because you didn't think of it."

"Why should I think of it? You're the boss."

"Sometimes I think you are," said Hal. "You're fifteen. It's time you started to think for yourself."

"I'd punch you on the nose if I could get my hand loose."

Hal laughed. "What are we getting into? You and I never quarrel. It's this blooming storm that is getting us down. Getting our nerves on edge."

Thunder and lightning joined the wind and the hail. And it was getting icy cold. Two days and two nights went by without food and without any pause in the violent storm.

Then the wind died, the whirling dervishes in the sky quit putting on their act and the boys emerged from their cocoon. They could hardly walk about, so cramped and stiff were their legs and so empty their stomachs.

The storm had wiped out the trail they had come by. The sky remained covered with cloud so the sun could give them no help. East, west, north, south, did not exist for them. They were completely lost.

"Someone will come along," was Roger's optimistic forecast. No one came along.

"At least we have to go down the mountain," said Hal. "We know that much."

"Yes, which way down?" Castle Mountain was only 3,700 feet high and they were at the top. Every way down but one would be a mistake.

With so many mistakes possible, it was not surprising that they stumbled at random down the rocks, hoping against hope that they would meet some human being. They met a bear, but he could tell them nothing. He didn't even try to eat them because he had already dined and these scrawny, starved humans didn't look like a good dinner.

They sat down occasionally, puffing and snorting and trying to get their strength and their breath back. Hal wished that he could carry Roger, but the boy would resent being carried like a baby and, besides, Hal was much too weak to carry 130 pounds in his arms or on his back.

Then they saw it – a cabin!

"Whoever lives there", Hal said, "will help us. We can get warm by his fire and he may even let us have a little food. What luck!"

The roof was covered with half-melted hail three or four inches thick. The walls were made of heavy logs that were too stout to have been destroyed by the storm. The furious wind had caved in one window.

Hal knocked at the door. There was no answer. He rapped again. Nothing doing. Roger was shaking with cold. He sat down on the steps.

Hal said, "The fellow who lives here must have gone to town."

Looking at Roger he thought, "I must get him in and

warm him up. If I don't, he'll get pneumonia."

He climbed in through the broken window, cutting himself with some of the loose bits of glass. He stepped down on to a table and from that to the floor. What a relief to be in a house again, even one so small as this.

He called. There was no answer. There was no one in the cabin but himself.

"Come in through the window, Roger. There's nobody home and the door is solidly locked."

Roger came in, scratching himself as Hal had done. He looked about. "Isn't this great. We'll start a fire and perhaps we'll even find some food. Do you think the owner would mind?"

"I don't think there is any owner," said Hal. "It's been cleaned out completely. The door isn't really locked. It's just been jammed shut by the years." He shivered. "It's as cold as a refrigerator. It doesn't even have a stove. All the dishes are gone, pots, pans, everything."

"Well, anyhow, it's ours for the time being," said Roger. "Isn't that the custom in the North? An empty house is for anybody or everybody. Isn't that the way it goes?"

"That's right," said Hal. "But it isn't of much use to us without food and without a stove."

"What are those tin cans in the corner? Piled up on

each other. There's a sort of pipe going up through the ceiling. I'll bet the person who made it thinks that he made a stove. Let's try it."

"We have to have wood," said Hal, "and there's not a stick in the cabin."

"But there was a sort of hump that I had to stand on to get in through the window. It's all covered with hail, but I'll bet there's some wood beneath," said Roger.

"Bright idea," said Hal. "Let's heave open this door. It's just stuck."

They threw their combined weight against the door and it popped open.

Roger attacked the hump with his mittened hands. He cleared away the hail. "There's a cord of wood here," he exclaimed. "Do you think he forgot it?"

"Perhaps. But it's more likely that he left it on purpose for anybody who wanted to use the cabin. People up here are like that."

They took some sticks inside and Hal whittled off some shavings with his pocket knife.

He put the shavings in the silly tin stove, put some sticks on top, and blessed the tin stove when the fire blazed up and began to warm the room.

It was wonderful to feel even the small heat from this

stove. They began to feel human once more. Roger's stiff joints relaxed.

"Now, if we only had some food. I'll bet there's some somewhere. The last people who were here left the wood and surely they would have left something to eat."

"Well," said Hal, "you can look for it if you like, while I patch up that window. We won't get very warm with a busted window."

"There's no way you can patch it up," said Roger. "There's not a towel in the house, not an old shirt, not a piece of board, nothing."

While Roger started his search for food Hal went outside. He faced an almost impossible task. If there had been snow he would have cut out a block of it and wedged it into the open space left by the broken window. But there was no snow. There was plenty of ice on the ground formed from hail that had frozen together into flat slabs. With his knife he cut out a section of hail-made ice and fitted it over the hole in the window.

Then he went in, expecting Roger to congratulate him. Instead Roger said, "That's no good. The heat from the stove will melt it."

"It will try to," said Hal, "but perhaps the chill air from outside will keep the ice from melting. We've seen ice windows in Greenland. They last for months. There's heat inside but the cold outside is stronger than the heat."

"I'll bet your window will melt," said Roger, "and it will be as cold as Greenland inside here."

But the window did not melt and the tin stove gave off enough heat to keep them half comfortable.

"I found some food," said Roger.

"You did? That's great. You're not such a dumb cluck after all. What kind of food?"

"Pemmican, and dried raisins, some pretty tired bread, and a can of milk frozen solid. May I serve you? Do you like your milk hard or soft?"

"Soft, if you please."

"Very well, sir," said Roger. "I shall put the milk on the stove and you shall have your milk not only thawed soft, but hot. Can you think of any greater luxury than that?"

When they had eaten Hal smacked his lips. "The best restaurant in New York couldn't have done better," he said.

Next morning the sun shone and they could tell which way was north. They went down the mountain to the river at its base. There was no bridge in sight. But there was hardly any water in the river.

"We'll have to walk across," said Hal. "We'll only get our feet wet."

On his second step Hal's right leg suddenly sank from sight. The other leg followed. He was terrified. He realized suddenly that he was facing death.

"Stay where you are," he shouted to Roger.

"What's the trouble?"

"Quicksand!"

He did everything possible to free his legs. But he couldn't get either leg loose. Every moment he was sinking further. Roger started out to help him. "Stay where you are," commanded Hal. "No use both of us getting caught."

Now the sand was up to his waist. He writhed and squirmed. The sand soaked with icy water was chilling him to the bone.

"Lie down," Roger shouted.

This seemed to Hal a ridiculous thing to say. Why should he lie down? Well, of course, if he lay down there would be so much of him on top of the sand that he might not sink more. It was worth a try. He lay flat upon the sand, and worked to get his legs loose. He was more dead than alive. He was cold and exhausted but he kept struggling until his whole body including the legs lay flat on the sand.

Then he began inching toward the land. With a final struggle he reached firm ground. He lay on the shore breathing hard, his heart going like a trip-hammer. His clothes were soaked and heavy and his caribou boots were full of sand and water. He felt he couldn't move an inch.

Roger knelt and took Hal's head in his hands.

"Don't be in a hurry," he said. "This is as good a place to rest as any." Kneeling in sand and water, he was as dirty as his brother.

So Hal rested for half an hour. Then he got up and staggered off with Roger, looking for a bridge. It was almost dark before they found one.

After they had crossed it a car going their way pulled up in front of them. The Eskimo driver had seen that these staggering, soaking wet, sand-pasted fellows were in need of help.

"Where are you going?" he said.

"To Barrow village," Hal answered.

"Hop in," said the Eskimo. "If there's any hop left in you."

"Mighty little," laughed Hal. And with the little hop he had left he climbed into the car.

Arriving in Barrow, he heartily thanked the Eskimo driver for his kindness, and with Roger's support he wobbled over to their lodging, where the proprietor stood in the door. He did not recognize Hal and said sharply, "This is a respectable place. We don't take any bums here."

Roger said, "Don't you recognize us? We're the Hunts."

"Oh, a thousand pardons." And he admitted these smelly, wet, dirty "bums" to his proud establishment, which was almost as dirty as the "bums".

31
Orchestra of the Elks

A telegram came from their father.

YOU ARE DOING GOOD WORK. WE COULD
USE ALASKAN ELK WHITE GRIZZLY GIANT KODIAK.

Hal went to the airport and showed the telegram to
his pilot friend, Ben Bolt.

"The best place to find those animals", said Ben, "is
down in that wonderful country called the Valley of Ten
Thousand Smokes."

"I've heard of it," said Hal. "That's where one of the
volcanoes exploded and sent clouds of smoke and gas around
the world."

"One of the two biggest eruptions in all history," said
Ben. "The other was Krakatoa."

"But isn't it still dangerous there?"

"Perhaps. But danger never stopped you."

"And we can find elk there?"

"Quite near there," said Ben. "Most of them are on
Afognak Island. It's just across the strait from the

225

volcanoes. I can't take you there because there's no landing strip. But I can fly you and Nanook to the volcano country and you can get a boat across to Afognak. Almost touching that island is another called Kodiak Island and that's where you will find the biggest and strongest bear in all creation, the Kodiak bear. How you will ever bag that ferocious monster I can't imagine, but that's up to you."

"And how about grizzlies?"

"You'll find them almost anywhere. Or they'll find you. They have a grudge against all two-legged animals such as you and your brother."

Hal said, "Our father wants us to get a white grizzly. I thought all grizzlies were grey."

"Most of them are," said Ben. "But he means the silver-tip."

"Just what is a silver-tip?"

"The tip of every hair is a silvery white so it looks as if the bear is wearing a white coat. A silver-tip is a very dangerous animal. It looks beautiful, but it has a devil where its heart should be. You'd better carry a gun."

Hal laughed. "I don't think Dad would appreciate a dead grizzly."

"O.K. It's your funeral," said Ben. "When will you be ready to go?"

"Tomorrow morning. Eight o'clock. All right by you?"

"Fine. I'll be ready."

The next morning after breakfast Hal paid the proprietor, who said, "I suppose you're out after more animals. I can give you some advice. I can tell you where you can find rabbits and woodchucks, and porcupines and skunks."

"Thank you so much," said Hal, "but we would be afraid to tackle such savage animals. Don't you know of anything that won't bite?"

"Well," said the proprietor, "there's the lizard and the toad and the frog."

Hal said, "You're giving us some very valuable information. We'll look for some lizards and toads and frogs. You're quite sure that they don't bite?"

"I've never laid hands on them myself. That's the best policy. Leave them alone – then they can't hurt you."

The landlord never suspected that Hal had been kidding him. Roger laughed when he heard about it. "Well," he said, "we'd better get after those toads and frogs."

The flight over hundreds of snowy peaks stabbing the sky was as exciting as it had been before. Nanook enjoyed the ride. He was not at all nervous, because he was travelling with the two humans he loved. They would take care of him and he would take care of them.

As soon as they had dodged one peak they faced another. It kept them a little breathless, not knowing at what moment they might collide with one of these towers of solid rock. Ben usually flew over them. But that was not so easy when he was toting half a ton of polar bear.

Smoke ahead told them that they were approaching the Valley of Ten Thousand Smokes. Martin Volcano was sending its white cloud of steam thousands of feet into the air. They passed over the great Katmai Volcano. A terrific eruption in 1812, which had spread a haze over half of the world's surface, was credited to Mount Katmai. The effects were felt in Europe, North America, Asia and North Africa. Volcanic ash a foot deep was laid down on Kodiak Island a hundred miles away. Violent earthquakes laid open the land and from the cracks there was a gigantic flow of red hot sand, which kept rolling fifteen miles, consuming everything in its path. Steam, boiling hot, spouted from the cracks, scorching anyone who happened to come near. That was the birth of the Valley of Ten Thousand Smokes.

Below them the crater of Katmai Volcano was eight miles wide. At its bottom they expected to see fire – instead there was a large lake.

The Valley of Ten Thousand Smokes had lost many of its smokes, but at least a thousand remained. The plane came down in the Valley, singeing the wings as they passed over a column of fire. If that fire had reached the tanks of gasoline there would have been an explosion that would end for good and all the Hunt expedition.

After visiting the fumaroles, as these jets of fiery steam were called, they flew back a few miles to Grosvenor Camp, named after the president of the National Geographic Society, which had originally explored this region.

Beside the camp was Lake Grosvenor and around it on all sides rose great volcanic mountains, Kaguyak still on fire, Griggs, Mageik, Martin blazing furiously, and many others, all well over a mile high.

The manager of Grosvenor Camp heartily welcomed the boys and their bear. Hal spoke to him about the great eruption.

"I was here when it happened," said the manager. "Of course I was a young man then. It scared me half to death. The days were as dark as the nights. The earth kept shaking and fire spouted from the volcanoes. Hot ash covered the houses several feet deep. But not one person died. Vesuvius buried a whole city. That didn't happen here because there was no city."

The boys spent a day exploring the Valley. Even where steam was not spouting up, the ground was so hot that they could not sit on it. Every once in a while there was a rumble beneath that shook the earth. There were deep gullies that had to be crossed. To go down fifty feet and climb up on the other side was exhausting. With every step their ankles sank into hot sand. At any moment their feet might start a burning avalanche that would carry them down with it. Nanook had less trouble. His clawed feet went down through the sand and clutched the rocks beneath. He climbed up the sliding slopes with ease. The boys found that the best way to get up was to hang on to Nanook.

Walking over the flat places, they found the earth so hot it nearly burned through the soles of their caribou boots.

They had brought along a can of food, but the food was cold. They attached a string to the can and let it down into a fumarole. After a few minutes it came up boiling hot. How convenient to have a stove waiting for you wherever you walked.

And if they wanted a cold drink, they had only to place their bottle, which had been warmed by the sun, upon one of the glaciers which came down from the mountains. In a few moments the drink was as cold as if it had contained ice cubes.

★ ★ ★

But this fascinating experience was not getting them an elk. The next morning they set out on a walk past Mount LaGorce to Hallo Bay. There they boarded a ferry which took them across Shelikof Strait to Afognak Island.

There was a dense fog. Roger said, "The island has a good name – Afog. Is it always foggy here?"

Hal said, "There's a lot of fog along this coast."

They could see no elk. But suddenly they heard them. The orchestra of the elks – bugles, trumpets, trombones, saxophones, and the deep thunder of the tuba.

Hal remembered what Theodore Roosevelt had said: "Heard at a little distance, it is one of the grandest and most beautiful sounds in nature."

He was right. The song of the elks was a sound never to be forgotten.

Hal said, "Any zoo would be tickled to death to get an elk just for its music alone."

"Why did we have to come way down here to find elk?" Roger asked.

"There used to be plenty of them in Alaska, but the Indians killed them to get their two upper teeth."

"Why in the world did they want them?"

"They used the teeth as ornaments to adorn their clothes. These were supposed to be charms to keep off evil. One Indian chief thought himself well protected because he had fifty elk teeth sewn to his garments. Thousands of elk were killed just for their teeth, and their bodies were left to rot. This island was off by itself and hard to get to so the elk that were here thrived and multiplied."

Roger said, "Since there are so few still alive I hate to take one of them."

"But taking them is exactly what will keep them alive," said Hal. "Safe in a zoo, away from the charm hunters, they can raise their babies in peace, they can have medical treatment when they need it, and they will no longer be an endangered species. I mean they won't die out like so many other fine animals that have disappeared from the earth."

Roger said, "I heard the pilot say these were Roosevelt elk. Why are they called that?"

"Because Teddy Roosevelt took a great interest in them and in their fine music. These are the largest of all the world's elks. In honour of a great president they were named Roosevelt elk."

The fog lifted a little and they could see the orchestra. It was a magnificent sight. More than a hundred of the great animals stood with their heads thrown back, pouring their music into the sky. Their splendid antlers almost touched their backs.

A man appeared. He strode up to the two boys and demanded, "What do you want?"

"Is that any business of yours?" said Hal.

"It certainly is my business. I'm here to guard these animals. We have no use for charm hunters."

"You're making a mistake," said Hal. "We are not charm hunters. We don't believe in charms to keep away the evil eye."

"That's just so much talk," said the guard. "We've had a lot like you. You just want to murder an elk and cut out pieces of his hide and get his upper teeth and sell them to the Indians. I know your kind. Get off this island. There'll be no killing here."

"Just what can we use to kill an elk? You can see that we have no rifles. I have a pocket knife – that's all. My brother doesn't even have that. I think he does have a toothpick. Do you think we could kill an elk with a toothpick?"

"Then why did you come here?"

"To hear the music. Also, we want to take one animal alive for a zoo. Our name is Hunt. Do you read the papers?"

"Of course I read the papers. Do you think I'm a dummy? Guess I owe you an apology." He smiled for the first time. "So you are the young fellows we've been reading about? Still I don't see how you are going to capture an elk with nothing but a toothpick."

"How many elk do you have on the island?"

"Only three hundred. Every day we lose a few."

"What do you mean – how do you lose them?"

"To charm hunters. And to these devilish wolves and wolverines and bears. They'd be much safer in a zoo. If you want one, take it – but I don't know how you're going to do it."

"We'll find a way," said Hal.

"Well, I must be getting on," said the guard. "Good luck to you."

The boys, now on their own, puzzled over the problem of what to do. Hal had a lasso, but a powerful elk would snap it as if it were a thread.

"How about the sleep gun?" said Roger.

"The sleep gun would put an animal to sleep. Then how the dickens could we get him to the dock and on a boat? He'd just lie there until he woke up and we'd be no better off. We couldn't carry him. One of these big bulls must weigh at least eight hundred pounds and he's nine feet long."

"If we had a helicopter," Roger said, "it would pick him up and carry him across the water to the Valley of Ten Thousand Smokes."

Hal felt in his pockets. "I have a handkerchief, and I have a little money, but, darn it, I don't seem to have a helicopter."

Then the answer to their problem appeared. It was a ball of black fur from which stared two blazing red eyes.

"A wolverine!" exclaimed Hal.

It leaped up on the back of a great stag and sank its claws into the animal's flanks. A bad smell came from the shaggy little beast. It was a powerful musky odour. Roger held his nose.

"That's why they call it a 'skunk bear'," said Hal.

The skunk bear fixed his large red eyes upon the boys as if daring them to do anything they could.

"He'll kill the elk," said Hal. "The wolverine kills just for the fun of it."

The wolverine growled at the two humans and his growl developed into a roar that was louder than a bear's. He was small, not more than three feet long, but his terrible strength and fierceness were known throughout Alaska. The boys felt very helpless as they watched this furious beast.

But how about the lasso? It couldn't be used on the elk but it might do nicely in the case of the skunk bear.

Hal threw it over the wolverine's neck. Both boys pulled with all the strength that was in them. The wolverine dug its claws more deeply into the suffering elk. The great bugler was not bugling now. He tried to scrape his enemy from his back with his horns but the wolverine had evidently taken that into account. He had positioned himself far enough back so that the horns did not reach him. When the elk grew weak with pain, his attacker would come forward and, clasping his sharp claws around the animal's neck, would choke him to death.

But this thing around his own neck – he didn't like it and tried to scrape it off. The boys could not pull him loose. Another bull came up. Roger had an inspiration. He made a loop in the other end of the rope and dropped it over the horns of the elk who had just arrived. Then he gave the animal a strong slap on the flank and the bull leaped away jerking the wolverine from the other bull's back. Hal flipped the lasso free.

The tortured elk was bleeding from the gashes made

in his hide by the savage claws of the wolverine. Hal went into his pockets and found more than money and a handkerchief. He took out a tube of antiseptic salve and doctored the wounds of the injured elk. The intelligent animal stood still. He knew who his friends were. Besides, he was too weak to do any galloping.

"Let's start toward the dock and see if he follows," said Hal.

The elk did follow, very slowly. He was trembling with pain. He kept looking from right to left, watching for other beasts that might do him harm. With these two humans who had saved his life, he would be safe.

With them he went out on the dock and followed them as they boarded the ferry for the Valley of Ten Thousand Smokes. The manager of Grosvenor Camp, being an animal lover, warmly received this four-legged guest and gave him a stall in the barn with plenty of fodder of the sort that he liked best. As soon as a cargo plane was available he would be shipped south.

In the meantime he began to bugle, weakly at first, but soon he was trumpeting what Roosevelt had called, "one of the grandest and most beautiful sounds in nature".

32
The Horrible Grizzly

"In Latin it is called *Ursus horribilis*," Hal said. "*Ursus* means bear and *horribilis*, of course, means horrible. And we have to get one."

They were hunting by helicopter. Ben Bolt had consented to fly the boys and their Nanook to Kodiak Island and stay with them until they captured a grizzly.

"It sure is a new way to hunt," said Ben. "But it has its good points. It might take you weeks if you walked. Flying, we may come on one in a day or so. They say Grayback Mountain is the best place to find them. We'll just fly round and round Grayback, up and down, until we spot one. Then we'll land and grab him."

It was not going to be quite that easy. They circled the mountain all day and saw nothing. At dusk they landed on the summit and put up their tent.

"Better luck tomorrow," said Ben.

They had their "better luck" sooner than that. A little past midnight Roger heard a snorting and snuffling just outside the tent. He nudged Hal. "Wake up! There's your grizzly."

Hal leaped up, grabbed his trousers, and was in such a hurry that he put both his legs into the same leg. He hopped out of the tent and fell over the grizzly who was so astonished that he ran away as fast as his legs could carry him.

Ben woke up. "What's going on?" he asked.

"Nothing much," said Hal. "Just taking a little exercise."

"At midnight?" Ben turned on his torch. "My word! A bear got one of your legs."

Roger began to laugh and Hal joined in as he pulled his legs free and got back into his sleeping bag. Ben, going to sleep again, dreamed that his friend Hal was going about on crutches with one leg missing.

At breakfast, Hal had nothing to say about his somersault over the *Ursus horribilis*.

Ben talked about grizzlies.

"If you come anywhere near one, he'll kill you. Grizzlies have terrible tempers. There's only one bear more fierce, and that's the Kodiak bear. Your father wanted a white grizzly. There are very few of them left but some may be found here. The grizzly is hump-backed. He has a pushed-in face. Alaska has perhaps ten thousand grizzlies left but few of them are white. The cubs are very much like boys. They do not reach a good size until they are ten years old. A male grizzly can weigh as much as eight hundred pounds. A lot more than the black bear, which weighs about four hundred. Of course your dad doesn't want a black bear because there are plenty of them down south. A black bear can do something that a grizzly can't do. He can climb a tree. The grizzly is too heavy to do anything like that."

"What does a grizzly eat?" asked Roger.

"He eats you, if he can get you. If he can't, he dines on chipmunks, mice, marmots, gophers and ground squirrels."

"Can he run fast?"

"Twenty-five miles an hour. Then he gets tired."

They spent the morning flying about Grayback. They saw squirrels and woodchucks, but no grizzly. It was almost noon before they spotted a big white rock. At least it looked like a rock. Ben was suspicious. He brought the helicopter to a halt fifty feet above the "rock". The rock got up on all four feet and turned his pushed-in face up so that he could look at this strange bird above him.

"That's our boy," said Ben. "His face is ugly but his snow-white body is a beautiful thing to see."

"But how are we going to get him?" Roger asked.

"I'll let down a net," said Ben. "It will lie flat on the

ground. Perhaps he will walk into it. Then we'll pull him up."

"How can you pull up eight hundred pounds?" asked Hal.

"Not by hand," said Ben. "By machine. We have a hoist."

The grizzly showed no desire to walk into the net. They waited patiently for a long time but it was no use.

"Someone will have to go down and attract him into the net," said Ben. "I have to stick by the helicopter. It's up to one of you two."

Roger spoke up before Hal could. It would be an adventure, and Roger thirsted for adventure.

"I'll go down the rope," he said.

"Wait a minute," said Ben. He moved the helicopter twenty or thirty feet away so that Roger would not descend directly upon the bear.

Roger went down the rope hand over hand. As he reached the ground the grizzly welcomed him with a savage growl. Roger placed himself so that the net would be between him and the bear. He still hung on to the rope so he could climb it at any moment.

The grizzly moved toward him, growling softly. He was hungry, and here was his dinner waiting for him. Now the grizzly was in the middle of the net.

Roger, who had had plenty of experience in climbing a rope, went up about fifteen feet. "All right," he yelled, "haul away." Then the net tightened around the bear and he began to go up toward the helicopter.

Roger got there first. Ben shut off the hoist. He had

no intention of sharing the cockpit with the horrible grizzly.

He changed the pitch of the rotor and the helicopter approached the airport. The net in which the bear was cradled swung about twenty feet below the aircraft.

Arriving over the airfield, Ben looked for a cargo van with an open hatch on top. When he found one he stopped the helicopter in mid-air directly above the hatch and let the net with the bear in it down into the van. The bear scrambled out of the net and the net was drawn up into the helicopter.

Mission accomplished.

The aircraft came to earth and Hal went to the office to arrange shipment of the van, locked upon the flatbed of a cargo plane, across Canada and the United States to a certain farm, where the *Ursus horribilis* would receive a hearty welcome from John Hunt.

33
Biggest Bear on Earth

"Now we just have to get a Kodiak bear and we're finished," Hal said. He was talking to a captain at the Kodiak Naval Station.

The captain replied, "You'll be finished all right if you tackle a Kodiak bear. He's a quiet fellow if you leave him alone. But if you interfere with him, you'll be sorry. Or, rather, you won't. You'll be too dead to be sorry."

"I'm afraid we have no choice," said Hal. "Our father is a collector of wild animals for zoos. He has asked us to get a Kodiak bear. We've never failed to get him what he asked for."

"Yes, but you've never tried to take the biggest bear in the world."

"Really the biggest?"

"Really. Let me tell you about Alaskan bears. The male blue bear weighs 200 pounds. The black bear, 400. The grizzly, 800. The polar bear, 1,000. The Kodiak bear, 2,000. That's an average figure. Some weigh 1,500, some weigh 3,000. But the average is 2,000 pounds – twice the weight of any other bear on earth. He's not only the biggest in the world, he's almighty strong."

"But you say he's quiet."

"When he's let be. But there's one on that hill just behind the Naval Station that is mad enough to chew your head off."

"Why?"

"A hunter shot his mate. Then somebody stole his two cubs. The big fellow went berserk. He's ready to eat anyone who comes near him. He was very fond of his mate and his young ones. Now he's just a big ball of wild, slashing fury. He's killing every person he can get his teeth into."

A young fellow not in uniform, who had been listening, broke in with, "Oh boy! What he needs is a bullet from this new gun of mine. Can I go with you?"

"No thanks," Hal said.

"But you can't stop me."

"No, I can't stop you. But if you get killed don't expect me to bury you."

At the foot of the mountain the road split into two branches. Which should they take? Hal rapped at the door of a farmhouse. The door was opened by a surly fellow who said sharply:

"What do you want?"

"Which road do we take to get to the top of the mountain?"

"The one on the left," snapped the farmer. "But don't go up there."

Hal said, "We know about the bear who has lost his mate and his cubs. Has he done any damage here?"

"Killed twenty of my cattle," said the farmer roughly.

"Have you any idea who stole his cubs?"

The farmer's face flushed. "How the devil would I know anything about that? I live here alone. I don't get any news and that's the way I like it. I can't stand here wasting time on three kids. I told you which road to take. Now, get along. I'm busy."

Just before the door slammed shut, the boys heard a small sound from inside.

As they started up the left branch, Roger said:

"Did you hear that? He said he lives alone. Then what could have made that sound?"

"A cat perhaps," said Hal.

But he wondered.

The boys followed the dirt road up Sharatin Mountain. That was the name given to it on the map. The captain had called it a hill. Well, perhaps it was more than a hill and not quite a mountain since its height was less than three thousand feet.

The boy with the gun followed. His name, he said, was Mark.

Hal kept hoping that Mark would tire himself out climbing the steep slope – then he would turn about and go home.

"I'll protect you if you get into trouble," said Mark.

"Your protection is the last thing we want," Hal said. "If you use that gun, I'll kick you all the way down hill."

"But what's the use of having a gun if I don't use it?"

"Go shoot a hedgehog – or a gopher," Hal suggested. "But if you value your life, leave the bear alone."

"Look!" exclaimed Roger. "Right here beside the road." He picked up a jawbone. "Some animal was killed here."

Hal looked closely at the jawbone. "That didn't come from any animal," he said. "That's human."

Near by was a skull, and it certainly was the skull of a man. They found the dead body. On his wrist was a watch.

Mark removed it. "I'll take that," he said. "Finders keepers."

"Wrong," said Hal. "If you find something that belongs to someone else, you have no right to keep it."

"But he won't have any more use for it."

"His folks will probably come to find him. Anything on him belongs to them."

Grumbling, Mark replaced the watch on the dead man's wrist. The body was spattered with dried blood. In the blood Hal saw brown hairs.

"Now we know what happened," said Hal. "This man was killed by that bear made crazy by the loss of his mate and cubs."

"How do you figure that out?" Roger asked.

"These hairs came from a brown bear. That's the Kodiak bear. And the ordinary Kodiak bear is too quiet to attack a man unless he had good reason. This is the work of the bear we are after."

A little farther on a whole tree had been torn up by the roots and lay on the ground, its leaves still green. Again there were brown hairs that told the story. Then they saw the remains of a black bear. It had been partly eaten. More brown hairs.

A small house had been completely wrecked. Some terribly powerful force had broken the walls and the roof had collapsed. A woman stood by the ruined house, weeping.

"He was always a good bear," the woman said. "Never hurt man, woman or child. But now something has got into him. He's gone plumb crazy."

They came to a tent. The tent had not been attacked. But when they looked inside, they saw a man lying on the ground. Hal felt his pulse. He was dead.

They came to an empty cabin. Nobody would use it again for a long time. The windows were smashed, the roof torn off, the bunk destroyed, the sheet-iron stove had been flattened and the floor was covered with beans, rice, flour and coffee.

Reaching the top of the mountain, they found the great bear. He was sleeping, his head on the dead body of his mate. It is said that animals do not love. This scene impressed them all, for this showed the deep affection one beast may have for another. Hal and Roger were too old to cry, but tears came to their eyes.

Mark felt differently. He was going to kill this monster. He put his foot on the bear and fired. The bullet went through his foot. Mark howled to high heaven.

The bear did not stir. The bullet had not penetrated his heavy hide. He was so completely lost in misery over the death of his mate that he paid no attention to the boys. He would take care of them later.

Hal felt inclined to give Mark a good beating. Instead, he looked at the injured foot. Luckily, no bones were broken since the bullet had simply gone through the fleshy part of the foot. After all, the bullet had been very small, coming from a low calibre .22 gun.

"Quit howling like a stuck pig," Hal said to Mark. "You're not badly hurt."

The boys set up their own tent. It was nearly dark now and they hoped that the bear would stay exactly where he was until dawn. Mark crowded into the tent with them. He had no sleeping bag, but the night was not cold.

In the middle of the night Mark heard a rustling outside the tent. It must be the bear. He reached for his trusty pea-shooter, and prepared to be a hero. He was going to save the boys from certain death.

He separated the flaps just enough to get the muzzle of the gun out and he fired. He could see nothing, and he was not to know until morning that he had shot not the bear, but a mountain goat.

Aroused by the report, Hal said, "You fire one more shot and I'm going to take that gun away from you."

Mark fired one more shot. Dawn had come and he ventured out, holding his precious rifle. This time he saw the great bear itself, and there was no mistake. What a great story for the folks back home if he could just kill this monster!

He fired. The small bullet did not penetrate the tremendous hide of the bear. The Kodiak's skin has an elastic quality and the bullet ricocheted, bounced back, and struck Mark on the jaw.

Hal leaped up, seized the little rifle, and broke it over his knee.

Mark was whining about his dislocated jaw, not to mention his punctured foot.

There was a small village of not more than a hundred people on top of the mountain. After breakfast, Hal went to the village to find help for the banged-up youngster. He entered the tiny one-room post office. The staff consisted of one man only, the old postmaster.

"We've had an accident," Hal said. "Is there a doctor in town?"

"No doctor. The nearest doctor is the surgeon down at the Naval Station."

Hal said, "A young fool of a boy has busted himself up. He needs a doctor."

"I'll take him down," said the postmaster. "I have to go down anyway to get the mail."

"Thanks a lot," said Hal. "That's mighty good of you."

He sat down and wrote a note. It was addressed to Captain Sam Harkness and it read, "Sending you a boy who has shot himself twice while trying to kill the Kodiak bear. Have Navy Surgeon fix him up and send him home before he makes a bigger fool of himself. I will pay any charges." And he signed it, "Hal Hunt."

So Mark was transported to the Naval Station and Hal fervently hoped that he would never see him again.

Hal went to the police station. The little village had only one policeman.

"Would you go down the hill with us," Hal said, "to the farmhouse where the road divides?"

"That's Spike Burns's place," said the policeman. "He's a rough customer. What do you want to see him for?"

"This Kodiak bear that has gone crazy because he lost his mate and his cubs – there's nothing we can do about the mate. She's dead as a door nail. But if we could give him back his cubs, perhaps he would quiet down."

"What has that to do with Spike?" asked the policeman.

"Perhaps nothing. Perhaps a good deal. When we talked with him we heard a sound inside that might have been made by a cat, or a bird – or by those cubs."

"You think he was the one who stole the cubs?"

"It's just a guess. I can't barge into his house and make a search. But you can because you're a cop."

"O.K.," said the policeman. "Here we go."

253

Roger joined them and they went down the road to the farmhouse. The policeman carried a search warrant. They rapped, and Spike came to the door. He was highly displeased to see the policeman. "What's up?" he said.

"May we come in and look around?" said the cop.

"You may not. You have no authority to do anything like that."

"Here's the authority," said the policeman, and he handed Spike the search warrant.

Reluctantly Spike let them in. They searched the house quite thoroughly and found nothing.

Then there was that sound again. "What was that?" said the policeman.

"Just one of the doors. It creaks," said Spike.

"Perhaps it's this door," said the policeman, and he opened the door of a closet. And there they were, the two cubs.

"You'll get a heavy fine for this," said the policeman. "Why in the world did you steal these cubs?"

"Well," said Spike, "I was just going to fatten them up and then kill and eat them. A man must live, you know. Besides, the bear killed twenty of my cattle."

The policeman said, "You'll live long enough to pay handsomely for what you've done. Pick 'em up, boys."

Hal took up one squirming little fellow in his arms, and Roger took the other. They climbed the hill and found the bear occupied in tearing down their tent. The great bear growled when he saw them coming. He was ready now to add them to his list of victims.

But when he saw the cubs his manner changed. They were set down gently in front of him. He licked both of them from stem to stern. He looked up at the boys and his eyes said, "Thank you." Most male bears pay no attention to their cubs. They leave that to the mother. But here there was no mother. And the great Kodiak was not only larger and stronger than others, but also more intelligent. When he lost his mate, he poured out his love on these little brats.

There was one telephone in town and that was in the postmaster's shack.

Hal telephoned to Captain Harkness. "We've got the big bear," he said. "He's torn things up pretty badly, but he has his cubs now. You wouldn't believe what a difference that has made. The happiest and sweetest old bear you ever saw."

"How are you going to transport him?" the captain asked. "Can we help? There's no war on at the moment and we have a lot of planes standing idle. You can use one if you wish."

"That's just fine," said Hal. "The only thing is, how do we get the bear and his cubs down to you?"

"No need to do that. We'll send a transport plane up there. Is there any sort of a runway?"

"Not a real runway, but there's a long straight stretch that might serve."

"I'll have a transport up there in half an hour."

They did better than that. In twenty minutes a transport plane settled down on top of Mount Sharatin. The Navy had all sorts of planes, and the "transport plane" was a boxlike affair quite strong enough to carry a 2,000-pound bear and his cubs, plus two boys whose work was done. The pilot was a brisk young fellow who had never seen New York and was delighted to have this chance.

"But how are you going to get the three bears into the plane?" he wanted to know.

"Very simple," said Hal.

He picked up the two cubs and put them aboard. The big bear promptly followed them. The sliding door at the rear was let down.

"Got room for us too?" asked Hal.

"Sure. Right up in front with me," said the pilot.

The great box, ten feet wide and as high as a room,

trundled bumpily over the ground to the edge of a cliff and then launched out into space. At first it fell dizzily. But soon it was under control and came down at the airport to pick up Nanook. This done, it rose into the sky, passed over the harbour and above the reef called Albatross Bank, where dozens of the great birds were fishing for salmon. Then in an almost direct line it flew over Juneau, Edmonton, Winnipeg and Toronto, over the skyscrapers of New York to come down at last on the Hunt Wild Animal Farm.

John Hunt looked with amazement at the great Kodiak bear.

"I always knew", he said, "that the Kodiak was huge. But he's bigger than I ever imagined. A number of zoos have asked for him. I'm not going to give him to the zoo that offers the most money, but to the zoo that can care for him best and bring up those cubs to be as great as he is."

He looked at his sons with great pride.

"You fellows deserve the best. These three bears will bring at least fifty thousand dollars. You've both told me you want to be naturalists. All right – that money will go into a trust for you so you can get the education you need to be wildlife scientists. You already know the outside of your animals. The time will come when you will know them inside out."

SAFARI ADVENTURE

Contents

1
Poachers' Paradise

They were heading for trouble. But Hal, nineteen, was too old to show fear and his brother Roger, thirteen, was too young to realize what he was getting into.

Both felt the tingle of new excitement as the small plane soared above the Mountains of the Moon and pointed its nose east by south-east for Tsavo. Tsavo, home of murder and mystery. Tsavo, Africa's largest national park, where animals should be safe – but were not.

Gangs of poachers were killing the elephants, rhinos, giraffes, hippos and other wild creatures of Tsavo by the hundred.

What is a poacher? In Africa it means a thief who kills animals without a licence and sells the tusks, horns, or other valuable parts.

Warden Crosby could not stop the killing. He had a force of only ten rangers. How could ten men hope to patrol eight thousand square miles of jungle?

Worry had bitten deep furrows into Mark Crosby's forehead. He sat in the pilot's seat with his hands on the controls, but he paid slight attention to Lake Victoria slipping by below, the source of the Nile, the spot where Stanley met Livingstone, the vast Serengeti lion country, the snow-capped Mount Kilimanjaro. His mind was on the land beyond – the scene of blood, horror, torture and death.

"It's a war," he said, "a war against big odds. We're losing it. We have ten men on our side. Ten men against hundreds of poachers. We no sooner drive them out of one place than they pop up in another. It's pretty hopeless."

"Have any of your men been killed?" Hal asked.

"We had twenty-two rangers. Twelve have been killed."

"Poison arrows?"

"Yes, all the poachers are armed – most of them with

bows and poison arrows, some with spears and bush knives, some with muskets. Two of our men were caught in traps that the poachers had set out to catch animals. Those two died a horrible death. We didn't find their skeletons until a month later."

"Skeletons?"

"That's all that was left of them."

"I suppose they died of thirst," said Hal. "Then the hyenas picked their bones."

"I doubt if it was that comfortable. Hyenas don't wait till you're dead. They're afraid of you as long as you can fight. But if they find you trapped and helpless, they gang up on you. Those two men were eaten alive."

Hal winced at the thought of the slow and terrible agony of the two unfortunate rangers. Roger shivered and began to be sorry that he had come.

"Why do you think it was hyenas?" said Hal. "Why not lions or leopards?"

"A lion is usually a good sport. He seldom attacks unless he is attacked. A leopard isn't such a gentleman. He might attack without provocation. But he has an odd little habit. After he has eaten as much as he can hold, he drags the rest of the carcass up into a tree where it will be safe from other animals until he comes back for another meal. He's very powerful. He could break a body loose from a trap and carry it up even if it was twice his own weight. But nothing like that happened. No, it must have been the work of hyenas. And perhaps vultures. They usually come round after the hyenas have finished and take any scraps that are left."

Hal and Roger exchanged glances. Their enthusiasm for this adventure had suddenly cooled. They had welcomed Warden Crosby when he had flown to the Mountains of the Moon to get their help. It had seemed a good chance to have a lively adventure, and to save wild animals from death at the hands of the poachers.

Besides, in a way, it was part of their job. Their father, John Hunt, was in the business of collecting wild animals and selling them to zoos where they would have good care and furnish education and entertainment to thousands of spectators. He had taught his sons to love animals and gone with them on their first take-'em-alive journeys. But what would be the use of such journeys if the wild game were all killed off by poachers?

So when the boys and their thirty black helpers had driven out a gang of killers from their hideout in the Mountains of the Moon, Crosby had come to them for aid in his battle against the poachers of Tsavo. They had phoned their father at his animal farm near New York and gained his consent. Now they began to wonder if they had bitten off more than they could chew.

Crosby guessed their thoughts.

"I hope I haven't scared you," he said.

"Scared us? Of course not," said Hal stoutly.

"When will your men get here?"

"Well, it's six hundred miles by road. Our jeeps and Land-Rovers aren't built for speed. But they should be here by noon tomorrow."

"I can't thank you enough for coming in with me on this job."

"Don't thank us until you see what we can do – if anything."

"There it is." Crosby pointed past an elbow of the snow mountain. "That's Tsavo."

It was a lovely sight. Who could believe that this beautiful land was a valley of death? It seemed a peaceful paradise of forest and plain, gentle hills, silvery rivers, quiet lakes, bright sun and dreaming shadow.

Roger, who had a keen appreciation of the beautiful, exclaimed, "Man! That's cool!"

His older brother said it a little differently, "Looks like a bit of heaven."

"It could be just that", said Crosby, "if we could get rid of those poachers. It should be a safe refuge for animals and a grand park for visitors. Now it's a deathtrap. Do you see that place where the river widens into a sort of lake? We have an underwater observatory there. You can go down into a submarine chamber and look out through port-holes and see crocodiles swimming under water and hippos walking on the bottom. But recently the poachers slaughtered dozens of the hippos and all you could see through the port-holes was a huge heap of rotting corpses. The decaying carcasses polluted the river, and the smell was terrible. Some hippo babies left alive were nudging their dead mothers and dying of starvation. But they didn't suffer long – the crocodiles snapped them up."

"What good did it do the poachers to kill the hippos and then leave them to rot?" asked Hal.

"Oh, but they got what they wanted. They took the heads – each of them would be worth a couple of thousand dollars. And strips of the hide had been cut off."

"What could they do with them?"

"Make whips. The hide is very thick. They dry the strips in the shade for several weeks. It becomes as hard as a board. Then each strip is sawed, like wood, into rods about three feet long. These can be used as canes. But generally they are shipped to South Africa where the Boers trim the edges to make them sharp and use them as whips, called *sjamboks*. A sjambok will cut the flesh like a knife. Cattle are afraid of it, and men too. You don't pick a quarrel with your boss if he's armed with a sjambok. Many a man has been killed by a hippo whip."

"It all sounds pretty cruel to me," Hal said, "murdering a hippo to make a murder weapon."

"It's a beastly business. And a *big* business. Of course poaching is as old as history. But it has always been a small business — until now. A native who needed meat might go out and kill an antelope. But now it's organized on a big scale. What they're after now is not just some meat for supper, but millions of dollars, and instead of a lone poacher here or there we now have armies of poachers directed by a man they call Blackbeard — because of his black beard and because he's a pirate like the original Blackbeard, only he steals tusks and tails, horns and hides, instead of gold. And he's guilty of more torture and killing than the first Blackbeard ever was."

"Who is this Blackbeard?"

"I wish I knew. He's a man of mystery. I don't believe he's a native. We've done a lot of guessing but we get nowhere. Perhaps you can solve the mystery. We've wondered if he might be a big merchant down in Mombasa, the port city. We know great quantities of hippo heads, elephant tusks, rhino horns, valuable skins of leopards, cheetahs, monkeys, pythons and all that are shipped out from Mombasa to cities all over the world. Somebody is making a fortune out of this racket. Perhaps he's *not* a merchant. Perhaps he's a military man who knows how to rule this army of poachers. Just guesses. We really have no idea who he is. Until he's caught, this thing will probably go on."

2
Poisoned Arrows

The plane was now gliding down towards the troubled paradise. It was a Stork – a German-made four-seater. It had dual controls – one joystick was gripped by the pilot and Hal, sitting in the co-pilot's seat, watched the other stick moving restlessly in front of him.

He longed to get his hands on it. But he wasn't sure that he could fly this crate. He had flown his father's Navion over Long Island, but that was a quite different machine. Here, every dial on the instrument board seemed to be in the wrong place. And everything was in metres and kilometres and Centigrade and European symbols, and words were in German.

Besides, every plane handles differently. One will be as steady as a cart-horse, another as skittish as a bucking bronco. He hoped that some time he would be allowed to pilot the plane, but first he must have full instructions and plenty of practice with Crosby at his side.

"That sharp-pointed hill with the pavilion on top," said Crosby, "is called Poachers' Lookout. A telescope is mounted in front of the pavilion. We keep a ranger there all day, every day, watching for poachers."

"How far can you see from that point?"

"Not far enough. You can spot anything within a few miles but then the hills and forests cut off the view. It would take at least a hundred such lookouts to cover our eight thousand miles of territory, and that would mean a hundred watchers. Of course that's impossible. So we do what we can with this movable lookout."

"You mean this plane?"

"Yes. But I'm the only one who can fly it. And I can't be in the air all the time – I have other things to do. When I locate some poachers I fly back to camp, get together any rangers who are not out on duty and we drive in a Land-Rover to the place where I have seen the poachers. If there are only one or two, we may be able to arrest them. But if it turns out to be a gang, we're lucky if we can get back to camp with only one or two dead rangers. Now you can see our camp – just beyond Poachers' Lookout."

Hal could make out a cluster of thatch-roofed cabins about five miles ahead. So this was the famous Kitani Safari Lodge where visitors from Europe and America might spend a few days enjoying the thrilling experience of being completely surrounded by wild animals. He was surprised to see that there was no wall or fence around the camp.

"How do you keep the animals out?"

Crosby laughed. "We don't. We could never afford to build a wall strong enough or high enough. Leopards or lions could scramble over the top of it. Elephants can push down big trees – they could push down a wall. Rhinos are irritated by anything that gets in their way – they would charge a wall and drive a hole straight through it. Buffaloes have heads as hard as battering rams. They smash heavy trucks and lorries. A stampede of buffaloes would make short work of a wall if they took a notion to see what was on the other side. No, a wall wouldn't be practical, and as for a fence, it would be trampled down in one night."

"So you let the animals come right into the camp?"

"Right. They seldom come in during the day. But every night we have visitors. We advise our guests not to go walking in the moonlight, but stay in their cabins after sunset. And keep their windows closed – leopards like to climb in. Elephants come looking for water. One wily old rascal has learned how to turn on the taps in the garden – but doesn't bother to turn them off again. He drinks his fill and wanders off and I have to go out and turn off the tap."

Roger's sharp eyes had been scanning the landscape.

"Speaking of fences," he said, "that looks like one over there – on the left. What could that be?"

The warden took one look, then swung the plane about and headed for the thing that looked like a fence.

"Nothing the matter with your eyes," he said to Roger. "You'd make a good ranger. That's a trap-line."

"Trap-line?"

"A line of traps set by the poachers."

"But it looks like a fence or a hedge."

"Exactly. The poachers pile up thorn bushes to make a fence. This one appears to be about a mile long. But you notice there are gaps in the fence. In every one of those openings they put a trap."

"What's the idea?"

"Well, suppose you were an animal. You come up to this fence and you want to get to the other side. It's too wide to jump over. You don't wish to plough through it because you know you'd get stuck by thousands of thorns, sharp as needles, each one about three inches long. So you run beside the fence hoping to find a way to get through. You come to one of these gaps. You dash in and suddenly find yourself in trouble. Your head passes through a wire noose that tightens round your neck. The more you pull the tighter it gets. You struggle and twist and the wire cuts deeper and deeper into your throat and the blood attracts the carnivores which proceed to eat you alive."

"But if I am eaten, then the poachers don't get anything."

"Oh yes they do. If you are an elephant, the chances are all they want is your tusks, or perhaps your feet to make waste-paper baskets, or your tail to be sold as a fly switch. The wild beasts don't eat those parts. So the beast gets its dinner and the poacher gets the rest and they are both satisfied."

They were now dropping fast towards the thorn hedge.

"What do you plan to do?" Hal inquired.

"Just give the poachers a good scare. Let them know that their camp has been located. Sometimes that's enough to make them pack up and leave. Of course, it may not work. There may be a lot of them and they know we have very few rangers. But they don't know that tomorrow we are going to have thirty more men — your men. We'll come out here tomorrow by road, the whole lot of us, and give them the surprise of their lives. Now I'm going to give you a good look at this trap-line."

The plane swooped lower. The beginning of the hedge was directly underneath. Looking down the line, the boys could see that almost every gap held an animal. Some hung still and lifeless. Some struggled fiercely and their screams could be heard over the roar of the engine. Packs of hyenas, jackals, wild dogs and other meat-eaters were enjoying a feast. The strange "laugh" of the hyenas, the yapping of the wild dogs, the yipping of the jackals, the occasional rumble of a leopard or roar of a lion added to the general tumult.

So that the boys could get a good look, the warden had cut the motor down to about thirty miles per hour. The Stork, with its flaps down, was quite capable of staying in the air at this slow speed, though its normal speed was one hundred and forty.

Now the temporary straw shacks of the poachers could be seen among the trees. Crosby, flying within fifty feet of the ground, examined the camp closely. "Bigger than I thought," he said.

Suddenly a swarm of black figures burst out of the forest, armed with bows and spears. A volley of spears and arrows came climbing towards the little plane.

If this were an ordinary plane, they would harmlessly pepper the bottom of the fuselage. But the cabin of the Stork is enclosed in a bubble of Perspex, which even curves in a little at the bottom towards the floorboards, so that the occupants of the plane can look straight down to the ground beneath. This is ideal for the purpose of complete visibility but offers little protection against ground fire.

Since Crosby was gripping the control, his elbow was well out into the bulge of Perspex. Suddenly he jerked it in with a little exclamation of surprise. He dropped the exposed arm beside him where Hal would not see it and held the stick with his other hand. Sharply he gunned the plane up well out of reach of ground fire, then levelled off straight for Kitani Safari Lodge.

3
Race with Death

Hal was unaware of what had happened. But Roger, sitting behind the warden, saw the black arrow that had gone through Crosby's arm just above the elbow. The arrow-head had passed through the fleshy part of the arm and come out on the other side.

"Hal, look," Roger said. "The warden – his arm . . ."

Hal leaned forward so that he could see the half-hidden arm and arrow.

"Never mind it now," Crosby said. "The important thing is to get you to camp before I go to sleep."

"You think the arrow was poisoned?"

"Probably."

Hal examined the arrow-head, looking for the black, gummy paste made from the highly poisonous Acocanthera plant.

"I don't see anything – except your own blood."

"You wouldn't see anything on the point. They don't put the poison there."

"Why not?"

"Because they might prick themselves with it. A man

279

tumbling around in the bush with a quiverful of arrows on his back with all the poisoned tips sticking up would be a great danger to himself and to his friends."

"Then where do they put the poison?"

"On the shaft, just behind the arrow-head."

"But that's the part that's in your arm. Shouldn't we get it out of there as quickly as we can?"

"You can't reach it." It was true. The front seats were almost two feet apart. The injured arm was on the warden's far side. Hal could not get at it without interfering with the control of the plane.

"I can reach it," Roger said. "Just tell me what to do."

Hal thought a moment. The arrow-head was barbed. "You can't pull it back," he said. "Try to break off the arrow-head. Then pull out the shaft."

Roger leaned over the back of the pilot's seat, gripped the arrow-head and did his best to snap it off. The wood was very tough. He put on more pressure. His hand was wet with blood. Sweat came out on his face and he felt faint – not that the effort hurt him, but he knew he was hurting the warden. Crosby said not a word.

Crack – the barbed head broke off.

Now for the most painful part of the operation. Roger hoped to make his patient suffer as little as possible. One good jerk and he would get the shaft out of the arm.

He laid hold with both hands, gritted his teeth, and gave one mighty tug. The shaft held fast. The plane staggered. Crosby at once brought it back under control.

"Must be wedged between muscle and bone," Hal said. "Give it another try."

Roger had once thought he would like to be a surgeon. Now he changed his mind. His body was streaming with sweat and it wasn't because this country, Kenya, is crossed by the equator. He knew the agony he was causing. He laid his bloody hands on the shaft again, gathered up all his strength, and yanked. No luck.

He worked the shaft up and down to enlarge the hole. He knew this must hurt like the devil, but he didn't know what else to do. Once more he yanked and the shaft came free.

The warden opened his mouth, and Roger expected him to shout something like, "You clumsy kid!" but all he said was, "Good boy!"

"Give me that," Hal said. He took the shaft and looked at the part that had been embedded in the flesh. Through the blood he could see a black sticky substance.

"I'm afraid that's it," he said.

What chance did the warden have? He might live, he

might die. Hal had seen Africans preparing this stuff. They themselves were deathly afraid of it. They took great care not to get a bit of it on themselves. They boiled it out in the bush, not in the village – that would be too dangerous. A drop might spatter out of the pot on to the skin of a man, woman or child. If there was a scratch on the skin, even though it might be no larger than a pin point, the poison would enter.

What happened then would depend upon the strength of the poison and the physical endurance of the person who was poisoned. A child might die in a few minutes. One woman died while she was being carried a few hundred feet to her house. Another died within twenty minutes. Hal had heard of a man who lasted three hours before he died. A strong man who had been struck by the arrow of an enemy tribe lay unconscious for two hours and then recovered.

It made a difference whether the poison was fresh or stale. If it was new it acted quickly. If it had been on the arrow-shaft for many days and had dried and been covered with dust it might not cause death.

The warden slumped against the stick, pushing it forward. Immediately the plane plunged towards the earth in a steep spiral.

Hal seized the stick in front of him and tried to pull it back. He couldn't do it – Crosby's weight against the other control was too much.

The earth was approaching at terrifying speed. "Pull him up," Hal shouted to Roger.

Roger had plenty to do to hold himself up in this crazy contraption whirling on its nose like a top. His seat-belt helped a little. He supported himself against the back of the front seat with one arm, got his other arm around the warden's neck and heaved. Crosby was not a light man and if Roger had not been big for his years he could not have budged the heavy body. He raised it a few inches, then a few inches more, and, with Hal pulling on the control at the same time, the plane hesitated in its dizzy dive and began to point upwards.

A few more head-over-heels revolutions and the wings steadied, the whirling stopped and the plane swooped upwards just in time to escape the reaching arms of a tall kapok tree.

Roger still held back the warden's unconscious body while Hal settled down to the uneasy business of flying a strange plane without either practice or instructions. He had to guess his way across the instrument board and some of his guesses were pretty wild.

Where was the gizmo that controlled the brakes? Or were they governed by the foot pedals? The most ticklish job would be landing. He must get ready for it. How did you lower the flaps? Any one of half a dozen levers might do it. He tried them until he found one that produced the right effect – the sudden check of extra lift and drag.

Once on the ground, he must apply the brake so that he wouldn't taxi right off the strip into a tree or a cabin. How to do that he couldn't tell until he was actually on the ground. Then it might be too late.

Meanwhile he peered ahead through the whirling propeller, looking for the landing field. His eye travelled all round the thatch buildings of the safari camp without finding an asphalt runway.

Finally he spotted a wind-sock. That must mark the airstrip, but where was the strip? The landing field appeared to be just that and nothing more – a field.

He was now directly over the camp. He circled the field, calculating the chances of getting down to it without striking the trees that blocked it at each end.

He was just about to come in for a landing when he saw something peculiar in the middle of the field. Something yellow and black lay on the green grass. Then a part of it moved and he knew what it was: a family of lions.

They were basking in the sun, quite undisturbed by the noisy plane. Hal knew that lions were not afraid of planes, trains or cars. More than once he had driven his Land-Rover close to a pride of lions and stopped within fifteen feet of them and they did not budge an inch. Kings of the animal world, they were not easily frightened.

He could not wait for them to wander off. They might not move for an hour or more. He had a patient on board who required prompt attention. He had to get rid of those lions, and fast.

He swooped down to within twenty feet of them. They were all stretched out comfortably in the grass. Some looked up at him lazily, others did not even open their eyes. One huge black-maned male lay on his back with all four paws in the air. He did not even bother to roll over.

Hal circled and came in again, lower this time. He kept the throttle full open in order to make as much thunder as possible. It was a dangerous business, roaring in at a hundred and forty miles per hour so close to the ground. This time one lioness with a brood of cubs decided they would be safer on the sidelines and led them away.

Encouraged by this success, Hal made another dive. This time he would really singe the fur of these haughty beasts.

He didn't quite do that, but he came so close that when he circled up again he saw that the lions were on their feet, the males roaring angrily, and even the upside-down animal had taken notice of this buzzing gadfly that was disturbing his slumbers. The whole pride moved away with slow dignity to the edge of the field.

Hal at once lowered his flaps, throttled down to a glide and came in for a more or less perfect landing. The brake linkage seemed to be as he had hoped, and he brought the plane to a bumpy halt within a few feet of the trees.

4
The Judge

The warden seemed dead to the world. Hal felt his pulse. The heart was beating, though faintly. So there was still a chance.

The helpless body was eased down to the ground. A man came running from the camp. He was dressed smartly in a light-coloured uniform that ended at his elbows and his knees and contrasted with his very black skin. His military-looking cap had an insignia in front and a thin cloth kepi behind hanging down over the back of his neck to keep off insects, after the fashion of the old-time French Foreign Legion. This must be one of the warden's ten rangers.

"What happen?" he asked, stooping beside the body in the grass.

"Poison arrow," Hal said.

The ranger put his ear to the warden's chest.

"No dead. We take to the judge. Judge, he fix."

"He needs a doctor."

"No doctor. Judge, he good, he fix."

Hal didn't wait to ask questions about the judge who

could fix. There was one thing that could be done at once. He whipped out a handkerchief and tied it round the arm above the bleeding wound.

Together, they carried the warden to the main building. The interior was furnished with comfortable chairs and a large desk. It evidently served the warden as both home and office. The unconscious warden was carried into his bedroom and laid on the bed. A little man came bustling into the room.

"This is the judge," said the ranger. "He fix."

The judge's slightly dark skin marked him as a native of India. There were many Indians in Kenya.

"An accident?" he said.

Hal explained briefly what had happened.

"Ah yes," said the little judge. "How fortunate that I was here. I know exactly what to do."

Roger, whose eyes had a way of seeing things that other people did not notice, saw the bright light that came into the judge's eyes. The judge seemed almost happy. Perhaps it was just his kindly nature. Perhaps he was happy because he could help.

"First," he said, "off with that tourniquet." He quickly untied it and flung it aside.

"But I just put it on," said Hal. "I wanted to stop the

poison from going through his system."

"You meant well," said the judge kindly. "But, you see, it's better to allow the poison to be diffused through the entire system than concentrated in one spot."

Hal had never heard this theory before, but it sounded logical.

"Shouldn't the wound be syringed with distilled water?" Hal asked.

"Wrong again, my boy." The judge spoke like a father gently reproving his foolish son. "What he needs is an injection."

"Ammonium carbonate?" asked Hal.

The judge's eyes narrowed. He seemed surprised that Hal should know these things, and a little annoyed. He covered his annoyance with a sweet smile.

"Yes, yes," he replied. "I'll see if there is any in the dispensary."

He left the room, walked across the lounge and into another room. Hal quietly followed him. He arrived just in time to see the judge pick up a bottle from the front row and put it back behind everything else on the shelf so that it could not easily be seen.

He turned and saw Hal. "No Ammonium here," he said. "Never mind. I know something better. Coramine. A heart stimulant. That's what he needs – something to keep his heart going."

Hal agreed. His confidence in the little judge was restored. He helped him search the shelves for Coramine.

"Hal!" Roger called. "Come quick!" Hal ran to the bedroom. "I think he's stopped breathing," Roger said.

The warden was as pale as paper. Beads of sweat stood out on his skin. Hal put his mouth to the warden's and breathed, slowly, powerfully, forcing air in, drawing it out, forcing it in, drawing it out, forcing it in, drawing it out.

He kept it up until the patient breathed again. But the breathing would die out once more if the heart didn't get a boost. Where was the judge with that Coramine?

The judge came in holding a hypodermic syringe. He inserted it into the wound. That was a strange place to put it. Wouldn't the thigh be better? Then Hal noticed that the liquid in the syringe was a blackish brown.

In a sudden panic he seized the syringe and drew it out before the judge could press the plunger. The judge stared at him with astonishment.

"Pardon me," Hal said, "but isn't there some mistake? That doesn't look like Coramine. It looks like Acocanthera."

The judge gazed at the syringe. "I do believe you're right," he said. "I am so happy that you noticed it. I know now how it happened. The two bottles were side by side and I got the wrong one."

Hal was already on his way to the dispensary and the judge followed. Hal was suspicious, but his suspicion faded when he saw that it was just as the judge had said. The two bottles, one labelled "Coramine" and the other labelled "Aco", the safari man's nickname for the deadly Acocanthera, really did stand side by side. That was natural,

291

for they were frequently used one after the other. When it was necessary to capture a large animal such as a rhino or elephant, a ranger might puncture the skin with a very light touch of Aco, enough to put the animal to sleep but not enough to kill it, and after the beast was caged it could be revived with an injection of Coramine.

Dismissing his unkind suspicions, Hal helped the judge find a clean syringe and fill it with Coramine.

"Permit me," Hal said, and himself took the syringe to the bedroom and injected the contents into the patient's thigh.

For half an hour he kept his fingers on the pulse. At first the heart-beat was so faint he could hardly feel it. Then it broke into a rapid palpitation. That was not a very good sign. But it finally settled down to a normal beat that slowly gained in strength.

All this time the judge was pacing up and down the room with every appearance of anxiety.

"A very fine man, the warden," he said. "We couldn't afford to lose him. We need him to help save our poor dear animals from the hands of the poachers. It's a cause very close to my heart. In fact I am one of the directors of the African Wildlife Society. Really, the tortures these poor beasts undergo would make you weep. No punishment is enough for those atrocious poachers. Of course as a judge I get at them through my court – when they come before me you can be sure they will suffer for their crimes."

Tears stood in the little judge's eyes as he looked at the helpless body of the warden.

"We are like brothers, the warden and I. If he should die it would break my heart." He dabbed at his eyes with his handkerchief.

Hal thought, He's either a sweet soul or a great actor. Always willing to believe the best of anyone, he decided that the judge was a sweet soul.

But Roger was looking at the judge with his face screwed up as if he smelt something bad.

5
Friend or Enemy?

The patient stirred. The judge rushed to his side. "I'll take over," he said. Hal stepped back and the judge took his place, his fingers on the warden's pulse.

So when the warden opened his eyes the first thing he saw was the anxious, tear-stained face of the sweet soul. And the first thing he felt was the pressure of the judge's warm hand upon his wrist.

He lay quiet for some time. When he did speak his weak voice gave some idea of the ordeal his strong body had suffered.

"Thank you, judge," he said. "I can always depend upon you." Then he noticed the boys. "You have met?"

"Not exactly," the judge said. "We were too concerned about you to take time to introduce ourselves."

"Then shake hands with Hal Hunt. And his brother Roger. Boys, meet Judge Sindar Singh, my dearest friend. This is not the first time he has saved my life. However did you do it, Sindar?"

"It was nothing, my friend," Judge Singh replied in

his softest, smoothest voice. "Just a matter of knowing what to do. Coramine and all that."

"The judge is a very modest man," Crosby said to the boys. "I hope you watched him closely so that you'll know what to do if you ever have a case of poisoning to deal with."

"Yes," Hal said. "We watched him closely."

It was on the tip of his tongue to add, "If we hadn't watched him closely, you would be dead now." But he didn't say it. After all, anyone could have made that mistake – getting the wrong dope in the syringe. It *must* have been a mistake. What possible reason could the pleasant little judge have for wanting to kill the warden?

Of course if anyone really wanted to commit murder that was a perfect way to do it. There was already Aco in the wound. If more were injected in the same place, no one would be able to tell, even in an autopsy, that it had not come from the arrow. Hal brushed away the evil thought. The beaming smiles of the little judge over the patient's recovery were strong evidence of his devotion to his friend.

"You'll be glad to know, Sindar," – the warden's voice was stronger now – "that the boys are going to help us round up the poachers."

"Very nice," smiled the judge. "But, with all due respect,

I'm afraid two boys won't get far against those gangs of killers."

"Ordinary boys would not. But these are not quite ordinary. They've already had a lot of experience. Their father is a famous animal collector and he has taught them how to get along in rough country. They've taken animals alive, even the big ones – don't you remember reading in the papers about their capture of the fifty-thousand-dollar white elephant in the Mountains of the Moon?"

"But catching an animal is a bit different from a war on poachers," suggested the judge mildly.

"They've had a taste of that sort of thing too. Anyhow, they'll have thirty men to help them – they're on the road now."

"When do they arrive?"

"Tomorrow at midday."

The news seemed to electrify the little judge.

"Well, well, I must be going. I just dropped in to see you on my way to Nairobi. I must move along or I won't get there before night. Take care of yourself, Mark. Sorry you picked up that arrow. Where did you say the gang is operating?"

"I didn't say. Their camp is due west, about seven miles."

"Good luck with your raid. I do wish I could be with

you but I'll be pretty busy tomorrow. Glad to have met you, boys. Watch your step. Remember, this isn't Long Island." He gave them a sweet smile, and was gone.

"You boys have had quite a day," Crosby said. "You'd probably like to rest. Don't bother any more about me — I'll be all right. Your banda is Number Three. It's unlocked. Just move in and make yourselves at home. If there's anything you want, ask a ranger."

As the boys left the building they saw a car driving away. It must be Judge Singh's.

But there was something wrong. The car was not heading north on to the Nairobi road. It was going west.

They squinted into the descending sun and watched until the car disappeared down the forest trail. Roger said uneasily, "There's something a little fishy about everything that guy does."

The banda — to use the African name for a cabin or cottage — was very comfortable. In fact, to the boys, who had been living in a tent during their adventures in the Mountains of the Moon, it seemed luxurious. It had a large living-room with big chairs. You could sit back and look up at the inside of the thatch roof where lizards clung upside down and every now and then pounced upon a fly. There was a small bedroom with two beds, a large bath, a pantry, and, best of all, a broad porch with camp chairs and a dining-table.

The kitchen was a separate small building about thirty feet behind the banda. A native boy came running from it to ask what they would like to have for dinner.

It was pleasant, having dinner in the open, looking out to the panorama of hill and valley and distant blue mountains. Highest of the peaks was Kilimanjaro, 19,000 feet, taller than anything else in the entire continent of Africa, topped with snow and glaciers.

"It looks like the Matterhorn," Roger said.

"Yes. But it's about a mile higher than the Matterhorn."

"Bet it's cold up there."

"To go from here to the top would be like travelling from the equator to Iceland – there'd be that much change in climate."

"Has anybody ever been to the top?"

"Oh yes. It's not so hard to climb – on the other side. But on this side it had everybody buffaloed until 1964."

"I don't wonder. It looks as steep as a wall. Who climbed it?"

"Two Royal Air Force men. It took them fifty hours – one way. A little over two days and nights. They went right up the face of that wall, clinging like flies, watching every foothold and fingerhold. They slept standing up – wedged into small clefts and tied to steel pegs driven into the rock. One of them had a nightmare – he struggled, and pulled the pegs loose. He woke just in time to save himself from falling five thousand feet straight down."

The sun had now left the valley of death but still glorified the snowy heights of Kilimanjaro. The white had changed to a warm pink and, as the sun sank lower, the pink snow turned blood-red which gradually became black under a canopy of brilliant stars.

The animals that dared to visit the camp at night began to arrive. The grass around the bandas was kept watered, and attracted grass-eating animals. There was a distinct chomping, chewing sound. Straining their eyes, the boys could dimly make out stripes.

Hal brought out the binoculars and looked in the direction of the sound. It was remarkable how much better one could see with these things, even at night.

"Zebras," he said. "A whole herd of them."

"What's that other noise?" Roger said. "Sounds like water." He took the glasses. As he put them to his eyes, a monster loomed in front of him. It seemed so close that he could almost touch it. "It's an elephant," he said. "He's turning on a tap."

"Come off it," said Hal. "That was just a story."

"No, it's true. Look for yourself."

Through the binoculars Hal could darkly see the huge beast actually turning the tap with the finger-like points at the end of his trunk. The dribble of water from the tap became a rushing stream. The elephant curved his trunk beneath the tap to catch the water. Then he threw back his head, opened his cavernous mouth, lifted his trunk and threw the water down his throat. He repeated this act over and over again. Hal estimated that he put away five or six gallons.

But after he had finished drinking, he was not done with the water. He tossed trunkfuls of it back over his body to wash off the jungle dust. When he had given himself a thoroughly good bath he grunted with pleasure, turned round, and ambled off into the darkness, leaving the tap still running.

"We'd better turn that thing off," Hal said. "If we don't, the warden will – and he shouldn't get out of bed."

"Isn't it dangerous?" Roger said. "You don't know what else might be sneaking round that tap."

"Nonsense. You scare too easily."

"Oh, is that so? And I suppose you're not one bit afraid. Then why don't you turn it off?"

"All right, I will. Just to show you what a fraidy cat you are."

Hal stepped off the porch on to the grass. He couldn't see so well without the binoculars. He could go back into the banda and get his torch – but why bother? He could tell by the sound where the tap was.

He didn't know that his mischief-loving brother had stepped off the porch on the other side and was circling round him.

Stepping carefully, Hal picked his way across the lawn to the tap, fumbled for the valve, and turned it off. He had no sooner begun the return journey to the porch than he was startled by the roar of a wild beast close behind him. It sent rippled of fear up and down his backbone. He leaped like an antelope back to the safety of the porch, his one instinct to get inside that banda and close the door. But he must pick up his brother first. He groped where Roger had been, but Roger was not there. Well, he must have heard the beast and gone inside. Hal lost no time in shutting the door between him and the angry animal.

"Roger," he said, "you here?"

No answer.

"Roger, where are you?"

An animal-like laugh came from the porch. A laughing hyena? No, it was that infernal brother of his.

"You young rascal, come in here."

Roger came in, still laughing. Hal couldn't help laughing too. "So it was you all the time, you scamp." But he wasn't going to let the kid off so easily. He grabbed Roger, backed into a chair, and tried to bend the boy over his knee for a good spanking. He used to be able to do that – but now Roger was too strong for him.

Roger twisted himself off the spanker's lap and overturned Hal's chair so that he went sprawling on his back, surprising a rat that scampered away squeaking with alarm.

"All right, young man," Hal laughed, picking himself up. "That's enough for now. I'll get you later. Just now I'm going to bed. We have a big day tomorrow."

When they were ready for bed, Roger sniffed the air. "It's stuffy in here. Smells ratty. Don't you think we ought to have a window open?"

"The warden said no. A leopard might climb in."

"I think he was just playing it safe when he said that. It's not really very likely, is it?"

"I wouldn't take a chance on it."

"How about this small window over my bed?" Roger suggested.

"A leopard could get through it."

"It's too high from the ground."

"You'd be surprised how high a leopard can jump."

Roger lay quiet for a moment. Another rat – or was it the same one? – scuttled across the floor.

"I don't like the smell of this place," announced Roger. "I'm going to open that window."

Hal answered sleepily, "Okay, you young idiot, open it. But don't be surprised if you have a visitor."

Roger opened the window, then flopped down under the covers and went to sleep.

303

6
Leopard Comes to Call

He dreamed that he was tussling with his brother. Hal sat on him, squeezing the breath out of him.

He woke with a start. Something *was* on top of him. A leopard? He was about to scream and wrench himself free when another thought came to him.

Hal had said he would get him later. He had scared Hal out of his wits by pretending to be a wild beast about to spring upon his back. Now Hal was trying to scare him – make him think that a leopard had pounced on him. He would fool the big boob. He'd just lie there as calm as you please.

"Ho, ho, hi, hum," he yawned. "Go back to bed, you big stiff. You're not fooling me a bit."

He felt hot breath on his face. Sharp points like claws pressed through the blanket on to his arms.

"You ought to cut your fingernails," he said.

The answer was a roar that sounded like a circular saw going through a knot.

Roger laughed. "Pretty poor imitation of a leopard. Now get off me – I want to sleep."

"What's going on over there?" came from the other side of the room.

Roger's blood froze. "Where are you, Hal?" he quavered.

"In bed, of course. Something woke me up. Sounded like a leopard."

There was a scampering sound on the floor. Whatever it was that had landed on Roger leaped off and went careering madly round the room. Hal dug under his pillow for his flashlight and turned it on. Roger saw spots before his eyes – black spots on yellow chasing a big rat.

The leopard caught the rat, gripped it between his teeth, jumped on Roger, squeezing out of that terrified boy one wild yell, then leaped out of the window.

Roger found himself shivering and sweating at the same time. Hal got out of bed and came over.

"Have you had enough fresh air?" he asked. He closed the window. Without saying anything more, he sat down on the edge of the bed, put his hand on Roger's arm and kept it there until the shivering died down. Then, with a final friendly pat, he went back to bed.

Roger lay listening to the sounds of the night. The animals had really taken over the camp. He recognized some of the sounds – the whine of a jackal, the hoot of an owl, and the familiar "ugh-ugh" of the animal he had come to know so well, most numerous of all four-legged creatures in the East African animal land – the gnu or wildebeest.

There was the "meow" that sounded like the voice of a house cat but came more probably from a beast twenty times as big, the cheetah. A rhino snorted like a car backfiring. There was a great clatter as the rubbish bin beside the kitchen went over. That might be the work of hyenas. He was more sure of it when he heard a loud chorus of laughter from those weird beasts – "tee-hee-hee-hee-hee-ha-ha". From the distant river came an answering laugh from the hippos, a deep sound, "wah-wah-wah", and, deeper still, "hoh-hoh-hoh-hoh".

And for every sound he knew there were a dozen he did not know. He enjoyed listening to them – until he heard one he knew too well – the leopard's saw going through a hard knot.

He buried one ear in his pillow, covered the other with his blanket, and slept.

It seemed only five minutes later when he was aroused by a knock on the door. He opened his eyes to the grey light of dawn.

The door opened and the warden, Mark Crosby, came in.

"You boys want to go on dawn patrol? It's the best time of day to see the animals."

The boys were surprised to see the warden on his feet. He must have a strong constitution. "How's your arm?" Hal asked. He saw the arm was bandaged.

"Not bad at all," the warden said. "See, I can move it. I was lucky that the arrow just went through the fleshy part. A few days in a bandage and it will be okay. Pull on your clothes and we'll have some coffee."

When they came out on to the porch they found the boy had already placed a coffee pot and cups on the table. Morning mists were rising. The lower part of Kilimanjaro could not be seen but the snow-crowned top rising above the mists floated like a white cloud in the sky. The sun had already struck the snow and glaciers. Here below it was still so dark that the shapes moving among the flat-topped acacia trees looked more like blobs of ink than animals.

Crosby saw Roger looking towards the kitchen as if he expected more than coffee. The warden laughed.

"Our ways may seem a little odd to you. The animals are out in full force in the early morning, so we get our guests up at dawn and take them out to see the wild life, then bring them back at about nine for breakfast."

307

"Speaking of guests," said Hal, "none of these other bandas seems to be occupied."

Crosby shook his head. "Very few tourists come here, now that the park has been overrun by killers. Tourists are afraid to come. That's one of the serious effects of poaching. It scares off visitors. And that means it scares off money that this young nation of Kenya needs. The country's biggest source of revenue has been the tourist business. Without the money the tourists bring in, the country will go broke. So if we can get rid of the poachers we'll not only save the animals – we'll save Kenya."

They climbed into the warden's Land-Rover and set out. They had not gone more than half a mile before the trail was blocked by a herd of buffalo. Almost a hundred of the great shaggy black beasts faced them, with heads lowered. Crosby stopped the car.

"I don't think we'll try to plough through that," he said.

A huge bull buffalo came out from the herd, advanced some twenty feet towards the Land-Rover and then stopped. He glared at the car and shook his big head.

"That's their leader," Crosby said. "If he takes a notion to charge us, they'll all follow."

"Will they go round the car?"

"Buffaloes don't go round anything. They go through it. Many hunters claim they are the most dangerous animals in Africa. They stop at nothing. Their heads are like iron balls. After they had finished there would be nothing left of this car but scrap iron."

"And they have the bad habit of coming back," said Hal, remembering his own adventures with these determined beasts.

"Yes," said Crosby. "Most animals do what damage they can and then call it a day. But the buffalo comes back to make sure that you are good and dead. Of course they aren't always dangerous. If nothing annoys them they may be as quiet as cows. That's why we're just sitting here, doing nothing. If they get it through their thick noddles that we mean no harm, they may wander off. It all depends on the poachers."

"What have the poachers to do with it?"

"If a poacher's arrow or spear has ever wounded that bull, he will hate everything human and he will very likely take it out on us. But I think I recognize him by that twisted right horn. I believe he's been around the camp and I gave him a drink. Let's see if he knows me."

He opened the door and prepared to climb out. At once there was an angry roar from the big bull. The herd behind him began to stamp and bellow. The bull started forward and Hal longed to get his hands on the gear lever and back away.

But as the warden stepped down to where the bull could see him from head to foot the bull stopped and appeared to be thinking things over.

Then he turned towards the herd and said something that might have been bull-language for "This two-legged one is okay." With great dignity he moved off into the woods and the herd followed him.

Hal and Roger breathed again.

"Next stop, Poachers' Lookout," said the warden as he climbed back behind the wheel.

They drove through some pleasant woodland where they saw long-faced heartebeest, waterbuck, gerenuk and the lovely, leaping impala, expert in both the high jump and the long jump. The clown of the woods, the warthog, humph-humphed out of their way and a family of baboons barked savagely as they passed.

They stopped to study a herd of a couple of dozen elephants who were breaking off branches from the trees and watching the approach of the car with much threatening spreading of ears and tossing of trunks. There were several huge bulls, also cows with calves. They were well off the trail, over humpy ground, and it was impossible to drive closer to them.

Hal, who wanted to photograph them, left the car, with the warden's permission, and walked towards them. The intelligent animals knew the difference between a camera and a gun and allowed him to come within a hundred feet. He took eight photographs. But when the world's biggest land animals found the fly-size human too annoying and seemed about ready to do something about it, Hal made a rather hasty retreat to the car.

Another half-mile and Crosby again brought the car to a halt.

"Now I'm going to show you something remarkable. You won't believe your eyes. Look over there."

What the boys saw was a broken-down tree. An elephant stood beside it.

"What's remarkable about that?" asked Hal.

"Watch."

The bark of the tree-trunk had already been torn off and the white wood was exposed. Presently the elephant raised his tusks and punched them deep into the wood. He exerted his great strength and, with a loud ripping sound, tore off a sheet of wood an inch or two thick and six feet long.

"What in the world is he going to do with that?"

311

For answer, the elephant coiled the end of his trunk round the board, lifted it from his tusks, and actually put it in his mouth.

Crunch, crunch – he chewed it up as if it were nothing but a potato chip. Within ten seconds the six-foot plank had disappeared into his great inside.

He tore off strip after strip, chewed, then swallowed. He evidently thought it a delicious breakfast.

"If he keeps that up," Roger said, "he'll soon be a wooden elephant."

The boys had often seen elephants eating the leaves of a tree or even the twigs. But they had never before seen one eating the tree-trunk itself.

This was surely a freak of nature. "I can't think of anything else in the world that eats trees," Hal said.

"There's one," Crosby replied. "The termite. But it doesn't take a plank at a time."

The elephant was so thoroughly enjoying his meal that he paid no attention to the car. He kept on filling himself with wood. Hal took photographs. People just wouldn't believe this unless they could see it in pictures.

"He was lucky to find a fallen tree."

"Lucky nothing," Crosby said. "He probably pushed it over himself."

"But that trunk is about five feet thick."

"Well, the elephant is more than five feet thick, and his strength matches his size. We lose a lot of trees to the elephants. If they can't push a tree over they have another way of getting it down. They attack the standing tree on one side and keep cutting into it until it falls. They are intelligent enough to step out of the way before it topples over. A young one who hadn't learned to do this was pinned under the tree when it fell. We found him three days ago still under the tree with his back broken. He died before we could get him out."

The car climbed a steep trail to Poachers' Lookout. In front of a small pavilion a ranger stood with his eye glued to a telescope. He snapped to attention and saluted as the warden stepped out of the car.

"See anything?" asked Crosby.

"No, bwana," said the ranger. "Except some birds."

Crosby looked through the telescope. He let Hal take his place, and then Roger. They could plainly make out some vultures circling over a spot at the edge of a wood. They flew round and round as they usually do over a dying or dead animal.

"Does it mean poachers?" Hal asked.

"I doubt it," said Crosby. "It's only about two miles from our lodge. Surely they wouldn't dare come that close. But we'll go down and take a look."

They drove to the spot. A large black hulk lay at the edge of a grove of trees. There was no sign of any poacher. As the men stepped out of the car a cloud of vultures rose from the black body and climbed to join the birds circling above.

"Dead rhino," said Crosby, and led the way to the side of the fallen animal.

The animal was more than dead. He was hollow. There was a hole in his side as big as a barrel and his insides were gone. Nothing was left but a big black cave — and a terrible smell.

The boys stooped and looked into the cave. "Poor brute," Hal said. "Perhaps he fell sick and died and the hyenas, jackals and vultures chewed this hole in him."

"Don't you think poachers might have done it?"

Hal stood up. "Look. There are the bandas in full view. The warden thinks the poachers wouldn't dare come so close to the lodge."

Crosby was studying the animal's head. "That's what I thought," he said. "But I was mistaken. Both horns are gone. No animal would chew them off — they're not good to

eat. Poachers took them. And the animal didn't die a natural death." He pointed to a ragged wound in the throat. "A spear did that. Now you get some idea of how bold these fellows can be. But you haven't seen the worst yet. Jump into the car and I'll show you something that beats all this hollow."

After only a few minutes' drive, the car stopped. "This is the Tsavo River," Crosby said.

The boys could see no river. There was nothing but a stretch of rough black rock.

"Have you ever walked on a river?" said the warden. "Now's your chance."

He led the way out on to the bare black area. He

315

stamped on the rock. It gave out a hollow sound. Hal studied the rock.

"It looks like lava," he said.

"It is lava. Some time or other it came down from Mount Kilimanjaro and covered the river. The river is still there – under your feet. Now let's walk downstream."

As they walked they heard a rushing sound which steadily grew louder. They rounded a corner and then saw the river, gushing out in great volume and thunder from under the roof of lava. They could feel the roof tremble from the violence of the current. Released from its prison, the stream broadened here to form a large pool or small lake.

"This is called Mzima Springs. The water is usually as clear as glass."

It was not clear now. It was reddish brown, and it stank.

"You've walked on top of the river," the warden said. "Now I'll take you under it."

He brushed aside the bushes and revealed a slanting hole in the ground. They descended the steep slope in the half darkness and came out into an underwater room.

This must be the underwater observatory the warden had mentioned. Through windows they could look out into the heart of the river and up to its shimmering sunlit surface.

They eagerly pressed their noses against the glass. What they saw made them sick. Hippos — but they were not walking on the bottom grazing on the river weeds, they were dead and their carcasses lay in great heaps pressed down by more carcasses on top. Some, inflated by gases, had floated to the surface. Blood still trickled from the deadly wounds made by the poachers. Tails had been cut off, strips of hide had been removed, canine teeth of solid ivory, more valuable for some purposes than elephants' tusks, had been torn out, in many cases the entire head had been chopped off.

A few baby hippos, still alive, but nearly dead from starvation, prodded their senseless mothers who could no longer feed them.

The babies themselves were food for the crocodiles which glided after them, their great jaws wide open. These tender young bodies made a delicious breakfast for the great reptiles. The crocs churned the water with their powerful tails and even fought among themselves for the choicest bits. Hundreds of fish gobbled up fragments of hippo flesh.

The boys were sober as they climbed out of the observatory. They had been told that such things were happening — but they had to see it to believe it. They had been eager before to help stop the killing of animals by poachers. Now they were determined.

They returned to the lodge at nine and had breakfast. They had seen so much — it hardly seemed possible that they had been out only three hours. Now they must impatiently wait another three hours before their men would arrive and they could make their first expedition against the killers.

7
Blackbeard Appears

At midday the fourteen lorries, trucks, jeeps and Land-Rovers of Hal's safari rolled in.

Hal's thirty black safari men, with smiling faces behind a red film of road dust, climbed down. They showed plainly their affection for their young masters and the boys were equally pleased to see them – these fine, stalwart fellows who had been their partners in so many adventures, capturing live animals of every sort for the world's zoos and circuses.

The tents of the safari team were erected behind the row of bandas. The kitchen boys of the lodge set up a long table in the open air and loaded it with food.

The men ate hungrily but hastily because they were eager to get on with the job that they had come to do.

Warden Crosby addressed them. He told them of the poachers' camp that he and the boys had seen from the aeroplane seven miles to the west. He told them of the terrible slaughter of animals. He stirred them until they could hardly wait to get at the poachers.

There were cries of "Let's go," "Break out the guns," "We'll murder them."

Crosby held up his hand to quieten the men. "I'm sorry," he said, "but that's the one thing you cannot do. You can't kill them. You will take no guns with you."

"But they will have poisoned arrows, and spears," objected big Joro, chief tracker. "They will try to kill us."

"Exactly," agreed Crosby. "And that's going to make your job dangerous and difficult. You see, there's a law against killing poachers. They have to be arrested and taken to court. They are tried and the judge fines them or puts them in prison. I know it doesn't seem fair — they will be well armed and you will not. You must not kill them — you must take them alive. You have had experience in taking animals alive. All right, these are animals — and you must capture them alive just as you would any other savage beast."

The men were not smiling now. This was going to be worse than they had thought.

Hal spoke. "Men," he said, "let's get one thing clear. This is not a part of your regular job. You were not hired for this. If you don't want to do it, you don't have to. Anyone who doesn't wish to take part has a perfect right to stay here in camp."

When the cars started off a few minutes later not one man stayed behind. Hal was very proud of his crew.

In addition to his men there were five of Crosby's

rangers. The other five were absent, looking for poachers in sections of the park more than a hundred miles away.

But there was one poacher-hunter perhaps as good as all of the five missing men. This one was not a man, but a dog – Zulu, the big Alsatian belonging to the safari man Mali.

Zulu had something that no other member of the party had – savage teeth. There was a law against guns. But there was no law against teeth. Zulu didn't know what this was all about, but he knew it was something great, and he barked excitedly.

Zulu's teeth would not be enough to win the battle. Crosby and the boys, sharing the same Land-Rover, discussed the problem as the cars bounced their way westward over the rough trail.

"There is a chance," said Crosby, "that they will take fright and run away when they see these fourteen iron monsters roaring in on them."

"But you don't want them to run away," Hal said. "You want to arrest them."

"Perhaps we can catch the ones who don't run fast enough. We may not be able to do all we want to do. We will just do what we can. I don't want to place your men in unnecessary danger."

"Our men are used to danger," Hal said. "But do you really think the poachers will run?"

"It all depends. If they have no leader, they will run. If Blackbeard is with them, he will make them stand and fight."

Hal had forgotten about Blackbeard, the man of mystery, whose real name was unknown.

"If we could nab him," the warden said, "that would probably end wholesale poaching in Tsavo."

But how to do it? Deadly weapons were not allowed. What weapons could be used that were not deadly? Hal reviewed in his mind the contents of the supply van.

"How about sleep?" he said suddenly. "Does the law say we can't put them to sleep?"

Crosby stared. "Of course not. But how would you do that?"

"We do it with animals all the time. I don't know why it wouldn't work with poachers. If you'll stop the car and let me out I'll flag down the supply van and see if we have all the sleep we need."

"I don't quite get you," said the warden, stopping the car.

Hal hopped out. "No time to explain now. See you later."

In the supply van he busied himself filling several dozen

darts with a thin white liquid. The darts looked harmless enough. They were only eight inches long and no larger round than your little finger. At one end of the dart was something like a hypodermic needle. At the other end was a tuft of feathers.

The van seemed to be twisting and turning. Hal put out his head. The cars had left the trail and were winding their way among termite hills ten to fifteen feet high built by the "white ants".

The fleet ground to a halt. Ahead was the thorn fence. The warden had stopped his car five hundred yards before reaching the fence and the other drivers had followed his example.

It would have been foolish to come close. Then the poachers could fire their arrows from behind the fence. Now it would be necessary for them to come out in front of it to attack.

Hal leaped out with a bucketful of darts. First he went to the warden.

"Will you help me distribute these?"

"What are they?"

"Darts — filled with dope."

"Aco? But I told you — we're not allowed to kill . . ."

"This won't kill anybody. It will just put him to sleep. It's Sernyl — a muscular anaesthetic. Our men have used it in catching animals. They find Sernyl a hard word — so we've taught them just to call it Sleep. I've made enough for us to give each man three darts."

The men had piled out of their cars and were looking for the enemy. There was not a poacher to be seen. Beyond the thorn fence among some trees were the poachers' grass huts, but there was no sign of life — except the life of suffering animals, struggling in snares in the gaps of the fence, raising pitiful cries of pain and terror.

The boys and the warden distributed the darts. But what good were darts if the poachers had fled?

The men lined up in front of the cars facing the fence. They were itching to get into action, disappointed at finding no enemy. A few of Hal's men became impatient and began to edge forward.

"Tell them to stop," said the warden. "All that ground is probably full of traps."

At Hal's command, the men stepped back into line, grumbling.

"Look," cried Roger suddenly, and pointed. Hal looked, and saw nothing. "He's gone already," said Roger. "I saw him plain as day. He struck his head out from behind the fence. A man with black whiskers. I'll bet it was Blackbeard."

Perhaps the kid had just imagined it, Hal thought. The boy had Blackbeard on his mind.

The waiting grew tiresome, but Hal would not let his men move. "If there are any fellows hiding behind the fence," he told the warden, "it's just as well to let them think we're afraid to come on."

Zulu, the big Alsatian, began to bark furiously. He started to run towards the barricade. His master, Mali, fearing the dog might be caught in a trap, called him back. The dog returned to the line but kept on barking.

Then a black head appeared in one of the gaps – then another and another.

"They're giving us the once-over," Hal said. "I hope we look harmless."

Seeing no guns, the poachers grew bolder. They crept out through the gaps past the dead or dying animals. They were all well armed with spears and bows and arrows. Doubtless every arrow carried its smear of deadly poison. Black figures continued to appear until there were nearly fifty lined up in front of the thorn barrier.

The poachers stared as if they couldn't believe their eyes. These fools who had dared to invade their camp held no rifles, no revolvers, no bows, no spears, nothing but some little sticks. One poacher broke out into a laugh. It was taken up all down the line. It grew louder until it was a roar of merriment. Men doubled up with laughter and slapped their thighs and slapped each other and danced. A few arrows came flying, but they fell short.

The poachers began to pick their way forward, stepping carefully to avoid the traps concealed in the long grass.

"Be ready," Hal called to his men, "but don't fire till I tell you." Joro repeated the command in Swahili for those who knew little or no English.

Someone else was giving orders. He was not in the line of advancing poachers. He stood in one of the gaps of the thorn fence. He was not bare-chested and bare-legged like the men he commanded. He was dressed in a bush jacket and safari trousers and his whitish face was half concealed by a black beard.

"There he is," Roger exclaimed. "I told you I saw him. Blackbeard."

"He's smart," Hal said, "to let his men do the fighting and save his own skin."

Another sharp order from the man behind. The poachers at once slung their bows over their shoulders and took their spears from the back straps.

"Why do they change to spears?" Roger wondered.

The warden said, "The arrow is for long-range fighting. At close range the spear is more deadly. They think we're unarmed – so they can come close. Watch out for those spears. They're poisoned too."

The safari men had their eyes on Hal, waiting for his command to let go. Hal delayed until the poachers were within twenty feet.

"Ready!" he shouted, and each man raised his dart.

It really looked very silly. The poachers laughed again. Here they were, armed with poisoned spears eight feet long, and their enemy had nothing but toys no longer than pencils.

It was lucky, Hal thought, that the Sleep darts which his men had used in taking animals in Uganda and the Congo were unknown in this part of Kenya. The poachers were in for a big surprise.

But at the last moment Hal's plan was almost ruined. The man with the black beard guessed the secret of those innocent-looking toys. He shouted something in Swahili. Joro said, "He's telling them to fall back."

It was too late. The poachers were too excited to obey their master's voice. Victory was almost within their grasp – why should they run now? The command did make them hesitate for a moment, and taking advantage of that precious moment Hal shouted, "Fire!"

The darts flew straight, guided by their tail feathers. The needle tips plunged into black flesh. They did not go in more than a quarter of an inch – they didn't need to. The shock was enough to send the liquid flying into the nerves beneath the skin, and these nerves telegraphed the bad news all over the body.

The first result was terror. "Aco!" yelled someone. The cry was taken up by others. They all knew Aco, the deadly arrow poison, and supposed at first that this was what had hit them.

They hastily plucked out the darts. They saw that the liquid dripping from the needles was white. They knew that Aco was a brownish black. So this was not Aco.

This discovery gave them no comfort. Probably this stuff was something new, even worse than Aco.

Whatever it was, it acted faster than arrow poison. It went straight for the muscles and turned them into dish-rags. Legs that were strong a moment ago became weak and refused to hold up the body. The drug – plus fear – paralysed the muscles.

Those who could run, ran – but soon fell in their tracks. Some blundered blindly into traps that they had set for the animals. Some who had not been hit at all were so overcome by the general fright that they fell where they stood and prepared to die. A few of the braver spirits plunged forward and seriously injured three of the safari men with their sharp spears before they themselves were overcome by the numbing effect of Sleep.

Presently the place looked more like a bedroom than a battle-ground. Everywhere sleeping bodies sprawled in the grass. Even those caught in the cruel traps did not cry out with pain, for they were unconscious.

Two who had run so well that they had almost reached the thorn fence were brought down by Zulu. Now they also were asleep.

"Into the Power-wagon," Hal ordered. "Into the cage."

The Power-wagon was the truck generally used for carrying captured animals. In it was a huge elephant cage. The happy safari men and rangers dragged the sleeping poachers to the cage and thrust them in.

Wire snares that had trapped some runaways were easily removed. It was not so easy to open the lion traps and elephant traps. These were like the bear traps sometimes used in American forests, but larger and stronger. The teeth of the trap caught a man's ankle and dug in fiercely.

The warden, trying to free a sleeper from such a trap, called Hal and Roger.

"You remember I told you about two of my rangers who were caught in traps and eaten alive? You may have wondered why they couldn't free themselves. After all, a man has something the average animal doesn't have – two hands. Well, try to open that trap with your hands."

Hal bent down, took hold of the two iron jaws and exerted all his strength to pull them apart. They did not budge.

"The spring is too strong," he said.

"Right. It has to be strong to hold a lion or elephant. It can't be opened without a tool."

Crosby saw Hal looking at the ten-foot chain that

connected the trap with an iron spike driven into the ground.

"I know what you're thinking –" he said, "that the ranger could have pulled up that spike; then he could hobble to his car with the trap still on his leg. Try to pull up the spike."

Hal laid hold of the spike. He pulled until he was blue in the face. The spike did not move. It was driven into the base of a termite hill and the termites came out to see what was going on.

"You may as well give up," Crosby said. "That was driven in with a sledge-hammer. About three feet deep into the hill. As you know, these termite hills are almost as hard as cement. Even an elephant couldn't pull that spike loose. Do you have a crowbar in your supply van? That would open the trap."

Hal brought the heavy iron bar. He inserted it between the jaws, pried them open, and Crosby drew out the bleeding foot. Roger went for antiseptic and bandaging. Hal doctored the wounded ankle of the man who would gladly have killed him.

8

Blackbeard Disappears

"Aren't we forgetting something?" Roger said, looking back at the thorn fence. "How about Whiskers?"

In the general excitement Blackbeard had been forgotten.

Hal leaped to his feet. "Joro, Mali, come with me. Bring your dog. Toto, take over while we're gone."

He set off at a run for the gap where Blackbeard had last been seen. The others followed.

They dashed through the gap and looked around. Nobody.

"Look in every hut." The huts were all empty.

Joro did not join in the search. When the others came back they found him squatting in the gap, studying the ground. He was Hal's best tracker.

The ground was covered with footprints, each ending in five dents made by the five toes, for the poachers went barefoot. There was one exception – a line of prints without toes.

"Made by boots," Joro said. "The boss – he wore boots. We catch him."

He started out with great enthusiasm, following the boot-prints. He had not gone a dozen paces before he stopped, puzzled. There were no more boot-prints. It was as if the wearer of the boots had suddenly gone up in smoke. Could he have climbed into a tree?

Joro looked up. There was no branch low enough to be reached.

"He was smart," Joro said. "Took off his boots — so we no can track him."

The ground was still covered with prints, but they all

had toes. Who could tell which were the tracks of Blackbeard?

"The dog," Roger suggested. "Try the dog."

Mali took his dog Zulu back to the gap. He bent the

animal's head down so that his nose almost touched the boot-prints. Zulu sniffed. He followed the boot-prints to the point where they disappeared. The dog sniffed about aimlessly, making little whining noises.

Crosby shook his head. "Your dog may be clever," he said, "but not that clever. Boots and bare feet don't smell alike."

"You watch," Mali said.

The dog went back and smelled the boot-prints – then the other tracks. Hal hoped against hope. It would all depend upon whether the boots were new or old. If they were new they would not have the smell of a man. But if they had been worn a long time in this hot climate they would have absorbed some of the perspiration and bodyodour of their wearer. It would be faint, but a hunting dog's keen sense of smell might pick it up.

Zulu barked. He had found something. He went back again to smell the boot-print. Then with an excited yelp he started off on a trail of bare feet.

"He's got it," cried Hal.

But the man who had made those tracks was not stupid. He had another trick to baffle his pursuers. A dead buffalo lay in a pool of its own blood. Blackbeard had walked straight through the blood. That should be enough to kill all man-scent. Where he had come out, who could say? – for the ground was covered with bloody footprints.

Crosby again shook his head, but Mali and the boys still had faith in Zulu's sharp nose.

Zulu took more time than before to make his selection. He finally picked out a trail but did not seem too sure about it.

Now the human tracker helped him out. Joro carefully studied and measured Blackbeard's prints leading into the blood and then the outgoing prints chosen by Zulu.

"Good," he said. "Dog, he got him. Foot, same wide, same long. Toes tight, boot."

"What does he mean by that?" the warden asked.

"I think he means," said Hal, "that the toes are close together. That's a sign that the man generally wore boots. The boot squeezes the toes together. If a man always goes barefoot, his toes spread apart."

Again they took up the trail. But again Blackbeard had a trick up his sleeve. The tracks led to the shore of the Tsavo River and entered the water.

Zulu howled his disappointment. He sniffed his way up along the bank, and then downstream, with no effect. Joro too was defeated. The hard river-bottom showed no prints. It was impossible to tell where the man had come out.

He might have swum across the river, he might have waded upstream or downstream, and he would be careful to step out of the water into brush where he would leave no footprints.

"He's long gone by this time," Hal said. "Chances are, he went to where he had hidden his car and now he's well out of the park."

Hal felt that his first attempt to help the warden had ended in failure. Crosby tried to cheer him up.

"Never mind. You caught the poachers. That's a good day's work."

"But we let the boss slip through our fingers," Hal said gloomily. "He'll just start over again somewhere else with a new gang."

9
The Tiger-Horse

Forty-seven poachers, sound asleep, were packed like sardines into the elephant cage.

They would stay asleep for about four hours – more than enough time to cover the hundred and thirty miles to Mombasa. They would wake up in the Mombasa jail.

Crosby wrote a note to the jail warden:

"Herewith, forty-seven arrested for poaching. Hold for trial."

He gave the note to the driver. The Power-wagon, with its unconscious freight, took off.

The other cars remained, for there was still a job to be done – a painful job. The hundred or more animals caught in the mile-long trap-line and in the separate traps in the grass must be set free.

Black clouds of vultures flew up as the men approached the animals. Hyenas and jackals, that had been sinking their sharp teeth into creatures still alive, skulked away. They went just out of reach and stood waiting for a chance to rush in again to torture the screaming beasts.

The animals still able to fight struggled fiercely to escape from the wire nooses that had pulled tight on their necks. Every jerk made the wire sink more deeply into the throat. It cut like a knife into the flesh. Blood streamed down the animals' heaving flanks.

Roger and the warden tried to rescue a zebra from the snare that was choking it to death. It was dangerous to come near the animal because it was so mad with fear and pain that it lived up to its nickname of "tiger-horse".

A zebra is usually harmless. Although striped like a tiger, he is more of a horse than a tiger. But this zebra was more tiger than horse. His pain had turned him into a killer. He was ready to murder anything that came near. His strong teeth snapped together like a trap when the dog Zulu came too close. He could and did kick out with all four feet.

An iron-hard hoof caught the warden in the stomach and sat him down on the ground with a jolt. With the wind knocked out of him, he was too weak to move and stayed where he was while hooves flew round him. If one of them struck him in the face he might be killed. Roger took hold of him by the shoulders of his bush jacket and managed to pull him back out of the way.

Shakily, the warden got up. An experienced animal man, he was ashamed that he had almost been laid low by a striped horse.

"First time I've ever been saved by a boy," he grinned.

Roger didn't tell him that it was the second time. The warden already owed his life to the boy who had pulled his helpless body off the control of the plunging aeroplane.

The warden pulled a wire-cutter from his hip pocket.

"We always carry these things when we go on rescue missions," he said.

"But how can you get close enough to use them?"

"It's not easy," Crosby admitted. He staggered a little. He was still dizzy. It wasn't just the kick of the tiger-horse.

He still felt the effects of his almost fatal experience of the day before. Perhaps there was still some Aco in his veins.

Roger knew he must help. But he had no experience with tiger-horses. He had tamed bucking broncos on his father's farm. He could leap on to a horse's back without benefit of saddle or stirrups. Then why be afraid now – wasn't this just a horse? Not even as high as a horse. It ought to be easy. He saw the dizzy warden pass his hand over his forehead.

"Let me have the cutters," Roger said.

"No, no," the warden replied. "I'll take care of this."

"Let's both do it. You get in front of him and attract his attention. I'll jump on his back and cut the noose."

Crosby shook his head. "Too risky."

"For you perhaps," said Roger. "Not for me. I'll be on top – where he can't get me with either his feet or his teeth. You're the one who will have to look out."

Crosby, half convinced, gave Roger the cutters. He went in front of the enraged beast, just out of reach of the huge yellow teeth that could snap off an arm and the sharp-edged forefeet that could split a man's skull right down to the Adam's apple. The frantic zebra lunged at him but was held back by the cruel noose.

Roger made a flying leap and landed neatly on the zebra's back. He leaned forward and snipped the noose. As it fell from the bleeding neck the animal plunged straight forward with a squeal of fury. The warden stepped out of the way. The zebra did not pursue him – he suddenly realized there was something on his back, something he had to get rid of.

He reared on his hind legs and tossed Roger upside down into the thorn barricade. The thorns went straight through the heavy bush jacket and safari trousers and tattooed the boy's skin. He struggled out to see the tiger-horse speeding away like a striped sail in a strong wind.

"Do you notice anything wrong with that zebra?" said the warden.

Roger studied the retreating figure. "Well, there seems to be something missing. I know – he has no tail."

"That's what made him so savage. Agony at both ends – neck cut, tail chopped off. That was all the poachers wanted – the tail. They lopped it off with a bush knife and left the animal there to suffer until he died. That tail is now a fly-whisk. Think of killing such a fine animal just so that some fool of a tourist can swat a fly. In the tourist shops in Nairobi you have probably seen trays full of fly-whisks made from the tails of zebras and gnus and other animals, and priced at a few shillings each — and you've seen tourists buying them because they thought they would make amusing presents to take home to Boston or London or Paris. Many of those tourists are kind and gentle people, but they just don't think. If they could see the agony these beasts must suffer so that they can swat a fly, they wouldn't buy that fly-whisk."

In the next gap were two snares, one set high to catch a large animal, one low to trap anything small.

In the lower one was a beautiful brown-eyed serval cat. In the upper snare struggled one of the handsomest creatures of Africa — the magnificent giraffe. Its throat was deeply cut by the wire noose. Plainly, it had not long to live.

Seven lions sat round it, licking their chops, waiting.

"I wish we could scare them away," Roger said.

"That would hardly be fair," said the warden. "They have a right to their dinner. Nature made them meat eaters — like you and me. They are no more cruel than you and I are when we eat a beefsteak."

"I know," admitted Roger. "It was the poachers who were cruel."

Roger and the warden stood at a respectful distance, for it is not quite safe to interfere with seven hungry lions.

It has been said that a giraffe has no voice. That is not quite true – a low moaning sound came from the throat of the tortured animal. If it had been a buffalo or a rhino or an elephant there would have been a bellowing or grunting or squealing loud enough to be heard a mile away. But the near-silence of the tallest animal on earth and one of the most graceful was no sign that he did not feel pain. His feelings were revealed in the jerky twisting and wrenching of the body. Death would be a blessed relief.

"How long will he live?" Roger asked.

"Not long. An hour perhaps."

"It's going to be a mighty bad hour for him. Can't we do something?"

"It's too late to save him."

Roger put his hand in his pocket. "I have one Sleep left. How about putting him out of his misery?"

"That's a wonderful idea," said the warden. "And it might work if you didn't have seven lions between you and the giraffe. Just how are you going to get round them?"

"I don't need to. I can throw the dart from here."

"The hide is too tough. The dart wouldn't go in. You would have to jab it in by hand."

Roger's eye followed the giraffe's neck up past the branch of an acacia tree.

"Why didn't I notice that before?" he exclaimed. "That's the way to do it."

Before the warden could reply Roger was halfway to the trunk of the tree. To get there he must pass within ten feet of the lions. Most of them were much too interested in the giraffe to pay any attention to him. But one, a huge male, evidently the leader of the pride, wheeled about to face him, laid back his ears, bared his teeth, crouched as if to spring, and let out a blast of thunder that tied Roger's nerves up in knots.

But he did not hesitate. He reached the tree and scrambled up. He could imagine the lion's claws sinking into his tingling back. Or the beast would catch one of his feet in its bone-crushing jaws.

He reached the lowest branch and looked down. The lion was standing on his hind feet with his front paws on the tree-trunk, and the look on the huge face was anything but pleasant.

Roger inched his way out on to the branch until he was close to the giraffe's head and neck. The great brown eyes with their remarkably long lashes looked at him appealingly.

He took the Sleep from his pocket and, with all his force, plunged the needle into the quivering neck.

He backed away from the thrashing head. He noticed a wire running down from the branch to the noose that held the little serval. Gently, he hauled the cat up out of reach of the lions and planted its feet on the branch. He took out his cutters and snipped the noose.

Crosby watched anxiously. The excited cat might turn on the boy and scratch him badly. But the serval's only idea was escape. It ran along the branch to the trunk, then up into the safe treetop.

Roger was happy to see that the lion had gone back with the others, waiting for dinner. He slid down the trunk and sprinted to join the warden.

"That was a good job," Crosby said. They watched as the drug took effect. The great eyes closed, the twisting and squirming stopped. The last hour of the great animal would be without pain.

Roger noticed that in this case too the tail was gone.

"To make a fly-whisk?" he asked.

"No. Some lady will wear the murder of that giraffe around her neck. They make necklaces out of giraffe tails."

"And is that all the poachers wanted?"

"That, and just one other thing. Look at the backs of the hind legs. The sinews have been torn out."

"What can they do with them?"

"Weave them to make a bowstring."

So for a necklace and a bowstring this magnificent animal must die. It was just too pitiful.

In the next snare hung the body of one of Africa's loveliest creatures, the impala. Every visitor to Africa falls in love with the impala. It is a gazelle, the gayest of all the gazelles, so full of the joy of living that it cannot stay on the ground. It is a flier that does not need wings. It happily soars over bushes and small trees, touches the ground, then soars, and soars again. The vision of a hundred of these sleek, streamlined animals all in the air at the same time is a sight never to be forgotten.

But this impala would never sail again. The lovely creature was no longer lovely. A deadly wound had been cut in the neck by the wire snare. Parts of the body had been eaten away and maggots an inch long squirmed through the rotting flesh.

Roger could not bear to look at it. Heavy-hearted, he went on down the wall of death.

But the next animal was not dead – it was a Thomson's gazelle, usually called a Tommy. The Tommy is a friend of man. He never seems to learn that it is not safe to trust man.

Beside the trapped animal was a smaller animal that had

not been trapped. It was a baby Tommy that had refused to leave its mother. The mother was kicking out savagely at some vultures that were tormenting the youngster. To the last she was thinking, not of herself, but of her fawn. The vultures flew away as Roger and Crosby approached. Crosby stooped beside the fawn.

"Too late," he said. "It's gone."

Roger snipped the wire snare and the Tommy was free. But she did not run away. With her delicate little nose she nudged her baby to make him stand up, but she got no response. She herself tottered as if she might fall at any moment.

"Do you think we can patch her up?" said Roger.

"We'll take her to the hospital," the warden said.

"Hospital?"

"Haven't you seen our animal hospital? We have a good many patients already but there may be room for a few more."

Roger took the Tommy up in his arms. The slender little body weighed only some thirty pounds. Her blood soaked his bush jacket.

As he walked towards the trucks, she struggled fiercely, looking back at her fawn.

Crosby went back and took up what was left of the

fawn. He carried it just ahead of Roger, and the mother Tommy was now satisfied and struggled no more. Her tired little head sank on Roger's shoulder. Her heart that had been beating violently against his chest slowed down and then stopped. Tommy had gone to the Tommy paradise, if there is one. At least the friend of man was beyond the reach of unfriendly man and his cruel traps.

Roger took a shovel from the truck and dug a shallow grave for the gallant little gazelle and her fawn. Then he set out to rejoin the warden who had already gone back to the trap-line.

10
Roger's Cheetah

The ground suddenly gave way beneath him.

He was falling. He clutched at bushes and grass but he kept on falling. It seemed he would never stop.

But Roger did stop, with a hard jolt, as he landed on the bottom some twenty feet below the surface.

He scolded himself. "How stupid can you get?" He had been told to watch out for elephant pits. Now he had walked straight into one.

It was very dark. At first he could see nothing. Gradually he could make out the details of his prison.

It was large enough for the biggest of elephants. The walls were straight up and down. The roof was of brush, criss-crossed, and sprinkled with earth so that it would look solid enough to fool an elephant – or a careless boy.

He bumped against something hard. He examined it. It seemed to be a wooden stake driven firmly into the ground and standing five or six feet high. His fingers ran up the length of it and came to a sharp point at the end.

A sticky something came off on his fingers. He looked at it, and then shivered. In the dim light he could see that the stuff was dark brown. It was Aco, the deadly poison the poachers used on their arrows.

He wiped his fingers on his trousers, hoping there were no scratches on his skin that would admit the poison to his system.

Now he could see that there were four such stakes in the centre of the pit. An elephant falling into the hole would be bound to land on them and they would mean his death. But before he died he would be in terrible pain. On so big a body the poison would not act quickly, so he might suffer for hours, even for days.

It was hard to believe that any men, even if they were poachers, could be so cruel. Most Africans were not brutal. He suspected that this pit of agony had been planned by the white man with the black beard.

Roger thought: Glad I'm not an elephant. I'd be on those stakes right now. Being considerably smaller than an elephant, he had fallen beside them, not on them.

A low snarl came from the darkest corner of the pit. Roger froze. It was bad enough to be in the pit alone – worse to be in it with the wrong kind of company. He thought of Daniel in the lions' den. But he didn't feel like a Daniel. He couldn't make friends with a lion that must already be furious at finding itself caught in such a trap.

Roger almost wished the lion had landed on a stake. But he repented of this thought immediately, for he wouldn't want his worst enemy to suffer that kind of death.

The beast stirred in its corner, still growling. Roger could see it a little more clearly. It was no lion. It was something much worse.

It was smaller than a lion, but more dangerous. He could see spots on its coat. It must be a leopard, and leopards were far more irritable than lions. Roger backed into the corner farthest removed from the angry beast.

Still the animal growled or snarled, but it didn't quite sound like a snarl or a growl. It reminded him of a cement mixer, or one of those chain saws the lumberjacks use in the Minnesota woods.

In fact it was very much like the purr of a house cat, only a hundred times as strong. As if puss were purring into a loud-speaker. Roger found it terrifying.

His uneasiness increased when he saw that the beast was coming towards him. Its big round golden eyes glowed as if they were lit from the inside. It didn't crouch like a leopard. It stood so high from the ground that it seemed to be walking on stilts. It had a bristling moustache and the hair on the back of its neck and shoulders stood up straight like that of a dog or cat that is angry or afraid.

Two black lines running from the eyes to the corners of the mouth made it look more savage.

Roger rubbed his eyes. Was it really there? He wondered if his nerves were still upset by his experience with the leopard the night before.

Now a little more light fell on the beast. It was real, but the craziest leopard he had ever seen. It was so high from the ground, and behind it, switching to and fro, was a bushy tail a yard long ending in three black rings and a white tuft of hair.

Those spots – they weren't a leopard's spots. Instead of uneven rings with light centres, these spots were round and solid black. Suddenly he remembered he had seen pictures of this thing and had read about it. It was sometimes called a "hunting leopard" – but it was no leopard. It was a cheetah.

The cheetah is a dog-cat. It is like a cat and like a dog and not quite like either. No dog, not even a Great Dane, has such long legs. No dog can run so fast.

In fact, nothing on four legs can beat it. The cheetah has been timed at seventy miles per hour. A Tommy gazelle can go thirty-seven, a Grant gazelle thirty-five, a zebra thirty, an ostrich twenty-nine, an elephant twenty-five, and a rhino has to stretch himself to do twenty. A cheetah quickly tires, but by that time he has caught what he is after.

And that buzz saw — it was really a purr. It was a purr to end all purrs. It made as much noise as a truck going uphill. But whether the truck-like purr was friendly or unfriendly, Roger still could not be sure.

The motor stopped and so did the cheetah. He cocked his head to one side and his blazing eyes seemed to look straight through the boy. Then an amazing sound came from his throat. You might have expected to hear the bark of a dog. But instead this was an ear-splitting "miaow"! It was followed by a few little bird-like chirps. To make them the cheetah puckered his lips as if about to whistle.

The dog-cat-bird seemed to be asking a question. Roger didn't know how to answer. Should he yell at the top of his lungs to scare the beast away? Should he growl like an angry lion? The cheetah was probably afraid of elephants — should he scream like a charging elephant?

He would have liked to run, but there was no place to run to. He had shrunk back into a corner of the pit as far as he could go and he had no weapon to defend himself if the animal attacked — except the wire cutters. But whoever heard of fighting a savage beast with wire cutters? Still, they might do a good deal of damage. If the cheetah

made a lunge at him, he might perhaps snip off that black nose, or plunge the cutters into an eye. The eye and the nose of any animal were particularly sensitive.

But what a pity it would be to spoil that handsome, savage face! Those wonderful golden eyes with sweeping eyelashes as long as the giraffe's, who could think of putting out for ever the light that shone in them?

Well then, there was only one thing left. Give the cheetah a polite answer to his question.

Roger tried to purr. It wasn't much of a success. It sounded more like a gargle. Perhaps he would do better with a chirp. He puckered his lips, but all he got was a whistle instead of a chirp. He said, "Chirp, chirp", but that was a failure too – it didn't sound a bit like the actual chirp of either a cheetah or a bird.

How about a miaow? It would have to be a supermiaow, as loud as the cheetah's. He put all his lung power into it. It was truly a noble performance, as miaows go, but it only made the cheetah cock his head to the other side and look puzzled as if trying very hard to understand this crazy two-legged creature.

Roger gave up the cheetah language and decided to try his own. He spoke in a low tone as he would to a pussycat.

"Here puss, here puss," he said softly with a smile in his voice. "Nice kitty, pretty kitty. Or if you prefer to be a dog, come Fido, here Fido."

The tone of his voice did the trick. With one bound, the cheetah reached him, jumped up on him like a dog, punched his fore-paws into his chest and jammed him tightly back into the corner. The super-dog's head towered above his own and the open jaws with their great jagged teeth were within an inch of his forehead. His lungs were pushed in by the animal's weight. He gasped for breath.

His arms were free and he could have punched the beast or struggled to get away. Something told him that it was better to stand still and let Nature take its course. He had to admit to himself that he was terrified. The hair stood up on his neck as it had on the cheetah's. Prickles ran down his backbone.

Two gold lamps were peering through his head like X-rays. The beast lowered its head and opened its jaws wide. Roger had never looked anybody or anything in the teeth at such close range. It seemed to him those canines were as big as a hippo's. They appeared to be about to do to him what he had thought of doing to the cheetah – bite of his nose. The animal's hot breath flooded his face.

Then it came – the long tongue licking his cheeks, dog fashion. But unlike a dog's tongue, this one was quite evidently made of coarse sandpaper. It would take the skin off his face in no time.

"Now, Fido," he said, trying to keep his trembling voice low and calm. "Down, Fido, down." He slowly raised his hand and scratched the animal's neck. Dogs liked that and so did cats. He wasn't so sure about birds.

The cheetah turned its head and seized his wrist in its jaws. Those terrible teeth could cut off his hand as easily as they could crush a rabbit. But he did not pull away. And the cheetah did not bite. The rascal was acting exactly like a dog that wants to play.

Roger put up his other hand and rubbed the beast behind the ears. The cheetah dropped the wrist and made a lightning change from dog into cat. It turned on its cement mixer. It rubbed its head against Roger's and its purr sent vibrations through his whole body.

Then it jumped down and went bounding about, chirping with pleasure. Its legs appeared to be made of steel springs. It could leap ten feet high with ease. Roger was anxious lest in one of its jumps it should come down on a poisoned stake. But every time it came down near a stake it skilfully twisted its body so as to avoid it. Then it would dash up to Roger and bunt him – and since it weighed more than he did, the bunt was nearly hard enough to knock him off his feet.

When he had had enough bunts he tried to give the playful animal something else to do. He pulled a root out of the earth wall and tossed it to the other end of the pit. The cheetah was after it in a flash. Roger thought he had never seen anything move so fast. The animal picked up the stick and raced back with it and laid it down at Roger's feet. Then it looked up at him, ears erect, eyes full of fun.

"That's a good dog," Roger said. "Nice pussy."

He began to see why the animal was called a "hunting leopard". It could very easily be trained to hunt game like a hound. Perhaps it would even hunt poachers – like a bloodhound.

11
Mischief

Roger heard voices.

"Where can that kid be?"

"When I left him he was digging a grave."

"Where was that?"

"Near the supply van. But he's not there now."

"Do you suppose he could have fallen into one of these pits?"

"Let's hope not. If he fell on the stakes he'd be dead by this time."

Roger recognized the voices – Hal and the warden were looking for him.

He didn't want to be rescued. He had been having so much fun with the cheetah that he hadn't bothered to think how he was going to get out of this pit. He just wanted to go on playing with his new pet.

"Roger – are you there?" Hal was peering down through the brush. Roger heard him say to Crosby, "I can't see a thing – it's so dark down there. But I thought I heard something move."

Hal sounded so distressed that Roger took pity on

him. He couldn't let his loving brother worry. He was just about to call back when he heard Hal say, "It would be just like the stupid little runt to fall into one of these things."

Just for that, thought Roger, I'll let you worry a little longer, you big clown. I don't need you. When I am good and ready I can get out of here all by myself.

He ran his hand over the wall of the pit, hunting for roots that would help him climb to the top. He found nothing that would bear his weight.

He heard Hal and the warden moving away. Sudden panic seized him. "Hal!" he called.

"Did you hear anything?" he heard Hal say.

"Not a thing."

"Just a moment." Crunch, crunch — Hal's footsteps as he returned through the brush. Then his voice, "Roger!"

"What can I do for you?" inquired Roger with mock politeness.

"You son of a gun! What a scare you gave us! Are you on a stake?"

The cheetah chose this moment to miaow. It sounded like a cry of pain.

"The poor kid is on a stake. We've got to do something fast. I'll get a rope."

"I'm afraid it's too late," Crosby said. "That poison works fast."

But Hal was already on the run to the supply van. He returned at once.

"I'm going to let this rope down to you. Do you have enough strength left to tie it round yourself?"

"I'll try," said Roger as weakly as possible.

Down came the end of the rope. A sudden mischievous idea struck Roger and he almost laughed aloud. He put the rope round the cheetah's body just behind the front legs and tied it.

"All right," he called.

The rope tightened. "Wow, he's heavy," Hal said.

"The stake is holding him. We'll have to pull harder to get him off it. Now, both together."

Up went the cheetah. For him this was a new style of travel and he didn't like it much. He snarled, and it was a real snarl this time, not a purr. It was an angry, growling, spitting cat whose head came up through the hole in the faces of the rescuers. They almost let him drop again, so great was their surprise. The cheetah scrambled out on to solid ground, showing an excellent set of savage teeth.

"A leopard!" cried Hal. Then he saw his mistake. "No, a cheetah."

Then he heard Roger's laugh, clear and strong. It was too hearty a laugh to come from anybody with a stake through his midriff.

Hal and the warden looked at each other grimly. "You young devil!" Hal called. "Wait till I get you out of there."

That sounded like trouble. Roger was tempted to stay down until Hal cooled off. But how about the cheetah? Perhaps it would run away. He didn't want to lose it.

He needn't have been afraid of that. His new friend came back to the edge of the pit and looked down, whining. It danced about, showing every sign of pleasure when Roger was drawn up to the surface.

If Roger expected to be greeted like a prodigal son and have his big brother weep on one of his shoulders and the warden on the other, he was disappointed.

"Bend him over," said Hal. "Let me get a crack at him."

The warden seized the young rascal behind the shoulders and bent him double over his knee. Hal spanked until his hand ached. He was stopped only by a sharp bite behind and a tearing sound as the cheetah laid open the seat of his trousers.

Then the three men sat down on the ground and laughed while the cheetah, seeing that things had changed for the better, pranced joyfully around them.

"He seems to have taken quite a liking to you," said Crosby. "It's lucky you got him before the poachers did. That gorgeous hide would be worth a couple of thousand dollars in New York. Cheetah coats are even more fashionable just now than coats of leopard skin."

"Nobody's going to wear his coat," said Roger, "except himself. I'm going to keep him for hunting."

"He'll make a wonderful hunter. A cheetah has a poor sense of smell, but marvellous eyesight – and he can go like the wind. He's easily trained – if he likes you. Never whip him. Never even scold him. He gets his feelings hurt very easily and then you can do nothing with him. Treat him well and he'll treat you well. He's nothing like a leopard – a leopard may become cross as it grows older. A cheetah doesn't. He's as faithful as a dog. You see, he's used to men – it's something that has grown into his nature because he has worked with men for more than four thousand years."

"Four thousand years?"

"At least as long as that. On ancient Egyptian monuments you see pictures of men using cheetahs for hunting. Even today in Egypt cheetahs are used as watchdogs. Indian rajahs put a hood over the cheetah's eyes just as a falconer blindfolds a hawk. They take the hooded cheetah with them on the hunt. As long as the hood is on, the cheetah is quiet. When they come within sight of wild game, they take off the hood. The cheetah looks round, sees the prey, and goes after it like a bullet. When it catches up with the animal, it gives it one pat on the side. It looks like a very little touch, but it's enough to knock the animal flat. Then the cheetah picks it up, even if it is a good-sized antelope, and carries it back to the hunter. It still hangs on to its prey. I bet you can't guess how they make the cheetah drop it."

"By saying 'Drop it'?"

"It might not understand that order. But there's something it does understand. Gently pinch its nose. That shuts off its breathing and it will drop whatever is in its mouth."

"Is it any good for catching poachers?"

"As good as any ranger. Better than a ranger — because it has better teeth. And gets over the ground three times as fast. We'll try it on the next poacher we see."

12
Rescue

The safari men set free all the animals that were still alive, and strong enough to stay alive.

The seriously injured were placed in the lorries to be taken to the hospital. Those nearly dead of starvation and thirst were given food and water at once.

The young, dying because their mothers had been killed, got special attention. A large cage was reserved for orphans. It was rapidly filled with as strange a crowd of babies as ever came together in one place – infant elephants, rhinos, wobbly little antelopes, lion cubs and fluffy little monkeys.

The men went down into the elephant pits, rooted out the poisoned stakes, put them in a pile and burned them. One wall of each pit was broken down so that if an animal fell in, it could climb out.

The rescuers went from gap to gap of the mile-long thorn fence and collected every wire snare.

They broke up every devilish trap – the 'drop spear' set in a tree and triggered so that it would fall upon an animal passing below; the crossbow so arranged in a tree that just a touch of an animal's foot to the trigger-line in the grass would bring a poisoned arrow plunging down into its back; the cruel spiked wheel that would let an elephant's foot in but not out and poachers could then take their time removing his tusks and tail, then leave him to starve to death; the "ant trap" set on the side of an ant-hill so that the angry, two-inch-long ants would swarm over the trapped animal and devour it, after which the tusks could be more easily removed; the "crippler" that when stepped on would fly up and break the animal's leg, making it impossible for him to escape the poachers — all the infernal devices that a diseased imagination could invent to inflict pain and death.

"Let's burn the fence," Hal suggested, and the warden agreed.

The dry thorns leaped into flame and soon a bonfire a mile long was blazing.

Now the poachers' camp must be destroyed. First the contents of all the grass huts were brought out and put side by side.

"Never saw anything like it in my life," Hal exclaimed as he looked at a collection of more than three hundred elephant feet that had been hollowed out to make wastepaper baskets.

In another pile were scores of leopard heads. Every one would have brought the poacher king several thousand dollars. The man from America or Europe who goes on a shooting safari in Africa hoping to get a leopard and mount its head on the wall at home to impress his friends, is apt to be out of luck. He is not likely to see a leopard, since it is a night animal. He gets tired of hunting for one. He finds it much simpler to go into a store in Nairobi and buy a head. Then he can take it home and mount it and claim that he shot it, and who will know the difference?

Here was a fortune in leopard heads. They would never get to the walls of would-be killers. Beside them was another fortune – a carpet of cheetah skins pegged out to dry. They would never adorn the backs of thoughtless women – sweet, kind women, quite unaware that they were the cause of the slaughter of beautiful animals.

Roger's cheetah, miaowing softly, nudged the skins with his nose as if urging them back to life.

"What in the world are those?" said Roger, staring at a large number of wooden bowls filled with curious curly hairs.

"Elephants' eyelashes," said Crosby.

Roger looked at him suspiciously. The warden must be joking. "You wouldn't kid me, warden?"

"Not a bit."

"But who would want an elephant's eyelashes?"

"They're very popular all the way from here to Singapore. Superstitious men think that if they carry a little bag of these eyelashes they will have as many children as there are hairs in that bag. They're supposed to give you all sorts of magic powers. One pygmy chief I know traded fifty-two hundred pounds of ivory for the eyelashes of a single elephant. Some gangs of poachers make a business of killing elephants just to get their eyelashes. Dhows sail across the Red Sea to get eyelashes – they can be sold for high prices in Arabia because of the belief that a bag of eyelashes worn on a string round your neck is a sure protection against bullets."

Near by was a pile of rhino horns that towered over Roger's head.

"What are they good for?"

"The Indians and Chinese pay big money for them. They grind them up into a powder. They mix the powder into their tea and drink it down."

"Whatever for?"

"They think it makes them as strong as a rhino and as brave as a lion."

"Does it have any such effect?"

"Only on the imagination. No physical effect. But the

effect is very serious in Africa — it means that the rhino is disappearing. The rhino is one of the most interesting animals in Africa. Too bad if it has to go."

"Look out," cried Roger. "You almost stepped on a big snake."

It lay in the grass, a gleaming stretch of brown and yellow more than twenty feet long.

"A python," Crosby said. "He's dead. The poachers hadn't got round to skinning him yet. Of course python skin is worth a lot of money. Shoes can be made of it, and belts, and handbags — all sorts of things. The flesh is good to eat — tender as chicken. But the best part is the backbone."

He stopped and smiled, while Roger cudgelled his brain to think what anybody could possibly do with a python's backbone.

"African women make a necklace of it."

"Just for decoration?"

"No. Another superstition. They think it's a cure for sore throat. Sometimes they make a belt of it. If you wear that round your tummy, you're supposed never to have indigestion."

"How wild can you get?" was Roger's comment.

"Pretty wild," admitted Crosby. "Look at the stuff in

those gourds. That's hippo fat – they use it as a pomade to slick down their hair. And that over there is lion fat. They rub it on for rheumatism."

The warden's attention was arrested by a plot of fresh earth. Not a blade of grass grew in it.

"If I'm not mistaken," he said, "some digging has been going on here. Perhaps something is hidden underneath."

He ordered men to bring shovels and remove the earth. Three feet down there was the gleam of ivory. The men threw out a beautiful elephant tusk. More tusks began to show up as they went deeper. Crosby counted as the tusks were tossed out on the growing pile. The total was five hundred and forty.

Crosby took out a notebook and did a little figuring.

"I'd guess that these tusks average about sixty pounds each. That comes to 32,400 pounds. Blackbeard has to pay his poachers about three and sixpence a pound – he can sell the ivory for thirty-six shillings a pound. That would give him a profit of over 52,500 pounds."

"I had no idea," Hal said, "that it was such a big business operation."

"And murder on a big scale," Crosby said. "Five hundred and forty tusks – that means two hundred and seventy dead elephants. Just in one camp. And there are hundreds of such

camps in East Africa. You think this trap-line a mile long is something. They are often five miles long, or ten, or fifteen. One discovered near Lake Victoria was seventy miles in length. In a single camp we found the carcasses of 1,280 elephants."

Hal knitted his brows. It was incredible. He could not grasp such figures.

Crosby went on. "Just in this one park we estimate that we lose 150,000 animals a year to poachers. In East Africa as a whole, poachers kill nearly a million animals a year." Crosby stopped and smiled. "Perhaps I'm drowning you in figures. But I'd like you to get an idea of how serious this thing is."

"Why don't the governments of these countries do something about it?" said Hal.

"More easily said than done," Crosby replied. "They can't afford it. It would take thousands upon thousands of rangers."

"But at this rate, soon the wild animals will all be killed off."

"Exactly. And that will be the end of the biggest zoo on earth. Ninety per cent of the tourists who come to East Africa come to see the animals. They bring in ten million pounds a year. These countries will be poorer than ever if that revenue is cut off. Man is the most deadly of all animals. During the last two thousand years he has wiped out more than a hundred species. And the rest are going fast. At present two hundred and fifty kinds of animals are on the edge of extinction. Once they are gone, we can never get them back."

13
Red Dust

The grass huts of the poachers were burned to the ground.

The tusks, tails, horns, hides, hippo teeth, elephants' feet, giraffes' sinews, leopard and lion heads, antlers of antelopes and gazelles, crocodile skins, lion fat, hippo fat, python backbones, feathers of egret, flamingo, ostrich and crowned crane – all the trophies, including elephants' eyelashes, were loaded on the trucks. With them went all the snares and traps.

"What will you do with all this?" Hal asked. "Sell it? It would bring a small fortune."

"What it would bring would be blood money," said Crosby. "We don't want to make a profit out of murder. Anyhow, I think we'll accomplish more if we put these things in our museum where visitors from all over the world can see them. I don't think anybody can look at them without being shocked into doing everything within his power to stop this slaughter of innocent animals."

Heavily loaded, the cars returned to the lodge. As Crosby and the boys entered the warden's banda they were greeted by smiling little Judge Sindar Singh.

"Well, my friend," exclaimed Crosby. "So good to see you again. Did you have a good trip to Nairobi?"

"Very good. On my way back to Mombasa now, but just called in to see how you got along with your raid."

"It was a great success, thanks to these boys and their crew. Forty-seven poachers are on their way to your Mombasa jail right now. You'll probably have them in your court tomorrow morning."

"Now isn't that just too wonderful," purred the little judge. "You can be sure of one thing – in my court they'll get what they deserve. We're going to stamp out this poaching – you and I. It's a disgrace and an outrage and must be stopped. I suppose you got their leader?"

"Blackbeard? No, I'm sorry, he escaped."

"Now isn't that a pity – a great pity," said the sympathetic little judge. "How I'd like to get my hands on him! He wouldn't get out of my court without the stiffest sentence that the law allows. How in the world did he slip through your fingers?"

"He was too foxy for us, I'm afraid. He was wise enough to stay behind his men and while we were arresting them he got away. The dog followed his tracks but lost them in the river."

The judge looked at Zulu. "He's a fine dog. That

375

Blackbeard must be pretty smart to outsmart such a fine dog." He reached out his hand to pat Zulu. The dog sniffed at him, then backed away, growling.

"Well, I must be going," said the judge brightly. "What a fine cheetah! He seems to be making himself at home already. How do he and the dog get along?"

"We hardly know yet," said Hal. "So far, they've politely ignored each other."

"We'll see you off," said Crosby, and they all walked out with the judge to his car.

Hal noticed something strange about the car. There was no red dust on it.

He had been over the Nairobi road several times. It was a dirt road with murram stacks along the edge – piles of red earth used to surface the road. You could not travel this road without getting your car covered with red dust.

Murram was not used on the roads inside the park. There too a car would pick up dust, but it would be white. There was a film of white dust on the judge's car.

"How did you escape the red bath?" Hal asked.

The judge seemed a bit surprised by the question, but he responded quickly enough. He laughed a silky laugh.

"Yes, yes," he said. "You certainly get plastered on that road. So I stopped at the petrol station just before entering the park and had the car washed." He smiled. "Any more questions?"

"No," said Hal, a little ashamed of having quizzed the good judge. But Singh did not appear to be offended.

He spoke to Crosby. "Goodbye, Mark. Take care of yourself. I congratulate you on having these boys to help you. Perhaps they'll even be smart enough to catch Blackbeard. Who knows?"

And he was off.

Zulu and the cheetah were getting acquainted. They were not very polite about it. They drew back their lips, each trying to show what a fine set of teeth he had.

Zulu barked. The dog part of the cheetah growled. The cat part spat.

Each was acting exactly as Nature had taught him to act. The Alsatian is a born police dog. He takes no nonsense from either man or animal. The cheetah is a born hunter of other animals including wild dogs. And this one looked wild enough.

"Zulu, come here," said Roger sharply. "And what's-your-name — I'll call you Chee — behave yourself."

Chee who had evidently been planning to make a meal of this dog changed his mind when he saw his young master patting Zulu. He came up on Roger's other side, nuzzling the boy's leg and miaowing softly. Roger patted him also.

The two animals were not quite ready to be friends. They suddenly made a lunge for each other between Roger's legs, tumbling him on to his back.

"Chee! Zu!" Roger jumped to his feet, caught Zulu by the collar and brought him face to face with Chee. Their muzzles were not an inch apart. He held them so, Zu by his collar, Chee by his silky mane. The dog in each of them whimpered. There was no barking this time, no spitting. These fine animals were not stupid. They got the message.

Roger let them go and each retired in a different direction to lie down and think it over.

"How are we going to feed Chee?" Roger asked. "No

telling how long he was in that pit. He must be hungry."

"That's easy," Hal said. "Just tap a vein in your wrist and let him drink the blood."

"You think you're pretty funny," said Roger scornfully.

"No," put in the warden, "your brother is right. There's nothing the cheetah would rather have than blood. But it doesn't have to be yours."

"We might let him go and hunt his own food."

"If you do that, you'll probably lose him. If you want him to stick to you, you had better feed him."

"But how?" Roger had a sudden idea. "Those animals we brought to the hospital — did any of them die?"

"No, and we mean to see to it that none of them will die."

"Then how . . . ?"

"Jump in the car," said Crosby. "I'll take you where you can get plenty of blood. And nothing will have to die to give it to you. Bring Chee."

Roger called Chee but the animal did not know his name. Roger went to him and tugged on his mane. Chee took this only as a friendly gesture, and purred.

Crosby laughed. "I see you don't know how to lead a cheetah. Take him by the teeth."

Roger stared. This time for sure the warden was joking.

"A cheetah has very long canine teeth," explained Crosby. "His incisors and molars are very short. You can slip your finger in behind a canine. The short teeth will close on your finger but, if he likes you, he won't close them tightly enough to hurt. Of course you're taking a chance – he may decide he doesn't like you after all. If it works, you can lead him anywhere."

"And if it doesn't work," said Hal comfortingly, "all you lose is a few fingers."

Roger gave Hal a savage look. His big brother was trying to scare him. He didn't need to try hard – the boy was already scared. The nerves crawled around in his back like worms as he very cautiously pressed Chee's lips apart, then slowly put his finger in between the short teeth and round the canine. This was the craziest thing he had ever heard of. Surely Chee would bite.

Chee did bite. But it was not a hard bite, only a squeeze. For a full minute, Roger kept his finger in place without making any further move. With his other hand he scratched Chee behind the ears.

Then he began to pull, very gently. Chee unwound himself and got up. Roger waited a moment – then began to move towards the Land-Rover. Chee tightened his grip ever so slightly and followed.

Getting into the car without jerking his hand or exciting his pet was an experience that Roger would not soon forget. Inch by inch, with frequent pauses, he sidled up into the seat, still keeping his fingers in the animal's mouth. In fact he could hardly have let go if he wanted to, the pressure on his fingers was so firm.

Luckily Chee had already had one ride in the car. No harm had come to him, so now he did not seem to be unduly nervous. He stood up on his hind legs with forepaws on the car floor. A light spring, and he was in the car between Roger's knees. His jaws relaxed and Roger withdrew his hand. The fingers were dented but not bruised. The powerful jaws that could crush a baboon's head as easily as a hammer can crack a walnut had been controlled by the animal's natural gentleness and intelligence.

14
A Cheetah's Dinner

Since the lodge was close to the park edge it was only a matter of minutes before the car left the park and came to a stop beside a thorn fence.

This was no trap-line. It was a wall of thorns round a small village.

"To keep wild animals out?" inquired Roger.

"No," said Crosby, "to keep cattle in. These Masai are cattle-men. You might call them the cowboys of Africa. Come in and meet them."

He led Roger and his cheetah through a thorn gate into the village. Roger had seen some strange villages, but never anything like this. The huts were more like ant-hills than houses. The only difference was that the homes of the ants were usually bigger and higher. The roofs of these were on a level with Roger's chin.

"Look as if they were made of mud," Roger said.

"That's about it. They make a framework of twigs, then plaster it over with clay and cow-dung."

"But the doorways are only three feet high. Are these people pygmies?"

"Far from it. Watch."

A man came out of the nearest hut. To get through the low door he had to bend almost double. When he straightened up he was more than six feet tall – almost as tall as the Watussi Roger had seen in the Mountains of the Moon.

"Why such low doors for such tall people?"

"They have a good reason for it," said Crosby. "If some enemy tries to enter your home, he has to bend far down to get in. He can't defend himself in that position. He can be knocked on the head or jabbed with a spear before he can get all the way through the door."

Other men came stooping out of the mud huts. They smiled when they saw Crosby, who was evidently well known to them and well liked.

Each man wore a cowhide cape over his shoulders and nothing else. His hair was plastered with red clay and worn in a short braid over the forehead and a long braid behind. His ears had been pierced and stretched so that they hung almost down to his shoulders and the hole that had been bored in the ear-lobe in childhood had been pulled larger and larger so that in a man of middle age it was big enough to carry a good-sized package. Which was lucky, since a man's cape had no pockets.

When any man smiled Roger could see that he had two teeth lacking in the lower jaw. He asked Crosby about it.

"These people sometimes get lockjaw. Then the teeth lock together so that they can't eat or drink. They knock out two teeth so that if they contract this disease they can still get food and drink into the mouth."

"But lockjaw can be cured. Don't they call a doctor?"

"They don't believe in doctors. In fact they don't believe much in anything that is modern. They stick to their own way of doing things."

A fine-looking Masai approached Roger with a smile and spat in his face. Roger wiped his face. He looked so astonished that Crosby had to laugh.

The Masai waited as if expecting something.

"Spit back," said Crosby.

Roger could not believe his ears.

"Spitting in your face is a sign of friendship," the warden told him. "Don't keep him waiting or he'll be offended. Spit back."

Roger summoned up all the saliva he could gather and spat back. The big Masai grinned from ear to ear.

Women and children began to emerge from the huts. They were too timid to come near. The little brown bodies of the children were bare. The women were dressed in metal – but their armour was not like that of the knights of old. Their arms were buried in metal bracelets, they wore necklaces of metal beads, huge metal earrings several inches wide hung from their ears, metal ornaments circled their waists, and their legs were completely buried from ankle to knee under wire spirals. The wire was the only thing that looked modern.

"Where do they buy the wire?"

"They don't buy it. They just steal it from the nearest telephone line."

Roger could not help noticing that these primitive people were not dirty. "For people who live in mud huts they keep themselves remarkably clean. They must bathe twice a day."

"Hardly," Crosby said. "They get only two baths in a life-time – one at birth and the other when they become adults."

"Then how do they keep clean?"

"Sand. Have you ever tried a sand bath? It will take the skin off you if you're not used to it. These people are used to it and it just takes off the dirt."

Crosby spoke to the Masai in their own language. He pointed at the cheetah and at one of the cattle that strayed among the huts. The men nodded vigorously, and one of them ran into a hut and came out with a bow and arrow.

"We're going to get some blood for your cheetah," Crosby said. "But without killing anything. We've come to the right place. The Masai are like the cheetah – they live on blood. Blood and milk. Perhaps it's the strangest diet of any people in the world – although some of the reducing diets in your country are just about as strange."

"You don't mean the Masai live on nothing but blood and milk? No meat, vegetables, fruit?"

"A few of the modern ones will take a little meat, perhaps on a holiday. Most of the people won't touch it. And never a vegetable of any sort, or a soup, or a salad, or a bun or biscuit or bread of any kind, or pudding or cake. No cheese, no butter, no eggs, no jam or jelly, nothing sweet, no fruit of any description."

"Just blood and milk," marvelled Roger. "How can they live on that? You'd think they'd dry up and blow away. But they look pretty strong."

"They are strong. And brave. A Masai will wrestle with a lion or a leopard. A young Masai must kill a full-grown lion with nothing but a spear before he can claim to be a man."

Roger looked at the cows. "That's where they get the milk. But how about the blood?"

"Come. We'll show you."

The man with the bow and arrow selected a cow. He came to within six feet of it, dropped on one knee, and aimed at the animal's throat.

So, thought Roger, that was all guff – about not killing anything. He's certainly going to kill that cow.

The cow did not seem to be alarmed. She peacefully chewed her cud. The bowman fired his arrow and it struck home. The cow went on peacefully chewing her cud as if nothing had happened.

Roger noticed that the arrow had penetrated only a fraction of an inch. A shoulder behind the tip had prevented it from entering further. The point had evidently been so sharp that the animal had not felt it.

The bowman pulled out the arrow and blood poured from the jugular vein. Another Masai caught the blood in a large gourd. The cow stood as patiently as if she were merely being milked.

When the gourd was full a sort of dirty-looking paste was applied to the small hole.

"A mixture of ashes and herbs," Crosby said. "You see how that stops the flow. It will also prevent infection."

The Masai spoke to Crosby and kept glancing at Roger. The warden nodded, and one of the men dived into a hut and brought out a small gourd. From the large gourd they poured about half a cupful of blood into the small container. Then one crouched beside the cow's udders and filled the small gourd with milk. With his finger he stirred the two liquids together – then offered the gourd to Roger. Roger looked helplessly at the warden.

"Drink it," Crosby advised. "They're trying to be nice to you. Don't let them down. You'll hurt their feelings."

"How about my feelings?" grumbled Roger.

"Never mind your feelings, young man," said Crosby rather sharply. "In Africa you show respect for the Africans. If you don't we have unpleasant incidents like the Mau Mau massacres when even our wives have to carry revolvers and no white man's life is safe."

"I get you," Roger said meekly and raised the gourd to his lips. He drank down the contents without stopping, trying not to taste the stuff. But when he got it down he realized that it had not been unpleasant after all.

The effect upon the Masai was magical. They chattered and grinned and patted his arm. Now they really accepted him as a friend.

It was Chee's turn — but for him, no milk thank you. He eagerly lapped up the fresh blood. In the meantime the Masai insisted upon tapping another cow so that Chee would dine well tomorrow.

On the way back to the lodge Roger had some questions to ask.

"Do the Masai raise cattle just to get their blood?"

"Oh no, they must have cattle to buy wives. A man must pay three or four cows to the girl's parents. The more cattle he has the more wives he can buy. A Masai's wealth is reckoned in cattle, not in money. He may not own one solitary shilling, but if he has a hundred cattle he is a rich man."

"Because he can sell them and make a lot of money?"

"No. He refuses to sell them. If he sold them, he wouldn't have them. He would have nothing but money, and he doesn't care a hang about money. All he cares about is cattle. That's what makes him such a problem."

"How so?"

"There are a hundred thousand Masai and they own about a million cattle. These cattle destroy thousands of square miles of land. They eat not only the grass above ground but the roots as well, so grassland becomes desert. Wild animals do not eat the roots, and grassland remains grassland. The Masai don't need so many cattle, but we do need plenty of food for wild animals if we hope to keep on bringing tourists here to see the greatest zoo on earth."

They stopped at the river to let Chee drink. Chee walked to the water's edge, looked upstream and down stream and across. He hissed loudly, then drank.

"A wise cat," said Crosby. "He hisses to scare the crocs away. A lion or a leopard or an antelope would probably just stick his nose into the water and drink. Then a croc might grab him by the nose and pull him in. A cheetah is too smart to take that risk."

Chee bounced back into the car without being led. He wasn't satisfied to stay on the floor. He tried to climb up on the seat beside Roger. Roger slid over to the centre to give him room and Chee sat up beside the open window.

The animal chose to thrust out his head just as the car

passed close to a group of tourists. A woman screamed, "Look! They've got a tiger in that car."

The warden grinned and stepped on the accelerator.

"The old story," he said. "Everybody knows or thinks he knows about the tiger or the leopard or perhaps the jaguar. But not one in a hundred has ever seen the cheetah – the friendliest of all the big cats."

Chee was sometimes almost too friendly. At night he insisted upon sharing Roger's bed. And since he was a good seven feet from nose-tip to tail-tip and his long legs reached three feet across the bed there was not much room left for the boy. To make matters more difficult, he purred like a grist mill in Roger's ear. But it would take more than that to keep a healthy young teenager awake after such a big day.

15
The Trial

"Something on your mind, Hal?"

Crosby had noticed that Hal was merely toying with his breakfast, letting his coffee grow cold. He had not joined in the conversation with the warden and Roger – and Chee, who was as usual purring so loudly that the others had to raise their voices to drown him. Hal's thoughts seemed far away.

He looked up and smiled. "You just caught me dreaming."

"Anything I can help you about?"

Hal hesitated. "Well – yes. It's about – your friend, Judge Singh. You think a lot of him, don't you?"

"I suppose I do," admitted Crosby. "He goes out of his way to be friendly and helpful. He's done all sorts of things for me. Even saved my life the day before yesterday – you saw him do that."

"It wasn't . . ." exploded Roger, then stopped as he saw a warning in Hal's eyes. He itched to say that it had been Hal who had saved the warden, not Singh. Singh had almost killed him.

"And the judge is my best ally against the poachers,"

Crosby went on. "We could really do nothing without him. We can catch some of them but we can't punish them. They are punished in his court – he fines them or sends them to prison. The law allows very heavy sentences for the crime of poaching."

"Does he give them all the law allows?"

"Yes, he says that he does."

"Have you been down to his court?"

"Oh no. I'm too busy here. I do my job and let him do his."

Hal went back to his eggs and bacon. He ate in silence for a few minutes. Then he said, "An interesting man, the judge. I'd like to see him at work. How about our hopping down there this morning to take a look at the trial?"

"I can't go," said Crosby. "But there's no reason why you shouldn't. Only trouble is – it's a 250-mile trip to Mombasa and back and the road is pretty bad. But then – what am I thinking of? You're a pilot. You proved that when I went to sleep on the stick. Take the Stork. Wait a minute."

He went to his desk and brought out a map.

"Now – here we are – and here's Mombasa. As you know, it's on an island connected with the mainland by causeways. Here's the landing field." He made a cross with his pencil. "You'll get a taxi there and go to the court-house – which is here." He made another cross.

On the airstrip, Crosby superintended the fuelling of the Stork, filling both wing tanks, also an emergency tank in the back of the plane. He pointed out the little hand pump that would transfer this petrol, if needed, to the wing tanks.

He translated the German instructions on the instrument board and explained some of the mechanical mysteries that had baffled Hal.

"Get full steam up before you take off," he said. "Otherwise you'll never clear those trees at the end of the strip."

Hal climbed aboard. Roger was about to follow but his brother stopped him.

"Stay out of it, kid. I want a little practice first."

"Can't you practise with me aboard?"

"Just let me take it up – and come down again. Then I'll pick you up."

Roger began to object but Crosby cut in.

"Your brother's right. It's a touchy take-off." Roger looked disappointed and a little angry. If Hal could take this risk, why couldn't he? The warden smiled. "I can't afford to lose you both, you know."

"I'll be back in five minutes," Hal said. "Sooner than that if I forget which button to push."

He looked at the wind-sock. It didn't give him much encouragement. It ought to be blowing up or down the strip. It was blowing across. On a narrow strip, walled in by trees, this could mean trouble.

He let down the Perspex hood, thus completely enclosing himself in the transparent bubble. Looks like a dummy in a store window, thought Roger crossly.

Hal started the ignition. He tested the booster pump and waited for the oil temperature to rise.

He taxied to the end of the strip and turned about. Down went the throttle. The plane moved, but too slowly. Hal gritted his teeth as if that would help the engine. He wished the strip were asphalt instead of grass. The plane stumbled on, gathering speed.

Now it was floating on the blades of grass. Now it was in the air.

Hal set the flaps at fifteen degrees for extra lift. The trees at the end of the strip were coming towards him at an alarming rate.

He was worried too about the cross-wind that kept pushing him to the right. This was a small plane, as planes go, but still its thirty-nine-foot wing span seemed too much in this narrow trap.

The end of the right wing was already tickling the

leaves of the trees. A small branch, no thicker than a finger, would be enough to send the whole contraption crashing to the ground.

He cleared the trees by inches. Now he had time to think of the things he might have done – give it a bit more flap, trim back the elevator a little farther, keep the nose closer into the wind – he would remember and do better next time.

He circled until his nerves settled down, then straightened out towards the strip and prepared to land.

Full flaps, speed down for the approach, ruddering to fishtail off the height – he skimmed the treetops, sank like a falling leaf and touched the grass. Now he knew where the brakes were, and used them.

The plane lumbered over the none-too-smooth ground and came to a halt. Hal opened his bubble.

"Good enough," said the warden heartily. Even Roger, still a bit sulky, had to admit it wasn't bad. He climbed into the co-pilot's seat.

This time the plane seemed to know its master. It rose as a plane should, levelled off at six thousand feet, and followed the Tsavo River eastward to the railway station at Tsavo.

Here Hal swung to the right. Below him was the red

road to Mombasa and beside it the railway.

This had been the scene of very tragic events. Years ago when the railway was being built, newspapers all over the world were running horror stories about the "man-eaters of Tsavo", lions that had developed a taste for human flesh and were killing and eating railway workers by the score in spite of all efforts to track them down.

On the left now was the gleaming ribbon of the Galana River on its way to the Indian Ocean. Northward stretched the wilderness of Tsavo Park for a hundred miles.

The foaming waters of Lugard's Falls flashed white in the morning sun. Around the pool at the base of the falls elephants, rhinos and giraffes were stooping to drink. Animals were clustered around a lake and several water holes. Herds of buffalo, zebra and wildebeest were mowing the grass in the open meadows. The day-loving lions were out looking for breakfast, but the night-loving leopards had retired into the darkness of the woods.

A thin spiral of smoke rose from the trees.

"A poacher's camp," Hal guessed.

"And there's a trap-line," exclaimed Roger. "Oh, boy — what a long one. It must be a good five miles."

Hal did some mental arithmetic. "That would come to around twenty-six thousand feet. And if there's a trap every fifty feet that would come to something more than five hundred traps. Suppose only half of them caught animals."

"Suppose nothing of the kind," said Roger. "Yesterday there was an animal in every single trap."

"All right. And the poachers clear the traps once a week. Five hundred dead animals a week — more than two thousand a month. I can't believe it. Must be something wrong with my figures."

"What does it matter?" Roger said. "Even a hundred a month would be a hundred too many. And don't forget, this is just one trap-line. And the warden says there are others two or three times as long. And hundreds of trap-lines all over East Africa."

It was easy navigation. All you had to do was to follow the road and railway. Actually the road could not be seen because it was concealed beneath a continuous cloud of red dust stirred up by traffic. The ribbon of red wound down to Mombasa, already visible on its coral island set like a jewel in the blue of the Indian Ocean.

The plane landed lightly on the broad airfield eight miles from town and the boys took a taxi across the causeway and through the busy streets of the island city to the court-house.

Hal stopped in the corridor outside the court-room.

He peered in through the crack between the double doors.

At the far end of the room behind a desk on a high platform sat Judge Sindar Singh. He did not look so little now. His black robe gave him importance and dignity. Before him stood the poachers, all of them. The rest of the room was full of spectators, also standing. There was no jury, no prosecutor, no defender. Judge Singh was the sole authority. This was not a criminal court — strangely enough, the murder of helpless animals was not considered a criminal offence.

"I'd rather the judge didn't see us," Hal whispered. "Let's duck out heads down and sneak in as quietly as we can."

They slipped through the door and stood behind the crowd.

An interpreter was questioning one of the prisoners in his native dialect, then passing on the answers to the judge in English.

"He says," explained the interpreter, "that he is a poor man. He has eight children. And four more on the way."

"Four on the way?"

"Yes. He has four wives."

The judge looked severe. "Does this man realize that I could send him to prison for ten years for poaching?"

"Yes, he knows that."

"But this court has mercy upon the poor and unfortunate. I will not punish this man. Any man with four wives is being punished enough already."

The crowd laughed. What a jolly little judge this was!

"Case dismissed," said Judge Singh.

But not everyone was amused. An intelligent young African standing next to Hal whispered angrily, "He's being too easy on them. You can never stop poaching that way."

Hal nodded. He thought of all the trouble and danger he and his men had gone through to catch these fellows. And now they were being let off with little or nopunishment. Of course they would go right back to poaching.

The judge was questioning the next man. "Don't you know it is wrong to kill animals?"

"No. My tribe has always killed animals. It is our custom. Our fathers killed, their fathers killed, for ever it has been so."

The judge meditated. "How can we ask this man to go against the custom of his tribe? Case dismissed."

The next man had a different excuse. "I am a kind man. I do not like to kill. But the black-bearded one, he makes us kill."

The judge nodded solemnly. "You do not do it of your own free will?"

"Never."

"This black-bearded one is a devil. You are afraid of him, are you not?"

"We all fear him."

"That is good. I mean," stumbled Judge Singh, "it is good that you do not do this willingly. How can I punish you if you do only what you are forced to do? Case dismissed."

The next prisoner when asked why he was guilty of poaching explained that he had a flock of goats, and wild animals were killing and eating his goats – so he must kill the wild animals.

"What wild animals do you kill?"

"Mostly rhinos, giraffes, elephants, hippos, zebras, antelopes."

"You cannot be blamed for defending your flock against these wild beasts," declared Judge Singh. "Case dismissed."

The African at Hal's elbow boiled over. "Every one of those animals eats grass and nothing else. Not one of them ever ate a goat. This whole thing is a farce and a fraud."

He turned and left the room.

16
Old Harbour

The boys also had had about enough. But they stuck it out – they listened to the lame excuses of all forty-seven prisoners. The judge, realizing that it would look too ridiculous for him to say "Case dismissed" every time, imposed a few light sentences.

One man was sent to prison, not for ten years, but for three days. He grinned when he heard his sentence. He could rest in prison and would get better food than he would have at home.

Another man who had a small farm on which he raised melons was fined one melon.

Another who raised chickens was ordered to pay a penalty of two eggs.

Most went scot free.

Hal and Roger left the court-room without having been seen by the judge. They were gloomy, angry and bewildered.

"We break our necks to catch poachers," grumbled Roger, "and he lets them off."

"And that means we've really done more harm than good," said Hal. "Now those fellows know that they can poach all they like and if they're caught they'll just have a nice trip to town at somebody else's expense."

"What's the matter with that crazy judge?" wondered Roger. "He had so many big things to say about what he would do to the poachers. All that big talk about protecting the wild animals. He certainly has the warden buffaloed. You know what I think? I think he's in league with Blackbeard. I'll bet they're in this thing fifty-fifty. They're splitting the profits right down the middle."

Hal shook his head. "He seems like such a kind sweet little man. And Blackbeard is such a devil. How could they possibly have anything to do with each other? Until we know more about it we'll have to give the judge the benefit of the doubt. Perhaps he really thought he could win those poachers over by kindness."

"Kindness my hat!" exclaimed Roger. "Is it kind to the animals to let a gang of killers loose on them?"

They walked slowly down the street. Roger, irritated because his brother refused to think ill of the judge, stopped short.

"Look here. We'll do some detective work. You say he's an angel and he's just trying to be good to the Africans. I say he's a devil and he's working with Blackbeard. We'll just see who's right."

Hal smiled and said nothing. He had a suspicion that they were both wrong. There must be some other explanation for the judge's strange conduct. He really didn't think that the judge was an angel. In fact he might be even more of a devil than Roger imagined. Time would tell.

In their aimless wandering they had left the main streets with their fine modern buildings and found themselves in the maze of narrow alleys of the old Arab town.

Open doorways led into dark, mysterious shops. From some came the odour of fruits and vegetables, from others the smell of fresh meat.

One had the peculiar scent of wire and iron and something prompted Hal to step inside.

He saw that he was surrounded by traps, traps of every description, but particularly the cruel wire snares like those he had seen in the trap-line of death the day before.

A long-nosed Arab came out of the gloom rubbing his hands. "You are interested in traps?"

"Very much interested," Hal said. "You sell these to poachers, don't you? Isn't that against the law?"

"The law," laughed the Arab. "In this country, now that the British have gone, we don't worry too much about the law. Do you run an operation?"

"What do you mean, an operation?"

"A poaching operation – like Blackbeard's."

"So you know Blackbeard?"

"Of course. He's our best customer. We sell him a thousand snares at a time."

"How much are they?"

"Well, the average snare requires two and a half yards of wire. The price is one shilling."

"And a thousand snares – how many animals would they catch?"

"It depends on the season. And every operator has his own figures. Now, take Blackbeard – he estimates that from January to July each snare should take four animals a month. For a thousand snares, that's 28,000. During the dry season, August to October, only one a month. That's 3,000. During the big migration season, November and December, ten a month for each snare, and that's 20,000. Total for the year, 51,000."

"Big business," said Hal.

"The biggest business in the country," the Arab said proudly.

"How do the animals like it?"

The Arab looked startled. "Don't tell me you're one of those animal-lovers." His face turned purple with anger.

"You've just been leading me on, haven't you? Get out of this shop before I throw you out."

Farther down the street, Hal paused again. From the doorway came a musty, leathery smell that reminded him of the piles of hides and heads at the poachers' camp.

Entering, he found himself in a large warehouse that reached as far back as he could see. On each side it was piled from floor to ceiling with heads of lions, leopards, cheetahs, giraffes, buffaloes, zebras, wildebeests, rhinos, elephants, hippos and antelopes; also tails by the thousands, elephants' feet hollowed to make waste-paper baskets or umbrella stands, rich stores of great ivory tusks, rhino horns beyond number, stuffed monkeys of every sort, and hides of everything from elephants to bush-babies.

The proprietor was an Indian. Hal picked up the beautiful antlered head of a Tommy gazelle.

"How much?" he asked.

"In what quantity?"

"How much for this head?"

"I'm sorry, sir, we can't sell you one only. We don't sell retail – just wholesale."

"You mean, by the dozen, or by the gross?"

The Indian smiled. "No, no. We don't deal in such small amounts. Our minimum order would be for about ten

thousand specimens. In fact we usually sell by the shipload. We outfitted three ships yesterday. They're sailing this morning."

"Where from?"

"The Old Harbour. Just down at the end of this street."

Mombasa's 'Old Harbour', nestling among the coral cliffs at the north-east corner of the island, was full of large high-pooped Arab dhows. Those ready to leave were easily picked out, for their great lateen sails had already been raised and were idly flapping in the breeze.

A dark-skinned Arab who looked every inch a pirate stood by the gangway of the biggest dhow.

"Are you the captain of this ship?" Hal asked.

The man nodded.

Hal looked up admiringly at the great sweep of sail. He pulled out his camera.

"May I?"

The captain nodded again. Hal took the picture.

"Where are you off to?" he asked.

"Bombay."

"A fine looking ship," Hal said. "I could get a better shot at that sail from the deck. Do you mind?"

The captain waved his hand towards the deck. Hal and

Roger went aboard. Hal took a couple more pictures. He turned to find the captain beside him. Hal took his picture and the piratical face lighted with a smile.

"Do you speak English?" Hal asked.

"Pretty good."

"What are you taking to Bombay?"

Hal did not expect an honest answer. But the captain evidently had no fear of possible spies, plain-clothes police, or customs officials.

"I show you."

He lifted the edge of a tarpaulin so it was possible to see below deck. The great hold was crammed to the limit with the same sort of specimens that the boys had just seen in the warehouse. The dark face beamed with pride.

"Good, no?"

"All of these — how many?"

The captain pulled out his bill of lading. The number of trophies of each kind was set down. The grand total of all specimens was 180,000.

And this was but one of three vessels to sail in a single day, all chock full of trophies representing the death of thousands of Africa's animals.

★   ★   ★

409

"I can't under-
stand it," said the
warden after Hal
had made his
report con-
cerning the trial
of the forty-
seven poachers.
"Why Sindar
was so easy on
them baffles

me. Perhaps it's just because he's so
tender-hearted — can't bear to hurt
either animal or man." He dismissed
the matter as if it were too painful and
puzzling to think about.

"Anyhow," he said, "I have another
plane trip mapped out for you. But
this time I'd like you to take two
passengers. One is a colobus and the
other is an okapi. Come over to the
hospital and I'll introduce you to
them."

17
Thirty Million Years Old

The animal hospital was alive with the grunts, groans, squeals and squawks of everything from baby elephant to crowned crane.

"Meet the most beautiful monkey in all Africa," said Crosby. "This is the colobus."

Truly it was handsome. It was pitch black and snow white. The rich black hair on its back contrasted with the flowing robes of white on its flanks and the picture-frame of white that encircled its black face.

"Its coat is gorgeous," Hal said.

"Yes," agreed the warden. "And that may mean the death of it. The fur is in great demand for women's garments. High prices are paid for it, so the poachers are hot on the trail of the few colobus monkeys that are left. If something isn't done to stop the poaching, the finest of the monkeys will soon be as extinct as the dodo."

"What a tail," exclaimed Roger, looking at the great white bushy plume that restlessly fanned the air. "Why, it must be longer than the monkey."

"You're right," replied Crosby. "The body is usually

411

about thirty-two inches long, and the tail forty inches."

"What do you want us to do with it?" Hal asked.

"Take it where it will be safe. If we turn it loose here it will soon be picked up again by poachers. It doesn't belong here. How it ever got here I don't know. Colobus monkeys do best in a higher altitude than this. There are some of them left in the Aberdare Mountains – they feel at home there in the very tall trees and the cool mountain air, and they are pretty safe. So it would be fine if you could fly this one up to the Aberdares."

"Okay. Is it ready to travel?"

"It got a nasty cut on the neck from the wire snare but we've treated it and I'm sure it will heal."

"How will it like being cooped up in the plane?"

"I don't know. It depends on whether it trusts you or not. You both seem to have a way with animals, so I think you'll get along all right."

The colobus cocked its picture-frame face to one side and studied the boys with its soft brown eyes. It raised one hand and stroked its white beard.

"No thumb," exclaimed Roger. "I thought all monkeys had thumbs."

"Practically all do. The colobus is an exception. It's a very intelligent animal, but it can't do what many other monkeys can do since it has no thumb. Do you realize how important the thumb is? Try picking things up without using it. You would have a lot of trouble using any sort of tool if you had no thumb. Man is very lucky because Nature gave him one. Much of our civilization is built round the thumb. Now come over here and meet your other passenger."

He led the way to a cage occupied by an animal about the size of a mule. But it didn't look like a mule, nor like any animal the boys had ever seen.

"You're looking", said the warden, "at the rarest of all African animals. The okapi."

"I've always wanted to see one," Hal said. "The okapi is listed at ten thousand dollars. Now I can see why it's worth so much."

Every inch of the animal was different from every other inch. It was dabbed with colours as if an artist had brushed it with every paint he owned. It was yellow, red, chestnut, black, white, blue-black, maroon, sepia, cream, orange and purple. All the colours blended perfectly in the wonderfully soft, glossy coat.

It seemed to be a combination of zebra, giraffe and antelope. It had the head and short horns of a giraffe, the stripes of a zebra on its hindquarters, the large broad ears of a wild dog, and it seemed to wear white stockings.

Suddenly it looked like an ant-eater when it put out its tongue a foot long and licked itself behind the ears!

"It's a stranger here," Crosby said. "Like the colobus. It will certainly get killed if it stays here. It belongs in the deepest, darkest jungle in the northern Congo, or close to it. No white man knew it existed until sixty years ago. The pygmies knew about it and told white hunters about it but no one believed them. I wonder how many other animals there are hidden away in the jungle that we know nothing about. The okapi is very shy. He never came out and showed himself. He hid for thirty million years."

Roger wrinkled his forehead. "Did you say thirty million?"

"Naturalists know now that the species is that old. The okapi has been called a living fossil. Most animals change, grow larger, or smaller, or become extinct. The okapi has stayed the same all that time. But now the poachers are after him and the chances are that very soon this thirty-million-year-old beauty will disappear."

"Where can we take him where he'll be safe?"

"Nowhere," said Crosby gloomily. "Nowhere will be safe. But there is a place that the poachers haven't found yet and perhaps won't for a while. It's a big island in Lake

Victoria. It's called Rubondo. It has fifty-five thousand acres of dense forest – just the kind the okapi loves. It has been set aside as a game sanctuary and it is protected by waters that can get very wild and stormy and poachers who try to get there are apt to be drowned. You could be drowned too. There's no airfield on the island. You would have to bring your plane down on the mainland and then charter a boat or raft to take you and the okapi over to the island. Perhaps you'd rather not try it."

"It doesn't sound too bad," said Hal. "I suppose it would only take an hour or so to ferry across to the island."

Crosby smiled. "More than that. Victoria is the second largest lake in the world. Your voyage to the island would take fifteen hours. And if you didn't have about five storms on the way I'd be much surprised. I can't ask you to take the risk – it's up to you."

"We'll go," Hal said. "If you'll show us how to get there."

Back in the office, Crosby spread out the map of East Africa.

18
The Treehouse

"The Aberdares are here, north of Nairobi. You land at Nyeri, then trek in to Treetops. You've heard of Treetops?"

"Of course. The hotel perched in the top branches of a giant Cape chestnut."

"Most of the forest trees there are giants. The colobus will love them. Stay overnight up in the treehouse. The next morning, fly three hundred miles south-west to Mwanza on Lake Victoria. Here it is. And there's Rubondo Island, a hundred miles across the lake."

"When do we leave?"

"If you want to leave now, you can make Treetops before dark."

"Let's go," said Roger.

The animal passengers were not quite so enthusiastic. The two rear seats of the plane were removed to make room for them. The okapi in a close-fitting bamboo cage was driven to the landing field and five men hoisted the animal aboard.

"Won't he be too heavy for the plane?" Roger wondered.

"No," said the warden. "You have a 250-horsepower

engine there. It will lift two and a half tons. That okapi can't weigh more than a quarter of a ton."

The zebra-giraffe-antelope had never been in a spot like this in all his thirty million years. He whinnied like a worried horse and banged his head about against the bamboo slats, which bent when they were struck, so they did him no harm.

Crosby stripped a leafy branch from a tree and laid it on top of the cage so that the leaves hung down between the slats. The okapi at once coiled a twelve-inch ribbon of tongue round the leaves and drew them down within reach of the grinding teeth. So long as he had his favourite food, he could tolerate his strange environment.

The mild-mannered colobus did not need to be caged. Roger climbed into the plane with the monkey in his arms. With the curiousity natural to an intelligent animal, it examined the instrument board closely, then climbed back over Roger's shoulder to the top of the okapi's cage from which point it made a close examination of every inch of the cabin. When the engine began to roar it plopped back into Roger's lap and peered about anxiously as the plane thundered up over the treetops.

Hal followed the red road north-west to Nairobi, then turned north towards the dazzling snows of 17,000-foot

Mount Kenya. Helped by a tail wind, he made the three-hundred-mile flight in two hours, then came down on a small but open landing field at the edge of the Aberdare forest.

Here was the Outspan Hotel where arrangements must be made to enter the game reserve and spend the night at Treetops.

They had scarcely touched the ground when they were greeted by the hotel's white hunter who introduced himself with "Call me Geoffrey."

The okapi was left in the plane with plenty of leaves for supper and breakfast.

"He'll be all right there," said Geoffrey. "We'll look after him. Now, if you'll climb into this jeep, we'll be off."

With Roger holding the colobus, the car slithered over a muddy forest trail for three miles, then came to a stop at the end of the road. Great trees towered all about.

"Now we have a quarter-mile walk to Treetops," said Geoffrey.

They followed a narrow track among the forest giants. The colobus was getting more and more excited. These tall trees offered it an ideal home. The air cooled by the snows of Mount Kenya was bound to please an animal with a coat of fur so warm and thick.

"What's that ladder for?" asked Roger, noticing a ladder nailed to a tree. Farther down the trail was another – and then another.

"I'm afraid you're going to find out right now," said Geoffrey. "Quick – climb that ladder."

"Why?"

"No time for questions and answers. Get up there fast."

Roger climbed, the colobus clinging to his shoulder. Close behind came Hal and Geoffrey. There was a crashing sound in the forest, then five loudly trumpeting elephants came charging out of the gloom.

"Higher," shouted Geoffrey.

They climbed until Roger reached the end of the ladder. The upstretched trunks of the elephants did not quite touch Geoffrey's feet.

"Now you know what the ladders are for," said Geoffrey. "I should have explained – it's a rule of this trail. Climb eight feet high in case of rhino or buffalo, eighteen feet if it's an elephant."

"Are they really so savage?"

"The rhinos and buffaloes can be. You never know about the elephant. He may be just trying to tease you – or he may mean business. If some poacher has pinged him with an arrow, he will revenge himself on any human he happens to see."

"What do we do now?"

"Just wait."

"How long?"

"It may be five minutes, it may be five hours. You can't hurry an elephant. They'll go when they're ready."

It was not the most comfortable place to wait, thought Roger – clinging to a ladder with a heavy monkey glued to your shoulder.

The elephants were in no hurry. They put in their time tearing up bushes and swallowing them, leaves, twigs, roots and all. They glanced up now and then to make sure their quarry was still there.

The colobus was getting restless. It threw back its head and stared upwards. Gradually Roger realized that there was something alive above him. He looked up and could see nothing at first but a little movement of the leaves at the top of the tree.

Then he saw a face peering down. It was a black face with a white ring all about it. It must belong to a colobus monkey. Other faces like it appeared. The animals chattered down an invitation for Roger's colobus to come and join them.

"Shall I let it go?" Roger asked Geoffrey.

"This is as good a place as any," said Geoffrey. "The colobus monkeys are a very friendly sort. They'll give your friend the red-carpet treatment I'm sure."

Roger was already fond of this gentle creature, but knew it would be better off with its own kind.

Hanging on with one hand, he used the other to shift the animal over on to a branch beside his head. The colobus sat on the branch and looked long and thoughtfully at Roger. Then it climbed up branch by branch to the welcoming party above. There was a new burst of happy talk when it arrived and there was no doubt that the stranger had at once been adopted as a full member of the Aberdare colony.

"Don't look so blue," said Geoffrey. "You'll probably see it again. The monkeys come down to drink every night at the Treetops lake."

The elephants had wandered off. The march to Treetops was resumed. Now they could see it through the trees, and it was a strange sight. A hotel floating in the air! It was perched fifty feet above the ground in the top branches of a big tree and it moved slightly backwards and forwards as the tree swayed in the wind. A wooden stairway something like a spider's web hung from the door down to the ground.

It was like a six-storey building with the lower five storeys removed. It was as if wreckers had destroyed all of a building for fifty feet up but had forgotten to take the top floor. There it seemed to float in the sky, defying the laws of gravity.

Directly in front of the hotel was a small lake completely surrounded by forest. The boys had heard much about this famous place. They knew that at night all sorts of animals came out of the forest to drink at the lake and root around in the mud for salt. You could look down on them from the balcony of the hotel and if you made no sound they would not be aware of your presence.

Many notable people had slept in this little hotel in the sky.

"Queen Elizabeth has been here, I believe," Hal said.

"Yes — but she was Princess Elizabeth when she came. During the night she got word that her father the king had died and she was queen."

"And Prince Philip?"

"He has visited us several times. Of course he is the strongest man we have in the whole movement for the protection of African wild life. Come along — we'll go upstairs."

They approached the cobweb. The boys were surprised to find that the lowest twelve feet of it were missing — or, at least, these steps had been drawn up out of reach.

Geoffrey pressed a button and the steps came down. After they had climbed them, he pressed another button and up they went like the companion-way of a ship when it is about to sail.

"What's the idea?" Hal inquired.

"If they're not up out of the way the big animals will smash them or the small animals will climb them. So we hoist that section out of reach."

"Like the drawbridge of a castle," Hal said.

They climbed the rest of the steps to this castle in the

clouds and entered the hotel door.

Geoffrey introduced them to the manager and they were assigned a room.

In comparison with most hotels, this one was tiny, accommodating only twelve guests – yet as a treehouse it was surprisingly large. It swayed when the tree swayed. If any guest stepped heavily the whole structure trembled.

Outside the boys' room was a balcony from which they could look straight down to the beach of the little lake. There was a stairway to the roof where one had an unobstructed view in all directions.

19
House of Whispers

It was a house of whispers. Signs warned that any sound would disturb the game. The white hunter whispered, the guests whispered, the servants whispered. Everyone wore rubber-soled shoes. It was the rule. Tackies (tennis shoes) could be bought if you did not have a pair.

"But there's one thing I don't understand," Hal said to Geoffrey. "Even though the animals can't hear us, surely they can smell us. We're only fifty feet away."

"If we were down on their level they would certainly get our scent – perhaps even if we were a quarter of a mile away. But here, fifty feet above them, the air currents carry our scent high above their heads. They don't know we exist – unless we make a noise. This is no place for a person with a cold. One cough, and all the animals scamper into the forest. But they come back. They love this place. The soil in that beach happens to be full of salt. All animals need salt – except the meat eaters. They get it from the meat they eat."

An excellent dinner was served at the long table in the dining-room. Then every one of the twelve guests slipped out silently on to the balcony and sat to look down on the pageant below. All wore heavy clothing, and some had wrapped themselves in blankets stripped from their beds, for the mountain air at an altitude of seven thousand feet was cold in spite of the fact that Treetops was almost on the equator.

Darkness veiled the scene. But suddenly a powerful floodlight was turned on. It illuminated the beach and the edge of the lake. Two bush pigs, a wart–hog, and a stately waterbuck had already arrived. They looked up into the light. Perhaps they were surprised to see the sun shining at that hour of the night, but they were not frightened. They could not see the balcony and the spectators, for the hotel was now completely dark. They went back to their search for salt.

Four rhinos came on the scene. They eagerly sucked up the salty mud. Others joined them. They quarrelled over the choicest mudholes, pushed and jostled each other, made angry blowing sounds and a peculiar blast that sounded like a loud snore. Their ears went round like radar screens picking up signals. A slight cough of one of the guests sent them galumphing off.

Soon they were back, or others like them, chasing each other about, making a puff–puff–puff like a steam locomotive. They also snorted like a horse, but with rhino power instead of horsepower.

Now came the elephants, great lumbering monsters, wading into the lake and throwing water up over their dusty hides, then coming out to insert the delicate tips of their trunks into deep footprints made by the rhinos. There they found salt and conveyed it to their mouths. They blinked now and then at the floodlight but evidently took it for the moon or for a sun that had forgotten to set.

Unlike the hot-tempered rhinos, the elephants did not interfere with each other. And when a baby elephant poked its trunk into a hole already being explored by an adult, the big one let the little fellow have it.

Five shaggy buffaloes now came on the stage and they proved as hot-tempered as the rhinos. Soon the beach was a battlefield where the weapons were rhino horns against the harder, sharper horns of the buffaloes, and the night resounded with their grunting and trumpeting.

The elephants didn't like the squabble and finally all joined in a screaming charge that sent the misbehavers flying into the forest.

A giraffe came out to drink. He had to spread his legs far apart to get his head down to the water. The lake was surrounded now by graceful antelopes of many sorts; impalas, Tommies, Grant's, kudu, waterbuck and klip-springer. These charming and dainty animals took care not to get under the feet of the monsters.

"Look. There they come," whispered Roger.

The visitors both boys had been eagerly waiting for slipped out of the forest into the light. They were the colobus monkeys. What lovely creatures they were with their white-ringed faces, their rich silky fur and magnificent white tails! No wonder they were so loved by fashionable ladies that they were being slaughtered at the rate of more than ten thousand a month.

Roger strained his eyes. Was his friend among them? He borrowed a pair of binoculars from Geoffrey.

Yes — there was no mistake about it — he could make out on the neck of one of them a line where the wire noose had rubbed away the fur and cut into the flesh.

The trusting creature he had held on his lap seemed to be equally happy with its new friends. Roger felt a pang of jealousy but was instantly ashamed of it. The pretty creature that might have made such a good pet was where it belonged, with others of its own sort, and among the great trees it loved.

The boys kept vigil most of the night — then retired to their cots to dream of what they had seen.

At breakfast Hal said to Geoffrey, "What a wonderful idea it was — to build a treehouse over this pool."

Geoffrey agreed. "Only a person with a good imagination would have thought of it. It was a woman, you know. A certain Lady Bettie Walker came here with friends long before this was made a National Park. She had been reading *Swiss Family Robinson*. You remember the tree-house described in that book. That gave her the idea for Treetops. It seemed a crazy idea to some of her friends."

"Crazy or not, it's great. I hate to leave but we'd better be getting along. We have a big day ahead."

Back to the plane and the patient okapi, nibbling a leafy breakfast. The flight over the great lion country of the Serengeti Plain to Mwanza on the south shore of Lake Victoria took two hours.

There, Hal chartered the only craft available, a clumsy raft with a wheezy outboard motor, and set out on the fifteen-hour passage to Rubondo Island.

Warden Crosby's prediction that there would be five storms during the fifteen hours proved wrong. There was only one storm – but it lasted fifteen hours.

A strong north wind sweeping down the 250-mile length of the mighty lake brought big waves that washed across the raft, sousing boys and okapi alike. The boys were not allowed to forget that among all the freshwater lakes of the world only Superior is greater than Victoria. This lake deserved to be named after England's great queen and had all the majesty one had a right to expect of the source of the mighty Nile.

The okapi had certainly never made such a trip before and whinnied his strong disapproval. The constant tossing of the raft made the animal seasick and up came the leaves. The cage had been firmly lashed to the logs, yet the force of the waves against it seemed about to tear it loose at any moment.

Victoria is a lake of hidden reefs, lying just below the surface. Time and again the raft stumbled to a halt on a sand-bar. Sometimes reversing the engine would back it off. Sometimes this was not good enough and the boys must jump off and push the raft free. If on these occasions a six-foot wave came along and completely buried you, that was just part of the game.

One must keep a sharp look out for the crocodiles and hippos that infest the lake. Several times there was a wild scramble back on to the logs as the swish of a great tail signalled the approach of a croc. The hippos did not like the stormy water and lurked in the lee of small islands. Not being carnivores, they preferred reeds to humans as their diet – nevertheless they were dangerous as the boys found out when one came up beneath the raft, hoisting it three feet into the air before it slid off edgewise into the water. Whether the great beast performed this feat just for fun, or with evil intent, the navigators did not stop to ask. They merely congratulated themselves that the raft had not been turned upside down.

The troubles of the day became a nightmare as darkness settled on the wild waters of the lake. A light far ahead marked Rubondo Island. Sometimes it disappeared entirely behind rain and mist. Then only guesswork steered the raft. After a time the light would reappear off one quarter or the other and the course could be corrected.

Three exhausted sailors finally brought their craft into a fairly quiet cove of Rubondo and heard a welcoming shout from the wharf.

The warden, who introduced himself with "Just call me Tony", helped them put the cage ashore. "What have you got in there?"

"An okapi."

"Wonderful. Male or female?"

It seemed an odd question. What did it matter?

"Male," Hal said.

"Good. We have just one okapi on the island and it's a female. Now we have a chance of breeding more. Mighty rare animal, the okapi. You can be sure we'll handle this one with kid gloves. Wait till I get a towel."

He ran to his small rustic cabin and came back with a towel. It was not for the shivering boys, but to dry the precious okapi. The cage was cautiously opened and the animal brought out on to the wharf.

Tony went over every inch of the hide with the towel, rubbing briskly to stimulate circulation. "There – he'll do," said Tony finally.

"Should we feed him?" said Hal.

"No need. He can't go ten feet in these woods without finding food. And as for water, he has a whole lake of it."

"So we just let him go?" inquired Roger, always sorry to lose a pet.

"That's the best thing for him. Just let him make his own way. He'll be pretty safe. He has no enemies on this island – no lions, leopards or poachers. A good many rhinos have been brought here for safe keeping, but they won't bother your okapi. This is as close to heaven as any okapi will ever get."

The okapi was already eagerly moving off into his heaven.

Hal had a pang of regret as he saw ten thousand dollars walking away. He and Roger had been sent to Africa to get animals for their animal-collector father who would then sell them to zoos. It seemed a pity to lose this one.

But Hal was aware that few okapi had ever survived the journey to America. The important thing right now was not to capture an animal or two for their father, but to do everything possible to stop the killing of the thousands of animals of East Africa. In the long run that would do more for their business of animal-collecting than anything else they could do.

"Now," said Tony, "come along to the cabin. It's your turn to get dry — and you must be starved."

433

20
Men Live, Animals Die

The night was half gone before the boys were dried, fed and bunked in Tony's cabin.

Roger was asleep in two minutes. Hal lay awake a little longer, worrying about the trip back — fifteen hours over the stormy lake, then two hours by plane. Impossible to get to Tsavo before dark. Impossible to come down on that tiny landing strip after dark.

Then he slept and did not wake until roused by the sizzle and smell of bacon and eggs. Tony had some good news for him.

"I'm going to take you back to Mwanza in our launch. It will cut the time from fifteen hours down to seven. The boys can take the raft back later. There's just one condition."

"What's that?"

"That you give me a lift to Tsavo. I have some matters to discuss with Crosby — about a shipment of four rhinos to Rubondo."

The hundred-mile dash to Mwanza by launch was pure joy compared with the painful and dangerous voyage by raft. By mid-afternoon they were aboard the Stork and flying again over the mysterious Serengeti Plain.

"See that deep cut in the plain? Looks like the Grand Canyon. Fly low over it."

Hal flew low. He was trying to remember what he had heard about this canyon.

"Is it Olduvai Gorge?"

Tony turned to him in surprise. "So, you know about Dr Leakey. With luck, we may see him and his crew at work."

Hal followed the twists and turns of the gorge. Then suddenly, straight below, could be seen a group of men at the bottom of the gorge digging into the rock wall.

The whirr of the plane made them look up. They waved and Tony waved back. Then they were left behind. It had been only a moment, but a moment Hal would always remember. For that single glance had carried his imagination back two million years.

Roger, who had never heard of Olduvai, was not impressed.

"What's so wonderful about that hole in the ground?" he wanted to know.

Tony explained. "This archaeologist, Dr Leakey, has been digging there for several years. He has found the fossil bones of men who lived two million years ago. Those are the oldest human bones that have ever been discovered anywhere in the world."

"How can they tell they're that old?"

"A chemical test. Perhaps you've heard of the Carbon-14 test. That's been used for a long time – the only trouble with it is that it can't tell the age of anything more than fifty thousand years old. But there's a new method now, the potassium-argon test. With that they can go back millions of years."

"And this two-million-year-old man – was he like man today?"

"Apparently he was. Dr Leakey has found the bones of sixteen men. They were all pretty much like ours, but with some differences. Those men were only about four feet tall. Their thumbs and fingers were not as well adapted as ours for picking things up and holding them. Still they could use tools – some of their stone tools were found. The weight of these men was only about half the weight of modern man – five stone five pounds instead of ten stone ten. The weight of the brain was only one pound. Modern man's brain weight is about three pounds. So, you see, man really has improved a bit during the last two million years."

"The thing that strikes me as remarkable," said Hal, "is that we have lasted that long. Think of all the animals that have died out during that time – the mastodon, brontosaurus, diplodocus, dodo, quagga, moa and hundreds of others. All gone. And we go merrily along – not only still living, but multiplying to beat the band."

"Multiplying too fast," Tony said. "And the faster we multiply, the faster we push the remaining animals off the planet. We seem to think we own everything. How about our fellow-animals – don't they have any rights?"

They passed over one of the greatest of the world's craters, with one of the strangest of names, Ngorongoro. The volcanic fires had long since died out. The surrounding rim of the crater stood up like a wall two thousand five hundred feet above the crater floor. The floor was a lush green expanse of a hundred and fifty square miles, dotted with woods and meadows and lakes and swarming with animals.

"Lots of life here," Roger remarked.

"Yes, but what kind of life? Let's get down a little closer."

Flying lower, they could see dozens of lions, elephants, rhinos – but most of the room was taken up by thousands upon thousands of cattle tended by tall, bare Masai herdsmen.

"This is the beginning of the end of this heaven for

wild animals," Tony said. "It used to be reserved for them. But now the Masai have invaded it and their cattle are crowding out the wild life. The Masai have no need for so many cattle – they keep them just to show off. The same thing is happening in the national parks, even in Tsavo. Herds of bony, scrawny, worthless cattle are driving out the wild life."

The crater was left behind and Lake Manyara appeared – a curiously pink lake, for on its surface rested millions of pink flamingoes.

"At least the lake is safe from the cattle," said Hal.

"Yes, but the flamingoes are having a different kind of problem. This lake has become very salty. The salt hardens on the flamingoes' legs and makes great heavy balls three or four inches thick so that the birds cannot walk or fly. They starve to death by the tens of thousands."

"Is anything being done about it?"

"Something fine is being done. See all those African youngsters down there wading among the flamingoes? They have been trained to save the birds by breaking up the ball of salt with a hammer so that the leg is once more clean and free."

"So African children really do care?"

"Yes. I only wish their parents cared as much."

A strong blast of snow-cold air struck the plane as it passed the glaciers of Mount Kilimanjaro. Then Hal brought it down skilfully on the Tsavo strip.

They found Mark Crosby at his desk. The two Englishmen, Tony and Mark, greeted each other heartily.

"Nice to see there's a bit of England left in Kenya," said Tony. "I rather expected that by this time I'd see an African behind that desk."

Crosby laughed. "It will happen one of these days. Now that this country has its own government, official jobs like yours and mine will sooner or later be given to Africans."

"Are you going to wait for it to happen? Or resign now?"

"I'll wait. For two reasons. One is that there's no African yet with enough training to take over my job. The other reason is personal. I'd rather take my chances here than face going back to England. What would I do there? I couldn't get a job. They'd ask me, 'What experience have you had?' 'Well, I've been a game warden in Africa.' What use is that in England?"

Hal thought that both men looked tired. They faced an uncertain future. They had given their lives to saving the wild life of Africa. Would all they had done go for nothing? It was only natural for an African government to give important posts to Africans. But would Africans care as much about protecting the wild life? For hundreds of years they had been used to killing animals, not protecting them. Would the national parks be split up into farms for the rapidly increasing African population? Was there no way that people and animals could live together in peace? Hal could almost see these thoughts running like a motion picture through the minds of the two Englishmen.

"Well," said Tony, "we can't moon around about what may be. We can only do the best we can right now. I understand you have four rhinos ready for Rubondo. I'll see them through. I'll need a cage for each animal, and two lorries. I'll take them by road to Mwanza, and I've chartered an old car-ferry for the trip to the island."

While the two wardens discussed the transfer of the rhinos,

Hal and Roger went to their banda. They found a note wedged under the door. Hal unfolded it and read it aloud.

"GO HOME, YANKS. THIS IS YOUR FIRST WARNING. IF ANOTHER IS NEEDED IT WILL BE WRITTEN IN BLOOD – YOURS."
  Bb

Somebody playing cops and robbers," said Roger contemptuously.

Hal did not take it so lightly. "I have an idea he means it. You know who it is, don't you?"

Roger studied the signature, Bb.

"I can guess," he said. "Blackbeard."

"Right. Don't brush it off. He's a man who would go to any limit, even murder, to save a business that is bringing him in millions."

"So you think we should go home?" said Roger sarcastically.

"No. Not until we get done with Bb. You remember that five-mile trap-line we saw from the plane? We'll go after it tomorrow morning."

"But what's the use? We nab a gang of poachers and send them to court and the judge lets them off."

441

"This time we'll try to nab Blackbeard, not his poachers. But we'll give them a surprise too – something they won't like. Perhaps it will make them think twice before they do any more poaching."

21
Tear Gas

"We'll be turning in early," Hal told the warden after reporting the delivery of the colobus to Treetops and the okapi to Rubondo.

"Good idea," said Crosby. "It was a hard trip. Thanks for doing a good job."

"Tomorrow morning we want to visit that trap-line we saw from the plane. We'll make another try to grab Blackbeard."

"Fine. Sorry I can't go with you. I certainly wish you the best of luck."

After they were in bed they heard a car drive up. Before they got up at dawn they heard a car drive away. They thought nothing of this coming and going until later.

After a sunrise breakfast the boys and their crew set out in jeeps and Land-Rovers for the trap-line. When they came within a mile of it Hal brought the cars to a halt and gave the men final instructions.

"You will find canisters of tear gas in the supply truck. Each of you take one." He went on to explain carefully the plan of attack.

The cars rumbled on. When they arrived at the trap-line they drew up in front of it just as they had done before. They blew their horns lustily to attract the poachers. But as the poachers began to come out through the gaps in the trap-line, Hal led a dozen of his men round through the woods to come up on the poachers' camp from the rear.

If Blackbeard behaved as he had before, he would stay safely behind his men and, when he saw them being defeated, he would try to sneak out the back way. But this time he would find himself trapped.

On the front line, arrows began to fly. The safari men did not fire back but stayed behind the barricade of cars.

The poachers grew bolder. Shouting insults at the men who seemed afraid to come out and fight, they came closer. The safari men looked to Roger for a signal.

When the poachers were within fifty feet Roger threw his canister and at once the air was full of the bombs which burst among the animal-killers upon striking rocks or the hard ground. Within seconds the poachers could hardly be seen amid the clouds of yellow-white tear gas. Choking, suffocating, weeping, they fell over each other in their mad rush to escape. They squirmed on the ground, and buried their faces in the grass. Some staggered back towards the camp. No arrows were flying now.

At the same moment Hal's men rushed in from the rear among the grass huts and into the gaps in the trap-line looking for Blackbeard. He was nowhere to be seen. Nor was there any sign of his boot-prints. The search was continued for half an hour, but without any results.

By this time some of the poachers were able to stand, but still could hardly see through their tears. All the fight had been taken out of them. They waited to be loaded into cars and transported to Mombasa.

But if they hoped to spend a few days resting in jail, they were disappointed.

"Tell them," Hal said to Joro, "to go back to their villages and stay there. Tell them if they are caught poaching again something worse will happen to them."

All the animals still alive in the snares were set free; some were taken to the hospital, the dead were left to the hyenas and jackals. The wire snares were collected, and all the trophies, some of them very valuable, some very odd.

Among the odd ones were bracelets made from the hairs of elephants' tails, and leopards' whiskers which had been gathered to sell to African witch doctors. When mixed with a drink and swallowed, the sharp, stiff little hairs pierced the walls of the stomach and caused death.

The grass shacks and the five-mile barricade of thorn bushes were burned to the ground.

Back at the lodge, Hal told Crosby the unhappy story. Blackbeard had not been caught.

"Never mind," the warden said. "You destroyed the camp, and you scared the poachers. That's something. As for Blackbeard, you'll get him yet. By the way, Judge Singh wishes you luck."

"Was he here?"

"He drove in last night after you had turned in. He left very early this morning – said he had important business."

"Did you tell him where we were going this morning?"

"Of course. He is always interested in these raids. He is very happy about the fine work you are doing."

Hal hesitated. "Warden, I hate to say this, because I know the judge is a personal friend of yours – but I've begun to wonder whether he is really with us or against us."

The remark took Crosby by surprise. He stared at Hal.

"That is a very strange thing to say about a man who has always been one of the chief supporters of the anti-poaching campaign. Of course he's a personal friend of mine. You remember, he saved my life. He's also a friend of the wild life. He never fails to speak up against poaching."

"Does he just talk? Or does he really do something?"

"He really does something."

Crosby opened a drawer of his desk and took out a cheque. He laid it before Hal. "The judge gave me this last night. I will send it on to the treasurer of the Wildlife Society."

The cheque was for two hundred pounds. It was made out to the African Wildlife Society and it was signed Sindar Singh.

"You see," Crosby said, "he does more than talk. In this country a judge's salary is very small. Two hundred pounds represents a real sacrifice for him. Now, do you doubt his sincerity?"

"I'm sorry," said Hal. "Perhaps I'm wrong."

"I am sure you are," Crosby said with a touch of severity.

Hal returned to his banda. He told Roger about the conversation and the cheque.

"He certainly caught me flat-footed," Hal confessed. "Perhaps we've been mistaken all along."

Roger was not ready to give in. "I still think he's a crook."

"Then how do you explain that cheque?"

"Simple enough. If he's really mixed up in this racket he isn't living on a judge's salary. He's making millions on the side. To him, two hundred pounds is nothing. It's just to pull the wool over the warden's eyes and make the society think he's on their side. I still think he's Blackbeard's buddy."

"You think so and I think so, but we can never convince the warden. We'd better give up trying. If we keep on, we'll only get him down on us. First we must get some real evidence."

"I guess we can't prove anything yet," Roger admitted. "But we're sure getting some evidence. There was that funny business about the Aco. If you hadn't stopped Singh, the warden would be dead now. And those silly sentences in court. And that warning signed Bb. How do you suppose it got here? I'll bet a plugged nickel Judge Singh brought it from Blackbeard."

Hal nodded. "Could be," he said. "And today we didn't find Blackbeard at the poachers' camp. Why not? Perhaps he'd been warned. The warden told the judge last night what we were planning to do. The judge left very early this morning. Perhaps he stopped at the poachers' hangout and tipped off Blackbeard." Hal brushed his hand wearily across his forehead. "But these are all perhapses. We've got to get some real proof."

"Well, we won't get it sitting round here. Let's go."

22
Massacre

Twice they had spotted camps from the air. It was worth trying again.

In the Stork they flew over hill and valley, scanning the ground through binoculars.

They looked for another trap-line. A trap-line would be a dead give-away. It was a sure sign of poachers, and easy to see.

But there was no trap-line. No camp of grass huts. No spearmen or bowmen searching for animals. Mile after mile, no sign of human life.

"Perhaps we've scared them off," Roger said.

"No such luck. Perhaps they're just hiding in the woods."

"Swing over to that waterhole."

It was solid with animals – elephants, rhinos, zebras, everything under the sun. But no poachers.

Suddenly the waterhole blew up in a mighty fountain of spray and smoke that reminded them of Old Faithful. The explosion made the plane bounce and stagger. Small animals and torn-off parts of large ones were shot into the sky. What had a moment ago been a source of cool refreshment for hundreds of creatures was now their grave.

"Dynamite," Hal exclaimed.

Out of the woods poured the poachers, spearing animals that were still alive, chopping off tails, horns, heads, anything that would bring a price.

Suddenly they saw the plane, and ran for cover. Hal circled and flew back at full speed to the lodge.

There he lost no time in mobilizing his men and their vehicles but, hurry as they might, it was nearly an hour before they could get through to the dynamited waterhole.

They were too late. The poachers had taken all they wanted and made good their escape.

The mangled corpses of animals filled the waterhole. If they were allowed to remain there they would rot and poison the water.

Hal's men with the help of a few rangers worked long and hard at cleaning out the spring. At nightfall they returned to the lodge, blue and moody. Roger expressed what they all felt:

"A tough day, and what have we got for it? One big fat nothing."

Early morning found the two scouts aloft once more. This time their flight took them far to the north, forty miles, fifty, sixty, but still over the wilderness of Tsavo Park. Then, another ten miles farther north, they saw a column of smoke.

Coming closer, they could see a milling madhouse of several hundred elephants surrounded by a ring of fire.

The poachers were at a safe distance. The elephant-grass in this plain was twelve feet high – they had set it on fire in a great circle round the elephant herd, and all they had to do was to wait for the animals to be roasted alive.

The crazed beasts charged into the roaring flames in a last desperate effort to escape and were so severely burned that they died lingering deaths of agony. Those that did not perish at once danced about curiously, because the soles of their feet had been burned away. Even if they should escape the flames they would not escape death, for they could not travel in search of food on the burned stumps of feet. They would soon be overtaken by poachers and killed.

Among the bare-skinned black poachers the boys could make out a black-bearded white face above a bush jacket and safari trousers.

"That's Blackbeard," Roger exclaimed.

They swept close to take a look. Blackbeard glanced up, smiled, and waved.

"The devil!" Hal said. "He knows he's safe. Before we could get back here with the trucks he could be a hundred miles away."

They did get back with the trucks, but it was as they had feared. The poachers had taken all they had time to collect and had fled.

The boys had failed again. But it was not a complete failure. In their haste the poachers had left behind the most valuable trophies.

They had had time to remove such items as tails, feet, eyelashes and some of the great ears — which would stiffen and could be used as table tops. But they had been in such a hurry to be off that they had left behind the most valuable parts — the tusks.

There is no quick and easy way to remove an elephant's tusk. It is strongly rooted in the great beast's bone and flesh. To chop it out with an axe is an almost superhuman task. The easiest method is to allow the carcass to decay for a week — then the tusk can be worked loose.

But it must have been evident to Blackbeard that he was not going to be allowed a week. In less than three hours the interfering strangers would be back with their cars and men. A few of the tusks had been chopped out but more than ninety per cent of them remained. It must

have been a sore disappointment for the poacher chief to
have to leave behind a store of ivory that would have added
perhaps a hundred thousand dollars to his illegal loot.

The killer king's operations became more secretive. He
and his poacher army seemed to have vanished. The Stork
scouted hill and dale, forest and plain, without spotting a
single trespasser. There were no more trap-lines, no more
explosions, no more fires. There were no more camps of
grass shacks. Perhaps there were no more poachers.

"Do you think we've really frightened them off?" Roger
wondered.

"No. But I don't understand where they can be. It's
almost as if they had gone underground."

Underground. It made Roger think. He remembered his
own experience underground, in the elephant pit. Had the
poachers dug themselves in? Tomorrow he would keep an
eye open for brush-covered pits.

Back at the lodge the boys found Singh.

"Well, my friends, have you caught your man yet?"

"Not yet."

"If I were you I'd give it up. We've been trying for years
to get hold of him. But he's just too smart for us. In some
ways I must say I admire him. The way he slips through

your fingers is quite amazing, don't you think? But of course you'll get him yet. You Americans are so clever."

Hal pretended not to see the hidden sarcasm in this remark.

The judge was evidently very well satisfied with himself. Hal encouraged his self-esteem.

"By the way," he said, "the warden told me of your contribution to the Wildlife Society. That was very generous of you."

The judge smiled expansively and waved his hand. "Nothing, my dear boy, nothing. I only wish it could have been more. Unfortunately, salaries are limited in my profession. But I am willing to do without some of the luxuries of life in order to help the poor dear animals."

"Quite noble of you," Hal said. "Too bad you don't have any income besides your salary. Some judges make out quite well, you know."

The judge's face darkened. "Whatever do you mean?"

"Well, take a purely imaginary case. Suppose you were not such an honest and noble judge. Suppose you were secretly in the poaching racket. When any poachers came into your court you could let them off with little or no punishment. You could close your eyes to what the big operators are doing — and they would make it worth your while. You could become rich – and all the time you could pose as a great friend of the animals. And every once in a while you could make a gift to the Wildlife Society just to keep everybody fooled."

The judge was flushing deeply and his usually soft eyes were like hard steel swordpoints. Then he forced a laugh.

"As you say, this is all purely imaginary," he said. "Quite impossible for a true lover of animals."

"Quite," agreed Hal, caressing Chee who had wandered in through the open door. Chee bared his teeth at the judge and snarled deeply.

Hal excused himself and went out. He looked back through a window screened with shrubbery. The judge's behaviour was remarkable. For the moment he seemed to have gone mad. He struck the desk a blow with his fist, then leaped up, strode backwards and forwards as if in a fever, came to where Chee was lying and gave the animal a vicious kick in the throat. Chee sprang up and came for him, spitting, biting and clawing. Singh kicked the animal repeatedly, then drew a knife. Before he could use it, the wrist of the hand that held the knife was between the cheetah's teeth. The knife fell to the floor and the judge collapsed into a chair. Chee, still snarling, walked out.

Hal went to his banda and thought about what he had

seen. So this was the great animal-lover! The cheetah evidently didn't think so and Hal trusted the animal more than the man. Hal was more convinced than ever that Sindar Singh was a colossal crook — otherwise why did he react so violently to Hal's 'purely imaginary' story?

But still there was no real proof.

23
Crash of the Stork

"I believe those are pits," exclaimed Roger, looking down through the Perspex bubble.

Hal, at the controls, scanned the earth below. He could see no pits — but there were many spots where the brush had been cut and was now lying in mats, and those mats might be the covers of pits. Were poachers hidden beneath?

Near by was a grove of baobabs, fantastic trees that looked like blown-up hippos. They were huge like hippos, bulged like hippos, had bark like the hide of a hippo. One might almost believe that a herd of the hefty animals had come up from the river and stood here until they took root.

There were none of the usual grass huts of poachers among the trees and not a sign of human life. Yet there was something suspicious about those brush mats. There might be a small city of busy men beneath them.

"It's worth investigating," Hal said. He swung the plane about and headed home. "We'll come back on wheels with our gang."

For ten minutes the plane flew steadily on the homeward course. Then it began to weave and wobble as if it were drunk.

"Pockets!" guessed Roger.

"I don't think so," Hal said. "It's not bumping the way it would if it were dropping into air pockets. Besides, why should there be up-and-down air currents here? You might expect turbulence over bad country, hills, cliffs — but not over a level plain like this one."

"Then what can it be? Are you waggling that stick?"

"Of course not."

"Do you think the rudder has gone haywire?"

"I don't know. But it's getting worse every minute. I think we'd better look for a place to land."

The plane was now bucking like a frightened horse.

"Your right wing," exclaimed Roger. "Look at it."

The wing was dancing. It seemed about to come off and fly away on a trip of its own.

Hal brought the plane down in a steep glide. He barely missed the top of a tall kapok tree. The plane rocked dangerously.

"I can't hold her," Hal said. "She's going to crash. She may burn. Be ready to jump clear."

He turned off the ignition.

The plane struck the ground and bounced. There was a ripping, tearing sound, the right wing disappeared, the Stork crashed into an ant-hill and lay still.

"Good," cried Hal.

"What's good about it?"

"No fire. We're alive. Isn't that good?"

"I suppose so," Roger said doubtfully. "What do we do now?"

They climbed out of the cabin and walked back fifty feet to inspect the torn-off wing.

"It doesn't seem possible," said Hal. "Why should that wing rip loose?"

Roger was inspecting the torn edge. "Looks fishy to me," he said. "Did this just tear — or was it cut?"

Hal studied the break, then stared at Roger.

461

"Monkey business," he exclaimed. "See this straight line? That's no natural break. Somebody has sawed part of the way through – just enough to weaken the wing. I suppose we can feel honoured. Somebody thinks us important enough to be worth murdering."

Roger was rubbing his knee. "What's the matter?" Hal asked.

"Just a bump I got when we landed. Now what do we do? No radio in this crate. How about a signal fire?"

"No luck. The lodge is a good fifty miles away. They wouldn't see it. The only ones who would be likely to see it would be the poachers. And we don't want them to come down on us. A fire would be an open invitation to Mr Blackbeard."

"Then what do we do? Just sit here and wait for somebody to come looking for us?"

"In a hundred miles of wild country? It might take weeks for them to find us. By that time we wouldn't be worth finding. There's only one way out of it. We've got to walk to the lodge."

They went back to the plane. Hal noticed that Roger was limping badly. "You'll never make it," he said.

"Never mind the knee," said Roger. "It will limber up."

"I'm afraid not. It will just get worse. Anyhow, one

of us should stay here to look after the plane."

"Why does it need looking after? What could happen to it?"

"Lots of things. A poacher might come on it and steal everything he could pry loose. Rhinos and elephants can get mighty curious. They completely wrecked a stalled plane up in Murchison a month ago. Hyenas have a taste for rubber – they'll eat the tyres off the wheels if you give them a chance. You can help most by staying right here."

"Okay," Roger said reluctantly. "How long will it take you?"

"Assuming we're fifty miles from the lodge – I'd say it'll be a ten-hour walk. Then it'll take about two hours to get back here by truck. Twelve hours altogether."

"But it's late afternoon already. You'd better wait until tomorrow morning."

"Cooler walking at night," Hal said. "And there's a good moon. Don't worry – I'll get through all right. So long – take care of yourself. I'll be seeing you round about five a.m."

He strode off. Roger's stomach called after him, "Bring a sandwich back with you."

As the sun went down the animals that had spent the heat of the day in the forest began to come out.

They were greatly interested in the plane. They gathered round it as if it had been the Ark and they were about to take a ride. Some of the smaller and more fearless ones tried to climb in with Roger. The baboons were determined to share the cabin with him. The vervet monkeys perching on the nose of the plane looked in through the Perspex.

Four rhinos looked the plane over carefully with many sniffs and snorts, perhaps thinking it was some new sort of beast. Then they retired to a short distance and held a conference.

They evidently decided that this strange creature had no business here. They lowered their heads and charged. Even one rhino could do serious damage to the fuselage. What might four do?

Roger threw open the hood and shouted. The rhinos stopped, blinking their weak eyes, tilting their ears to locate the source of the sound.

They held another conference. If they had been wise old elephants they might have reached an agreement. But being rhinos, irritable by nature and not very wise, they broke up the conference by fighting each other.

Gazelles and giraffes paraded round the plane examining it carefully. The famous jumpers, the impalas, had great fun leaping over it. A lurking leopard selected a waterbuck as its evening meal and broke its neck in one violent attack.

A terrifying scream ripped the air. It was loud enough and strong enough to come from a bull elephant — but Roger, when he got over the chill it gave him, remembered that it was just the night cry of the tree hyrax, a nocturnal animal only a foot or so long.

He was sorry to see the light go. The plane was left in shadow, and the shadow was climbing up the slope of Africa's highest mountain. Now it was a mile high, now two miles, now it reached the snow line, now it blotted out the brilliant glow of the glaciers, and now having climbed almost four miles it left the peak of Kilimanjaro in darkness, just a pale grey ghost against a blue-black sky.

24
Fall of Blackbeard

Roger tried to sleep.

He soon gave it up as a bad job. The seat was uncomfortable. He would be better off on the ground.

He climbed down and stretched out on the grass under the remaining wing. He depended upon the wing to scare off any inquisitive animals. It was so low that no rhino, elephant, buffalo or hippo could get under it.

But he had forgotten about another dangerous wild animal. The ant.

News of his presence spread to the occupants of the ant-hill against which the plane had crashed. He woke up with a start when he felt some sharp nips on his arms and legs. Before he could get fully awake the nips had spread under his clothes over his entire body and he was one trembling jelly of pain.

He leaped to his feet, tore off his clothes, danced and brushed and slapped and for every ant he got rid of two others arrived. His audience of animals looked on in amazement.

Then one of them came to his aid. It was really not at

all interested in aiding him, but just in getting a good meal.

The ant-bear known also as the aardvark (meaning earth pig) cannot pass up a chance to dine on ants. It sleeps all day. At nightfall it wakes and goes out hungrily searching for food.

It is a beast about four feet in length, weighs something like one hundred and forty pounds, has bear-like claws for digging, a tail like a kangaroo's, long pointed ears that shoot off in different directions like those of a donkey, a snout like a pig's and – most amazing of all – a sticky tongue eighteen inches long.

Roger's visitor immediately began thrashing that remarkable tongue into the army of ants that streamed from the ant-hill to Roger's trembling hide. The tongue, loaded with ants, was flicked back into the mouth, and down went the wriggling insects into the animal's paunch. Out darted the glue-covered ribbon to get a new load.

The ant has an intelligence far greater than one would expect in so small a creature, and the marching column promptly turned about and tried to escape into the ant-hill. But there were still numerous ants feasting upon Roger. Suddenly he felt a light stroke up his leg. The ant-bear was quite accustomed to tongueing ants from the hides of other animals. And to this bear Roger was just another beast, a table spread with food.

The boy stood perfectly still in order not to frighten his rescuer, and let the sticky, tickling tongue caress his hide. The moon must have laughed as it looked down on the strange spectacle. Roger himself laughed, as the tongue tickled, and at once the ant-bear took fright and clumsily galloped off.

Roger dressed and decided to spend the rest of the night in the co-pilot's seat, no matter how uncomfortable.

The ant-bear had one more surprise to give Roger. It

stopped short as it saw a lion approaching. The ant-bear is a favourite food of the lion.

The lion also stopped. He was in no hurry. Being just a big cat, he acted like other cats. A cat chasing a mouse does not pounce upon it and eat it at once. It plays with it, turns its head away, pretends to take no interest in it, keeps it worrying for a while before finishing it off.

So the lion dilly-dallied, evidently sure that his victim could not escape. It's true, the ant-bear cannot run as fast as the lion. But the ant-bear is a powerful beast in its own way, equipped with strong curved claws with which it can dig a hole and vanish from sight within one minute.

And so, while the lion gazed off into space and thought about the good meal he was about to have, the ant-bear silently and swiftly scooped away the earth. When the lion looked back the bagful of ants had disappeared and nothing was left but a hole.

The lion walked over to it, looked down into it, scratched at it, and then walked off with a disappointed grumble.

Roger slept fitfully. Twice he was roused by the peculiar laugh of hyenas under the plane, probably nibbling at the tyres. He scared them away by stamping on the cabin floor.

Then he slept soundly, undisturbed even by the squawling *Peeyah! Peeyah! Peeyah! Wah-wah!* of the bush-baby, so named because its cry is much like that of a very bad-tempered child.

He dreamed that he was being gored by the horns of a rhino, and woke to find that it was dawn and Hal was prodding him in the ribs.

"Come alive," said his brother. "Are you going to sleep all day? Here's your sandwich."

With difficulty Roger got his eyes open and saw that with Hal was Warden Crosby, and behind them all the safari men and the cars.

"Pile out," Hal said. "We're on our way to the poachers' camp."

"How about the plane?"

"Just have to leave it here. The warden telegraphed the Nairobi airport for mechanics. Let's get going and see what's under those brush mats."

It was a little over twenty miles back to the grove of big-bellied hippo trees and the suspicious-looking mats.

Not a soul was to be seen. But the muffled sound of voices came over the morning air.

If the pits were really full of poachers they would be armed with bows and arrows.

"Just raise one corner of this mat so that we can get a look," Hal said.

The men lifted the corner of the brush roof. Hal peered down, half expecting to get an arrow in his face. There was no one in the pit.

And still there was that sound of voices.

The other pits were examined, one by one. There were animals in a few, but no humans.

Hal hushed his men. "Keep quiet and listen."

There was no doubt about it. Somewhere men were talking. The sound seemed to come from the trees. But there were no men among the baobabs. They could not be concealed by foliage, for there was no foliage – the trees were bare.

Hal led the way back among the trees. Again he hushed his men. But now there was no sound of talking. Nothing but a breathless silence. Either there were no poachers here or they had become aware that they were having visitors. Hal looked under the trees, behind the trees, up into the branches. Not a soul. Hal was ready to give it up as a bad job.

"Wait," the warden said. "They could be right here – all round us."

"How could they be here without our seeing them?"

"You notice how big these tree-trunks are. The baobab doesn't grow more than about fifty feet high – but it grows sideways. Like a short fat man, a 'five-by-five'. Many of these trees have a waist measurement of sixty feet. That's a pretty big tummy. They are old trees – anything from five hundred to a thousand years old. Now the peculiar thing about an old baobab is that it gets hollow. Any one of these trees could hold twenty men."

"But how would they get in and out? I see no holes."

"The opening is usually up there where the tree branches, about twelve feet above the ground."

"Joro," Hal said. "Stand close to this trunk. Give me a hand up."

He mounted to Joro's shoulders. There he could just reach the lowest branches. He pulled himself up. Now he could see the hole, just where the branches radiated from the trunk.

He crept to the edge of the hole, very cautiously so as not to invite a shower of arrows. He looked down into the gloom. The trunk was full of men. They stared up at him solemnly but made no move to attack him. They acted more like small boys who have been caught doing something naughty.

He drew back as the poachers began climbing out of

the hole and dropping to the ground. They left their weapons behind them. Hal came down. Why weren't the poachers prepared to fight?

"Joro, ask them what this is all about."

Joro spoke in Swahili. When one of the poachers replied Joro translated.

"They don't want to fight. They give up."

"Why?"

"Every time they try to make a camp, we spoil it. They are tired of following Blackbeard. He isn't paying them — because he's getting no trophies. They say if they're not paid they won't work."

Men were now pouring out of the other trees. Among the last was Blackbeard himself. But he was not ready to surrender. He carried a revolver in each hand, his beard bristled, and his face was contorted with rage. He screamed at his men, urging them to fight. He acted as if he had gone stark staring mad. He fired shots into the air, and when that did not terrify his men he levelled his guns upon them and blasted away at them, killing six.

Now the poachers were really stirred into action — against their own leader. They rushed him, losing two more men to his bullets before they pinned him to the earth and took away his guns. They might have killed him if the warden had not stopped them.

"Get up," commanded the warden. Blackbeard, still blustering, rose to his feet.

Chee, who had come along with the safari men, was acting strangely. He sniffed at Blackbeard, then bared his teeth in a savage growl. Why, wondered Hal, should the cheetah behave so towards a man he had never seen or smelled before?

Blackbeard viciously kicked the cheetah in the throat. Hal remembered someone else who had attacked the animal in exactly the same way – Judge Singh.

Chee lunged at Blackbeard but was checked by his young master's voice. "Stop it, Chee," Roger commanded, fearing that in a fight between man and beast Chee himself might be killed.

The warden faced Blackbeard. "Your game is up," he said. "We've been after you for years. Now we've got you — thanks to two boys."

"There's nothing you can do to me," said Blackbeard defiantly. "I have money."

"We'll see about that in court. You will stand trail for the murder of eight men. Sindar Singh himself will be your judge — and you will find him a pillar of justice. All your money cannot buy him off."

Blackbeard broke into a loud laugh. At the sound, Chee leaped upon him. His teeth closed on the killer king's throat. Not exactly on his throat, but on the beard that covered it.

The false beard came off in the animal's jaws.

And there, stripped of its disguise, was the face of Sindar Singh. Crosby gazed at it in amazement.

Judge Sigh was still laughing. "Now you see why I am not afraid of your Judge Singh," he said. "Ha, ha — it is really too funny. What a fool you have been."

He changed his tune when he was bound hand and

foot, transported to Nairobi, and delivered to the police.

There Singh alias Blackbeard did his best to buy off the judge who was to try him. He failed. When he was sentenced to life imprisonment he realized that not all judges were as corruptible as Judge Sindar Singh.

His wealth was confiscated and turned over to the African Wildlife Society to be devoted to the protection of African animals.

So the boys had been right – and wrong. They had guessed Singh was a crook. They had not guessed he was Blackbeard himself.

As for Warden Mark Crosby, the discovery that the soft-voiced little Judge Singh and the killer Blackbeard were one and the same person was a shock he would never quite get over. He had been fond of Singh. He was still fond of what Singh had seemed to be. He mourned the loss of a friend.

25
Man-eaters

The morning after the capture of Blackbeard, a ranger brought the boys a note from Crosby.

"Would you drop over to my office? Urgent."

When they entered the warden's banda they saw that he already had a visitor, a black man in the uniform of a railway official.

Crosby introduced him as Gazi Tanga, station master at near-by Mtito Andei where the Nairobi–Mombasa railway cuts through Tsavo Park.

"Tanga brings serious news," said Crosby. "Last night five of his men were killed and eaten by lions."

The boys were goggle-eyed. "I thought man-eating lions were a thing of the past," Hal said.

"Far from it. Every year more than a hundred people are killed by man-eaters in East Africa. Of course that isn't many, compared with those killed by cars in your country. But if lions kill the Africans the Africans are going to kill the lions. Now we want to protect both the people and the lions. Tanga's men are out this very morning killing every lion they can find. We can't allow that. The lions –

the innocent ones — have a right to live. Visitors come from all over the world to see our lions. We can't have them wiped out. Most lions are peaceable. There are just a few bad actors. The thing to do is to find the bad actors and leave the good lions alone."

"How can you tell by looking at a lion whether he is good or bad?"

"It isn't easy. That's why I called you in."

"But we've had no experience in this sort of thing."

"Perhaps not just this. But you've had a lot of experience with animals. And you seem to be good at solving riddles. You've done so much for me that I can't ask you to do anything more. But if you volunteer . . ."

He looked so hopeful that it was hard to refuse. Hal looked at Roger. Roger nodded.

"Of course we'll do what we can," Hal said. "We're lucky to have a good crew. Being Africans themselves, they know more about African animals than we could learn in a lifetime."

"That may be so," admitted the warden. "But they're not inclined to do much about it. Put their know-how along with your energy and I believe you'll get somewhere."

Hal turned to Tanga. "What do you think? Perhaps you feel we cannot help you."

"It is not so, bwana," replied Tanga respectfully. "We know you stopped poaching in Tsavo. We know you caught Blackbeard. It is all we need to know. We will do as you say."

"Good. Then go back and tell your people to kill no more lions. We will come with our crew in an hour. With your help we'll catch those bad actors."

If you enjoyed this book, you might like to read
the other **Willard Price** books in the series:

SOUTH SEA & VOLCANO
ADVENTURE DOUBLE

Dive into two action-packed adventures!

In *Volcano Adventure* Hal and Roger Hunt's research
into the volatile volcanoes of the Pacific erupts
into an awesome adventure when they join forces
with a world-famous volcanologist.

And they sink even deeper into danger on
a top-secret mission in *South Sea Adventure*, where
they're not the only ones looking for the treasure
of Pearl Lagoon ...

'Willard Price makes the pulse-rate soar'
INDEPENDENT ON SUNDAY

ISBN 0 099 48774 8

DIVING & AMAZON
ADVENTURE DOUBLE

Dive into two action-packed adventures!

Hal and Roger Hunt are plunged into the
depths in *Diving Adventure* when their
specimen-collecting trip to the Undersea City
takes a deadly turn.

And in *Amazon Adventure* the brothers are
on a mission to explore uncharted territory
in the Amazon, but when they go off course
in the greatest jungle on earth, it's the
survival of the fittest.

'Willard Price makes the pulse-rate soar'
INDEPENDENT ON SUNDAY

ISBN 0 099 48773 X

ALPHA FORCE

Mission: Survival

SURVIVAL

Alex, Li, Paulo, Hex and Amber are five teenagers on board a sailing ship crewed by young people from all over the world. Together they are marooned on a desert island. And together they must face the ultimate test – survival! Battling against unbelievable dangers – from killer komodo dragons to sharks and modern-day pirates – the five must combine all their knowledge and skills if they are to stay alive.

The team – Alpha Force – is born . . .

ISBN 0 099 43924 7

If you enjoyed this book, you might like
the Alpha Force series:

ALPHA FORCE

Target: Drug Rat

RAT-CATCHER

Alpha Force are an elite team of five highly-skilled
individuals brought together to battle injustice.
Together they join a covert SAS operation in South
America, fighting to catch an evil drugs baron. To gain
information, they infiltrate a tight-knit community of
street kids then head into the isolated mountains where
a terrifying and twisted hunt is to test their individual
skills to the max . . .

ISBN 0 099 43925 5

ALPHA FORCE

Target: Ivory Hunters

HUNTED

Alpha Force head to Namibia to compete in an extreme
sports contest. When they discover a horrifying threat to
the local wildlife, they snap into action, only to find
themselves facing a desperate flight across the African
plains, pursued by a group who are prepared to shoot to
kill. The team freefall into danger . . .

ISBN 0 099 46425 X

ALPHA FORCE

Target: Toxic Waste

HOSTAGE

Alpha Force have flown to Northern Canada to
investigate reports of illegal dumping of toxic waste.
The team must dive into an icy river, cross the harsh
landscape on snowmobiles and mobilize their caving
skills to complete their mission. But they need all
their courage and determination when they come
face-to-face with a man who is ready to kill
– or take a hostage – to stop them.

The team face their toughest challenge yet . . .

ISBN 0 099 43927 1

ALPHA FORCE

Target: Terrorist Hostage Taker

RED CENTRE

The five members of Alpha Force train hard and are
prepared to go anywhere in the world to combat injustice.
Recruited to help on a survival show in Australia, they
are suddenly thrust into a terrifying ordeal when a hunted
terrorist takes desperate measures to escape capture.
Alongside the Australian SAS, Alpha Force must act
quickly to save lives – even if it means facing the
terrifying heat of an out-of-control bushfire . . .

ISBN 0 099 46424 1

ALPHA FORCE

Target: Child-Slavers

DESERT PURSUIT

Alpha Force are a unique group of five individuals, each with special skills, each ready to go anywhere in the world to help others in need. Undercover, they head for the Sahara Desert, resolved to gather evidence of young landmine victims. But they are catapulted into a desperate race across the desert when they discover a terrible evil – a gang of child-slavers operating in the area.

The team is in pursuit . . .

ISBN 0 099 43926 3